NAILING JESS

TRIONA SCULLY

For my mother, Teresa

ONE

MONDAY

'Sucking razors,' Wayne muttered, tossing the offending item into her sink. She applied some toilet paper to her bleeding chin and retreated from her bathroom.

Wayne felt like shit. Suck that! She felt like three-day-old shit that had been left to fester in the blistering sun. Wayne checked her coat pockets in search of painkillers. She found her fags instead and lit one, inhaling greedily. Almost immediately, phlegm rose up her throat and she spat a mouthful of green bile into the remnants of her evening meal—if a reduced-to-clear microwaveable shepherd's pie counted as a meal. She scanned the room searching for her badge and wallet.

Five minutes later, she bounded from the house without any money and frantically hailed down a taxi.

'Withering Police Station,' she barked at the tired-looking Asian woman who drove her cab. 'And step on it.'

She mentally rehearsed what she was going to say to O'Keeffe: *"Ma'am, I am so very sorry for having broken protocol, swearing at a senior officer and groping one of the canteen boys, but, you know, I caught an armed robber and was responsible for the safe return of half a million quid's worth of gems, so why the suck don't you just thank me, eh?"*

Wayne sighed. Even in her head, she couldn't sound contrite. Politically correct bullshit! That's what was going on here. That's what her suspension had really been about.

'Twelve pounds fifty, mate.'

'About that, pal. I've no cash on me, but I'm a D.C.I. at this station and you wouldn't want to fall out with a senior officer for a figure that small, eh?' Wayne said, climbing out of the taxi.

'Sucking pigs!' snorted the driver, speeding off.

Wayne paused outside and lit another cigarette. The old building had been given a fresh lick of paint in her absence. The couple of coats of white deflected nicely from the cracks and tiny holes that had started to form on its flecked surface. Thus, like much else in Withering Police Station, it appeared to be in better shape than it actually was. This point was proved as she pushed open the varnished entrance door and heard it squeak. She walked down the badly lit corridor to the information desk. The desk sergeant smiled, his pearly whites gleaming against the red of his lipstick.

'Good to see you, Wayne. You've been missed around here.'

As he spoke, he was busy filing the previous night's paperwork in the cabinets behind his desk. He bent down to put half a dozen files in a bottom cabinet, and Wayne whistled. 'Be a dear and get me a large black one, love.' Wayne winked at him and the young P.C. sprang into action.

Wayne smiled to herself as she waited for her coffee, soaking up the familiar atmosphere of her workplace and anticipating getting back in the saddle. Out of the corner of her eye, she spotted O'Keeffe walking towards her and she quickly rearranged her facial features into a sombre expression.

'Morning ma'am,' she said to her boss, who gave Wayne a curt nod, before continuing to stroll down the corridor towards her office. As she opened her door, O'Keeffe shouted back to her, 'For Christ's sake keep up! Do you think I have all day?'

Wayne sighed and swallowed the fresh coffee she'd been handed moments earlier in three mouthfuls, swearing as the piping hot liquid burned her throat.

'Wish me luck,' she whispered to the desk sergeant.

Even though the door was open, and she'd been summoned, she still knocked on it. O'Keeffe was big on protocol and she hoped this small act of deference might win her a few brownie points.

Her boss looked up from behind her desk and signalled for Wayne to sit in one of two soft black leather chairs that were positioned either side of her hand-carved mahogany desk. Everything in O'Keeffe's office was either antique and overpriced or ultra-modern and overpriced. The walls were covered in sterling silver framed awards; pointless awards bestowed on O'Keeffe by her golfing cronies in exchange for other pointless awards that said cronies hung on their own walls, or by way of reward for O'Keeffe turning a blind eye to all the illegal, immoral and unethical acts her swing buddies regularly committed.

Dead centre, right above her own chair, her boss had suspended the stuffed head of a deer hind. A wedding present from her mother-in-law, O'Keeffe had confided in Wayne, when asked about its origins. Like every person that sat in her chair, Wayne's eyes were drawn to the lifeless deer. She would have given a month's wages to see it fall and knock O'Keeffe out. All she needed was a claw hammer and ten minutes, but to date the combination had eluded her.

'Internal affairs have concluded their report,' O'Keeffe said.

'That's nice,' Wayne replied.

'Nice?' O'Keeffe snapped and Wayne instantly regretted

3

her flippancy. When the suck was she going to learn? O'Keeffe did not possess a sense of humour.

'No, not nice,' Wayne agreed.

'That's right!' O'Keeffe confirmed. 'It's the polar opposite of nice—it's shit! Shit that's landed on my desk. Does my desk look like it needs more shit on it?'

Wayne knew the question was rhetorical, but she was desperate to make a smart-ass retort and probably would have, had the desk sergeant not interrupted them, with an urgent request to speak to O'Keeffe. Wayne could tell from the junior officer's flushed face that something major was going down.

'I'll be right with you,' O'Keeffe told the desk sergeant.

Turning her attention back to Wayne, she thrust the internal affairs report in her lap. 'Read it,' she instructed. 'Sit right here and read it over and over until the words penetrate your tiny pea-sized brain. When I come back we can talk about what it says, and what it means for your future here at Withering.'

D.C.I. Jane Wayne is a relic. She is a product of a different time with ingrained sexist views. She shows no willingness to change and no real insight into the fact that her opinions are offensive and outdated.

It is my considered opinion that if D.C.I. Wayne continues working for the police she will bring not only Withering Station into disrepute, but quite possibly the entire force. I would therefore recommend

```
early retirement and a generous severance
package, in view of her many years of
service and her outstanding record in
closing cases.
```

Blah! Blah! Blah! Wayne thought, having read alternative versions of this report at least half a dozen times over the years. When the suck was someone going to write something interesting about her, or even something a bit more complimentary? It was all bullshit anyway, because O'Keeffe wasn't going to fire her. They would do the same dance they did every time Wayne sucked up. O'Keeffe would scream at her. She would apologise. O'Keeffe would make demands, backed up with threats. She would make promises that neither of them believed she'd keep. O'Keeffe would finish with a warning that this was her last chance and Wayne would get back to solving crimes.

She tapped her foot on the floor and checked the clock on the wall. O'Keeffe had been gone at least half an hour.

'Suck this!' Wayne fired her report in the bin, and headed out of the office, in search of whatever was keeping O'Keeffe away from her plush leather chairs and her underfloor heated carpet.

'Shit! Shit! You're back half an hour and you're already causing me trouble!' fumed P.C. McCarthy, or Peachy as he was known, on account of his very impressive arse.

Peachy was supposed to be going to Parkhouse Loan to investigate a domestic and instead found himself in the driving seat of a car going in the opposite direction.

He was next to Wayne, who was relishing the fact that Peachy was wearing a skirt and a pair of low pulls, which definitely weren't standard issue.

'Thought there was rules against that kind of footwear at work?' Wayne asked.

'Don't you go changing the subject! I'm pissed Wayne. I'm supposed be to working with Murphy today and you know what she's like. You better tell her that you ordered me to take you.'

'Yeah, about that, Peachy. You should probably know that I'm not actually officially back yet. I never managed to speak to O'Keeffe, what with that call coming in...'

'What? Suck! Suck! Suck! You're a sucking cunthead!' shouted Peachy. 'Are you trying to get me fired?'

'Calm down, sugar, and don't get your knickers in a knot.' Wayne smiled at him.

'Don't you be telling me to calm down!' Peachy fumed.

'Actually, don't calm down, toots. You're sexy as hell when you're angry.'

Peachy rolled his eyes in exasperation, but Wayne could tell he was secretly pleased. That was the trick with men, all you have to do is tell them they're sexy and they'll forgive you anything, and in this case, it was an absolute fact.

Peachy was about to turn into Buckstone Drive when Wayne instructed him to stop. 'Here's fine, love. I wouldn't want to get you in trouble.' Wayne patted his knee firmly as she got out of the car.

Detective Inspector Ben Campbell surveyed the crime scene and stifled the urge to gag. It brought to mind a scene from Macbeth. *"Who would have thought the old woman had so much blood in her?"* Or words to that effect. Only it wasn't a woman—it was a boy. *Probably Simon's age*, Ben thought and then shivered.

The victim had been stabbed brutally dozens of times and his blood was spattered all over the floor and walls. He'd been posed like Jess on a wooden cross, but face down. There was a silver implement protruding from his anus. *What kind of sick bitch does this to a kid*? He put his hand across his mouth to stem a wave of vomit.

'First time, love? That's always the hardest.'

Ben looked up to see a large woman with a round face and round glasses, dressed in a white coat, standing over the body.

'You must be the medical examiner, Dr Baker?'

Martha Baker smiled and extended her hand warmly,

'And you must be this city detective we've all been hearing about. How are you finding life in Withering? Not quite as fast as the Big Smoke, I imagine?'

Ben took his hand from his mouth and shook the doctor's hand limply. 'It's not my first body. I've seen several in my last post.'

'That's great, love.'

'Is there anything you can tell me?'

'About this murder? No, doll, I just got here.'

'Yes, of course,' Ben nodded, embarrassed. He stepped away from the body and allowed the doctor to examine it.

He glanced around the room, trying to decipher clues from the chaos. The place had been completely ransacked. Two empty bookcases had been toppled over, one knocking a mirror off the wall and smashing it into the living room table, resulting in the cream carpet being covered in shards of glass.

A book had been ripped up and its pages were spread all around the body, creating a circle. Despite the upheaval, Ben could sense an order to the scene. He paced the floor several times, taking in every detail. As he grabbed a pen and paper from his rucksack, he was conscious of Baker staring at him. *What's the matter, Doc? You never seen a bloke with a beard before?* he wanted to ask, but didn't. Instead, he scrawled some words and hastily sketched pictures in his pad. He bent down to retrieve one of the pages on the floor. A hand slapped it out of his.

'Not without gloves, you don't! You'll contaminate a crime scene. Or didn't they teach you that on the *How to be a Detective* weekend course they sent you on?'

Ben looked up to see a dishevelled, older woman in a long beige trench coat and a pair of tanned, worn-out cowgirl boots. Her short dark hair was thick and wavy and crowned a lined, but still handsome, face. Her breath smelled of cheap mints and her hair stank like an ashtray.

'I'm sorry, who are you?' Ben asked.

'D.C.I. Wayne,' Wayne replied, her tone implying Ben should already know who she was.

Ben was taken aback. She didn't look like a D.C.I., more like a D.U.I. He knew he should ask for I.D., but he didn't want to create animosity with a senior officer.

'Fast tracked, I suppose. Have you ever even seen a corpse before, pet?' Wayne asked.

'I worked the beat in central London for six months; I've seen several corpses.'

'Six whole months!'

'I was told I was in charge of this investigation.' Ben's voice veered towards a whine.

'And so you are, so don't go getting your lacies in a twist. I'm only here to observe, act like I'm not here.' Wayne replied.

Ben had a sense that this would be impossible. He

scrawled some notes in his pad then approached Baker, who was still kneeling over the dead boy, her face deep in concentration.

'Can you tell me anything about the body? Has it been moved?' he asked.

'I can tell you he had a cute little tushie,' Baker laughed. 'And, of course there were jewels on his jewels.'

'What the hell does that mean?' Ben asked.

'He was pejazzled,' Wayne explained. 'Don't tell me we have to explain to a city boy like you what pejazzling is?'

Ben blushed. 'Do you have an estimated time of death?'

'I'll know when I get him back to the lab.'

'Can't you hazard a guess?'

'She could, but she's a scientist, she'd prefer not to,' Wayne interrupted. 'Look, love, I appreciate that your entire knowledge of forensics was gained by watching a C.S.I. Miami box set, but here in the real world, it's a tedious labour intensive business. Why don't you go touch up your make-up, or dare I say it—apply some—and Baker here will have a report by say, one-thirty?' Wayne glanced at Baker for confirmation.

Ben stared at the two women and counted back from ten silently. By the time he got to three, he could speak. 'I'll see you after lunch then.'

Using the desk sergeant's hand drawn map, Ben struggled to locate the morgue and by the time he got there it was almost two o'clock. Engrossed in her work, Baker appeared indifferent to his lack of punctuality. The victim was naked on a white table in the centre of the room. Either side of him were two white trolleys. On one, the doctor had carefully laid out a row of small knives and scalpels. The other had a weighing scale and a bowl with a thick brown, rank-smelling liquid. Baker picked a scalpel not much larger than a nail file, and used it to slice a line from the victim's neck to his navel. Ben recoiled, grateful he'd skipped lunch.

'So,' he gulped, 'What can you tell me, Doctor?'

'Death was caused by strangulation.'

'Strangulation, but all those stab wounds?'

'Post mortem. And the crucifix that we fished out of his anus, mercifully that was afterwards too.' Baker's matter of fact tone served to highlight the sinister nature of his subject matter.

Ben flinched. 'What was he strangled with?'

'I can't be certain, but probably piano wire or something very similar.'

'Time of death?'

'I'm giving it a window between two and four a.m.'

Ben was scrawling frantically in his notebook. 'Anything else you can tell me?'

Baker laid down her scalpel and fixed Ben with an intense stare. 'She's done it before.'

Ben's eyes widened.

'And she'll do it again.'

'I don't understand. Are you trying to say this is the work of a serial killer? In Withering? Oh be serious! Now which of us has watched too much TV? And also, can we stop referring to any possible suspects as "she"? It's prejudicial and limiting.' Ben continued to note take as he spoke.

Baker's mouth curled into a snarl. 'Look, I'm as open-minded as the next, nearly retired, rural, medical examiner, but let's be clear on one thing, pet, when a death is dark enough and depraved enough and desperate enough, it's always a woman, and in forty years as a medical examiner

I've never seen anything as dark, depraved, and desperate as these murders.'

'Murders! What other murders?'

'We had two similar murders six months ago, two months apart.'

'How similar?'

'Well, you've seen our crime scene. She's got her own unique stamp, I'd say. I mean, what are the chances of there being more than one knife-wielding, wire-strangling, anus-defiling maniac with a wet cunt for ancient religious texts in Withering?'

'Religious texts, what texts?' Ben's wrist hurt, from speed scrawling every detail into his notepad.

'The pages surrounding the body are taken from a copy of the Bhagavad Gita. If it's like the other two, it will be a generic copy, and random pages.'

'So the other crime scenes were identical to ours?'

'Right down to the miniature Jess.' She handed a bagged crucifix to Ben, who paled.

'Who were the suspects? There must have been suspects.'

'Too many and none,' remembered Baker. 'These boys were from the street and they both had long lists of unsavoury clients, but nothing stuck out. We thought it was one of the boys' mothers at one point, but the lead investigator wasn't convinced, so we didn't run with it.'

'Who was the lead investigator?'

'You met her this morning.'

Wayne sat opposite her boss once again, this time affecting her most remorseful face to date. With the return of the Wringer, the stakes had shot up considerably and she was determined to be on her best behaviour.

O'Keeffe was giving her the silent treatment, focusing on her paperwork, a pair of designer reading glasses perched on her skinny nose. Wayne could see flecks of grey creeping out of the roots of her boss's hair and she yearned to point it out to her. O'Keeffe was notoriously vain and any criticism of her personal appearance really pissed her off. *Another time,* she promised herself.

'Where the suck did you go today?' O'Keeffe asked, removing her glasses and fixing Wayne with her hardest stare.

'I forgot to put money in my parking meter, didn't I?'

'You don't have a car, Wayne, and if you did, you could park it at the station for free.'

'Well, I'll keep that in mind ma'am, if I ever get one. Anyway, about today, I was actually…'

'Shut it!' O'Keeffe interjected. 'I don't want to hear any more ill-conceived lies. I know exactly where you were this morning. We'll get back to that. Let's start with your report, which I'm assuming you read before tossing it in the bin. Would you say it's a fair evaluation?'

'Funny you should ask that, I found it a bit harsh, to be honest, a bit one sided, all stick and no…' Wayne stopped mid-sentence, aware that O'Keeffe's nostrils were starting to flare.

'Maybe you need a bit more time off to reflect,' O'Keeffe's voice was barely a whisper.

'No,' Wayne replied quickly, 'Let me finish. Harsh, yes, but fair. I do need to buck up my ideas and scale back my attempts at humour, which I can see might offend some easily offended people.'

'For Jess's sake, is that your idea of an apology?' O'Keeffe's voice was beginning to rise.

'What do you want me to say ma'am?' Wayne clenched her hands as she spoke, digging her nails deep into her palms.

'I want you to say that you realise it's the twenty first century and that you are willing to drag your Neanderthal arse into it.'

'Absolutely, right away, ma'am.' Wayne gave her a respectful nod. 'So, when can I start back?'

'It's not as simple as that. Upstairs don't want you back.'

'But you do, eh? I know you, Kathy; if you were going to fire me, you would have spared me a lecture. The Withering Wringer is back and you know you won't close this case without me.'

O'Keeffe winced at the killer's in-house nickname; it was only a matter of time before it was splashed across the tabloids.

'I know nothing of the sort, you arrogant bitch! I'll tell you what I know. You're a good copper, Wayne. You've got the nose for it—and the cunt. I know that you get results and I personally, am all about results. I'll tell you what else I know. Times have changed and if we don't change with them, then we'll all be put out to pasture. Upstairs are gunning for you now, and let me be absolutely crystal about this, Wayne, you won't take me with you if you go.' O'Keeffe leaned forward, pointing her finger. 'Do you get my meaning? One suck up, one hint of a cunt-up, one throwaway comment in the pub or in the press, and I'll have your badge and your pension and your home. When you're reduced to sleeping in a car, I'll send the girls round to beat you into a coma, and when you are lying in a hospital bed, I'll come and pull the plug myself! Do you hear me, Wayne?'

'Loud and clear ma'am, one suck up and it's ruination,

bankruptcy and a violent death at the hands of my colleagues. So, can I have my badge now?'

'Once again, Wayne, it's not that simple.' O'Keeffe cut her off.

Wayne bit down on her tongue so hard, she drew blood. 'I see ma'am, so what's the problem?'

'I can't be seen to do nothing. I can't be seen to condone your behaviour...' O'Keeffe began.

'Ah, say no more,' Wayne interrupted her boss. She stood up, walked over to the door and opened it. 'You start shouting and I'll stand here, looking scared.'

'Sit down, you stupid fool,' O'Keeffe snapped. 'Do you really think I need you to keep my girls in line? Find me one among them that isn't terrified of me!'

Wayne conceded her boss was right, as she slunk back to her chair. 'So, what the suck do you want from me?' The words were out before she could stop them.

'You're going to have to accept a demotion, I'm afraid.'

Wayne cast her eyes down towards her feet. She knew the next sentence she spoke would either secure or annihilate her chances of being part of the investigation. 'Okay,' she nodded, 'But I still get the Wringer case?'

'You can work on it, yes, but you won't be in charge.'

'So who am I answering to? Ah Jess, no! Not the new guy? Seriously? I have to take orders from some city-slicking bloke, with the sort of face that'll scare the general public. Come on, boss, you should have seen him today. He turned green at the sight of our vic...' Wayne stopped abruptly.

'So, we've solved the mystery that was no mystery regarding your whereabouts this morning?' O'Keeffe took off her designer glasses and placed them neatly beside the telephone, before locking eyes with Wayne. 'Listen to me.

Securing D.I. Campbell is actually a coup for this station. He scored top of the class on his inspectors' exams—and that was out of everybody—not just the men. He's a smart cookie. Fourteen different rural police forces were head-hunting him. We should feel very pleased he decided to come to work for us.'

'Fourteen different forces, eh?' Wayne didn't attempt to hide the scorn in her voice. 'Was that because he ticks all the diversity boxes? Male, single father, ugly... Is there a box for ugly? Does he have any experience at all?'

O'Keeffe paused before replying, 'What he lacks in practical experience he more than makes up for in innovative, new thinking. He's a meninist, you know. In fact, he's been tasked with setting up a meninist reading group right here in this station. You should sign up; you might learn something.'

'A *meninist*,' repeated Wayne, 'Well, that explains a lot.'

Ben undressed slowly, methodically and sorted his clothes as he went. Socks, pra, knickers, blouse for the wash. His grey trouser suit was hung up neatly, as it would last another day.

He stepped into the steaming shower and allowed the water to heal his tired but taut body. Nobody would guess to look at Ben that he possessed such a lean, luscious body or that his penis when erect was so suckable. Ben worked hard to hide his body beneath layers of clothes, in the same way he kept his angular, beautiful face hidden behind years of hair growth. He'd stopped shaving when Anna walked out and, when he got over the initial stage of self-disgust, he came to love it. It was liberating to be concealed in a nest of hair. Women hated it, which was definitely part of the attraction. Anna's departure had rounded off a lifetime of being loved and lusted after, used, abused, beaten and always left by a long line of useless sucks.

Ben came to embrace the misogynist he'd always known he was. *"Meninism isn't about hating women,"* his well-meaning associates said at meetings. *Oh but it so is*, he thought, *because to not hate them was surely to miss the point.*

'Dad, are you going to be much longer?'

Drea was banging on the door. Ben turned the dial to blue and allowed stark, cold water to envelop his whole body. He shivered, but sixty seconds later when he emerged, he looked and smelled fresher and ready for the night ahead.

A quarter of an hour later, he was draining pasta at his sink and shouting at his kids to come to the table. A quarter after that, he was picking fusilli off the floor and yelling at his youngest to get her pyjamas and at his oldest two to get their homework out. He filled the dishwasher and the washing machine.

'Dad, you need to read me a story,' Val bawled from her bedroom.

'Drea, go and read your sister a story,' Ben told his eldest daughter.

'Not Drea. You, Dad!' Val screamed.

Ben swore under his breath, hit the 'on' button on the dryer and headed upstairs, retrieving an armful of Val's toys that were strewn across the landing as he went, and swearing some more.

Val was sitting up in bed, holding her book upside down and reciting its contents from memory. Ben's anger dissolved and he felt a surge of absolute love for his make-or-break baby.

It had been his ex-wife's idea to have a third child and not one that Ben had particularly warmed to, knowing that if their older children were anything to go by, he'd be doing the lion's share of the parenting. How right he'd been. Val had been a particularly difficult baby, and within weeks of her birth, Anna had reneged on her commitment to be more involved this time around. In the end, she'd been even more useless than she had with the other two, finding excuses to work late and to work away, eventually abandoning them altogether; no explanation offered.

'Why are you sad, Dad?' Val asked, tossing her book on the bed and stroking his face.

'I'm not sad!' Ben replied, his face breaking into a wide grin. 'How could anyone with a little girl as special as you ever be sad?'

Val grinned back, 'Are you going to read my story now?'

'I absolutely am,' Ben said, settling himself down beside her and picking up the well-worn copy of Gretel and Hansel. He read the book through and started again, and when his second reading was interrupted by faint snores, he gave his sleeping daughter a light kiss on the forehead, before switching off the light and tiptoeing out of the room.

'Dad, can you help, please?' Simon called from downstairs.

'Keep your voice down, Simon,' he hissed. 'What do you need? I've a lot of work to do tonight.'

'It's my Second World War project. It's to be in by tomorrow and I haven't even started. But if you're busy, maybe you could give me a note?'

'Nice try!'

The next two hours were spent printing and pasting pictures

of swastikas and warships into Simon's history folder. Ben looked at the clock on the wall. It was almost eleven. He could see Simon was barely conscious. He ran his fingers through his brown, curly locks and told him to get to bed.

'But what about my project?'

'I'll finish it, love. You need to sleep.'

It was after midnight. The last pictures of battlefields had been glued into Simon's folder. The night's washing was hanging to dry. The kids' clothes and lunch boxes were ready for the morning. He put five pounds in Drea's pencil-case and poured himself a strong, black coffee, before spreading the three separate files across his kitchen table and becoming immediately overwhelmed with the sheer volume of information.

Ben picked up the first case—Johnny Devlin. Terror danced in the young boy's eyes, as the life was squeezed from him, and captured forever in the mortician's camera. He sped-read his vital statistics and a brief bio, and the image of an unstable background started to emerge. On the streets at thirteen, the kid never stood a chance. Scanning through the interview list, he noted a boy's life and death amounted to ten hastily compiled informal chats. At first glance, not one of the conversations seemed intelligible, laced in innuendo surrounding the dead boy's work as a prostitute.

His doorbell rang and his head jerked. Ben didn't know anyone in Withering. Edging his way towards the front door, armed with the huge golf umbrella that hung in the hall coat stand, he opened it slowly, and was hit with the stench of whisky and tobacco.

'It took you long enough to answer, doll,' Wayne slurred. 'I'll get frostbite out here!'

'Sucking cock!' Wayne muttered to herself, staggering away from Ben's house. 'Who the suck does he think he is? Mister first-day-on-the-job, straight from behind a desk in London, wouldn't recognise a dead body if it came with its own coffin...' Her rant continued unabated, as she weaved her way through the empty streets of Withering. More than once she got lost and found herself wandering aimlessly down the wrong lane, but the town was small and she'd walked every inch of it, so could quickly get back on track.

Turning into the street where Baker lived, she heaved a sigh of relief, as she saw the living room lights were on. Baker was an insomniac, which was downright inconvenient for her, but frequently suited Wayne's purposes.

She stood outside Baker's house, shivering, and had a brief moment of awareness that she was far too drunk to be in public. She tapped lightly on her friend's window and waited. The outside light came on, as did the hall light, and Baker's ample frame, swathed in a deep purple dressing gown, came into view.

'Sorry,' Wayne muttered.

Baker gave her a wide smile and ushered her inside. 'Maybe take off your boots,' she suggested as she guided Wayne towards her living room. Wayne ignored the request as she relaxed onto Baker's crushed velvet sofa, oblivious to the trail of dirt she had spread across the recently cleaned pure wool rug that covered most of the wooden floor.

Baker tutted under her breath and she decided to ignore that too. She allowed her head to rest against a feather-filled cushion and was almost asleep when the clanking of a tea tray forced her eyes back open.

'I'd rather whisky,' she told Baker who seemed fairly

adept at the ignoring game herself. She poured a large cup of fresh Brazilian coffee and added several lumps of sugar and a large splash of milk to it, before placing it on a saucer and putting it on a small glass table bedside Wayne.

'No whisky in this house, but you could be the first to try my beetroot infused macaroons.' Next to the saucer she placed a side plate piled high with round purple biscuits. In true addict style, Baker had replaced alcohol and drugs with sugar, and swapped debauched, lost weekends for high intensity, all day baking courses. Ironically, these classes cost more than the Class As they substituted.

Wayne smiled at the perfectly symmetric snack and marvelled at how much dexterity lay in such chubby-fingered hands. Then she shook her head and moved the plate back to the tea tray.

'Too drunk,' she explained whilst patting her coat down searching for her tobacco tin. 'The last of Big Bertha's stash, I'm afraid.' She shook the small bag of blueberry bud and then set about skinning up, resting the papers on her tin that was perched on her knee.

'Use this, please,' Baker shoved the tea tray at Wayne, almost knocking the remains of her weed all over the couch.

'Careful now, there's not another raid planned 'till next Thursday.' Concern flashed across Wayne's wasted face.

'Then here, let me do it,' Baker snapped, taking the tray back from her before she had time to argue. She lay back on the cushion and struggled to keep her eyes open as Baker quickly and quietly put together the sort of spliff that teenage dope fiends, in competition with each other, take fifteen minutes to make.

'It's a damn shame you can't smoke anymore,' Wayne said, sparking the perfect joint that tasted even better than it looked. 'Never met anyone else who puts that much artistry in a spliff.' She laughed and coughed simultaneously. 'This is good shit.'

'Right, now that you're good and stoned, you going to tell me what's bothering you?'

'What do you make of your man?' Wayne asked.

'Ah,' Baker smiled, 'You feeling a bit threatened by the new boy?'

'Threatened? Who said anything about feeling threatened? He's a menenist, you know. Don't you think it's strange that one of them would choose to work with us pigs?'

'Well, they have to work somewhere, I suppose. It's back in fashion, you know. They reckon there are menenists in every field now.'

'But what do they want? They have the vote. They can work. They can divorce you in a heartbeat and take your car and kids? What more are they after?'

'You're asking the wrong woman,' Baker replied, a wry smile spread across her cheeks. 'I'd have stopped at the vote.'

'Or maybe even before it,' Wayne laughed, as she inhaled the last toke of Baker's perfect spliff and ground the butt into her saucer. 'Let's face it, what do men know about politics?'

'Probably more than they know about policing.'

'I went round to give him a briefing on the case so he doesn't sound like a complete dick tomorrow and he wouldn't let me past the front door, said I was drunk and should go home and sleep it off.'

'Which you are, but it's still bad form to point it out,' Baker said.

'Exactly! I didn't go telling him he was ugly!' Wayne replied.

'Which he isn't, by the way.'

'How's that?' Wayne gave her friend a bewildered look.

'Campbell's not ugly. You're focusing on the beard, which admittedly isn't pleasant, but give that man a sharp razor and a fitted outfit, and you would be panting about him like a bitch in heat.'

'Campbell? The guy we met today?' Wayne's expression had changed from surprised to shell shocked.

'The very one,' Baker nodded. 'Trust me, Wayne, I work with the dead, I'm used to seeing what lies beneath, what a body really looks like when you strip away all the covers and paintwork. I see bone structure and symmetry of features, length of leg, width of hip and I'm telling you, if Campbell was on my table you'd realise he's hot enough to be a model.'

'If Campbell was on your table, then I'd be back in charge of this case, where I belong,' Wayne replied and both women chuckled.

TWO

TUESDAY

Ben dropped his two eldest at the school gates and sped off towards the station. He was going to be late. The morning had started so smoothly, but descended into chaos when Val went on hunger strike, refusing to eat breakfast and throwing her lunch box out of the car window. She hadn't wanted to eat her school dinner the previous day, as the fish fingers were beside the peas, not the mashed potatoes, and her teacher had forced her to. Val recalled the episode to an exasperated Ben, as he tried to force her out of the car, and he knew he'd have to deal with it.

The next half hour was taken up with finding a staff member and formulating an action plan to prise Val off her father's leg and into a classroom. It had worked, insofar as Ben managed to leave the building, but not before she'd put up one hell of a fight. Turning the corner of the long corridor and heading for the main exit, he could still hear the tormented wails of his youngest child.

'We've got an I.D., boss,' Peachy said, handing Wayne a printout.

'I'm not the boss on this one.'

'What? I thought your suspensions had been lifted?'

'It has, but I've had to take a demotion, sad to say.'

'Shit Wayne! That's not fair. So, who's top bitch now? Not that city slicker?'

'Inspector Ben Campbell is indeed in charge of the

investigation.' Wayne's words held a mock haughtiness.

'A man! Seriously? They're putting a man with zero experience at the top of this one,' said Peachy. 'That's political correctness gone way too far.'

'I expect they wanted someone PR savvy, and my joint degree included media studies,' explained Ben, marching into Wayne's office and putting his handbag on her desk.

Wayne eyed her new colleague suspiciously. A night's sleep hadn't done much to improve his appearance. Baker was so off the mark on this one. Campbell was the least attractive bloke Wayne had ever seen and that was saying something. Maybe if he'd put some of that facial hair on his head to mask the thinning top and invest in a good beautician... No! Wayne still couldn't see it. He has nice skin colour, she conceded, but focusing on his wrists, she was immediately drawn to the small dark hairs peeping out from beneath his shirt and she felt like gagging. There was something so wrong about a hairy man.

Forcing her eyes away from the excess hair, for fear she might witness it growing, she stared instead at his feet, his vast feet, covered in plain, black, standard issue, police man brogues. Wayne had never actually seen a pair on someone's feet before, except in the uniform catalogue, where the model wearing them was caked in make-up and a tight-fitting jacket and skirt, to compensate for the plainness of his footwear. Well, however else he got here, he sure as hell didn't sleep his way to the top, Wayne reasoned, and vowed to have it out with Baker the next time they spoke.

Leaning back in her chair, her feet spread carelessly across a desk already weighed down with paperwork, she gave Ben a wide grin. Wayne's beige trench coat was fully open and revealed a once white shirt and some wrinkled black trousers, which had been bought when she was a medium, and now were stretched to bursting beneath her expanding gut. Her cowgirl boots had trodden in a puddle of muck earlier, and there were flakes of dried dirt distorting the fresh scene of crime photos Peachy had placed on the table.

Ben remained standing opposite her, in a clean, pressed grey suit. It was a size twelve and hung off his perfect ten frame, even with a belt pulled tight. He too was wearing a white shirt, but his had been washed and ironed. Ben pulled up one of four folding chairs stacked against a wall and sat down.

'O'Keeffe briefed me this morning. I'm in charge and you'll be assisting me. How do you think that's going to work for you?' Ben asked.

Wayne continued to grin.

'I want us to be able to work together. I appreciate your seniority both in chronological and experience terms and I see us as equals.'

'Only, you're in charge.' Wayne interrupted.

'Yes, equals, with me in charge,' Ben blushed. 'And with that in mind, I'm going to be taking the office over, temporarily, for the duration of the inquiry, if that's okay?' Ben waited for a nod from her.

Wayne's grin didn't waver.

'Right, so if that's clear, then maybe we could swap seats.'

As Wayne removed her boots from the desk, she shook each leg and even more dirt and debris dropped all over the paperwork. She stood up, shook herself again, and came round the opposite side of the desk. Ben, in turn took his seat at the helm and a round of eyeballing began.

'Right,' declared Ben, after his fourth blink, 'I'm calling

an incident meeting at ten-thirty. I thought you could talk us through the first two murders and I'll bring us up to speed on our latest victim.'

'Fine by me,' Wayne said, searching in her pockets for her fags and smiling when she found them.

The incident room at the back of Wayne's tiny office was one of the best and brightest in the decaying building. The previous January, the BBC had commissioned a documentary on rural policing, and Withering had been picked as an archetype. O'Keeffe blew a year's budget on the few areas she granted them access to. The incident room was one such space. Its walls were painted off-white and its floor had been stripped down to wood, and then varnished. The twenty or so chairs scattered around the space were an eclectic mix of colours and styles, thus creating a warmer, homelike feel and *"allowing a more natural flow of creative and intuitive ideas between the team"* as O'Keeffe had told Copper's Digest in an exclusive interview.

The smell of percolated coffee and the sound of a whistling kettle added to the relaxed atmosphere, which was completely at odds with the gruesome photographs that Peachy was pinning to the three free-standing boards at the top of the room. Peachy dropped a pin, and his bend to retrieve it elicited yelps of approval which were silenced by the entrance of Ben. Breathing deeply and walking tall, he strolled to the front of the room, his hands safely in his pockets. He could feel eyes boring into him from every corner.

'Go home, city boy, you're not welcome here,' someone shouted.

'Who said that?' Ben croaked, his eyes darting around

the room.

'It was me,' cried a voice, to his left.

'No, it was me,' said another, from the opposite side.

'Actually, it was me,' said a third.

Ben could feel tears stinging his eyes and he pulled himself swiftly into check. He pitched his voice as high as he could get away with, and addressed the hostile crowd.

'Good morning, I'm Ben Campbell, the Senior Investigating Officer on this case. I'm not from around here, but you give the impression of being a tight-knit unit and that's a good thing. We've been asked to track a very violent, very dangerous serial killer and our team needs to work together to achieve this. Some of you clearly have problems with my appointment, but we are all going to have to overcome those and focus on what's important here: stopping this maniac from doing it again. Our victim yesterday brings the total number of victims to three and means that we are now dealing with a serial killer. As most of you will know, the first two investigations were headed up by D.I. Wayne, who is now going to talk us through them.'

As Wayne stood up the room broke into spontaneous applause. Someone at the back began to chant, "Wayne, Wayne". She grinned, and silenced the supporter with her hand. Wayne pointed to the first photo on the board.

'April the fourth this year, our first victim, Johnny Devlin, was found in a three-bedroom rented house in Meadowfield Road. He had been stabbed several times, but the actual cause of death was strangulation with an unknown instrument. It was thought to be piano wire. He had been posed, face down, on a heavy wooden cross, his hands and feet bound with industrial strength rope. A crucifix had been inserted into his anus. This fact wasn't noted until Baker fully examined him. The rope and wood were common generic brands, difficult to track. We traced the crucifix to a religious relics company in Southern Ireland. They sell ten thousand crosses a month, including to three major suppliers in Withering.'

As Wayne spoke, Ben stared at the crime scene photos. There were over a dozen of Johnny's naked, mutilated corpse.

'Surrounding the victim was a total of thirty-six pages ripped from the Bhagavad Gita, an ancient Hindu text,' Wayne continued. 'A few words and phrases had been highlighted, but the girls at the lab could do nothing with it. Whoever had handled it had been very careful. The victim was a sixteen-year-old prostitute; whose employer we were unable to confirm, though we strongly suspected it was Harriet Hagan. What we did find was his little black book, which was full of names and telephone numbers. A diverse array of clients, including some very important women, were interviewed.'

Wayne paused, and checked her note-pad. 'The victim was originally from London and stayed in a squat off Billington Green, a few miles away from where the body was found. We contacted his father, who hadn't heard from him since he'd remarried when Johnny was thirteen. He was of no help whatsoever, having no idea how or why Johnny wound up in Withering. We brought in the two boys he was sharing a flat with. They were also runaways and too scared to give us anything, even when we threatened them with conspiracy and accessory charges.

In the end, the trail ran cold, until the body of Orlando King was discovered in a house in Clarkston Avenue, two months later, on June the eighteenth. King was a missing person. He'd absconded from his home, also in London, about six months previous.

When his father heard he was in Withering, he said King's mother might be based here. King was the same age as Devlin and the m.o.'s identical. Both boys were found in the exact same freaky pose, surrounded by the same freaky props, right down to the freaky crucifix. We drafted in a much bigger team for the King murder, and had a very promising start when we identified him as one of Hagan's hookers.'

Ben was listening intently. He hated to admit it, but Wayne had a way of collating the information available and summarising it seamlessly. She had condensed the hundreds of pages that he had read the previous evening into a few fact-filled paragraphs. Maybe I should have asked her in last night, he thought. He turned his attention back to the moment, where Wayne was pinning a photograph of Withering's most notorious pimp to the board.

'As most of you will know,' Wayne continued, pointing at the picture, 'Harriet Hagan runs two local strip clubs and a half a dozen massage parlours. She's already done a stretch inside for strangling one of her boys. The problem was the victim had been dead about a week before the body was found and Hagan's passport showed she had been in Croatia for the previous fortnight. We established a list of club regulars and tried to link them to Devlin's clients but we were unable to find any serious matches. We looked at King's mother for a bit. She's a drunkard with a rap sheet, but nothing too major: breach of the peace, domestic violence—'

'Seriously?' Ben interjected.

'Is there a problem, boss?' Wayne asked.

'Domestic violence is a very severe crime, you know that, right?'

'It absolutely is, sir, but I'm sure you can appreciate that if we treated every woman in Withering who'd given their old boy a slap as suspects, there would be a very wide pool. King didn't strike me as a plausible homicidal maniac. She was too messy; her house was too messy. The woman we're looking for never drinks too much, never leaves a dish until morning, never wears a shirt that has not been freshly pressed.'

'What exactly are you basing this on?' Ben scowled.

'Twenty years of senior policing and three crime scenes, where we have found almost zero forensics. I'm guessing yesterday's scene has thrown up nothing?'

'No,' Ben conceded, 'but I won't have you dismiss suspects based on anything less tangible than cold hard facts. This is a triple homicide and the buck stops with me. I want King brought in.'

'Right away, sir, I'll send a car for her now, sir!' As Wayne spoke, she saluted Ben. She gave the nod to one of the team to pick up King, and was rewarded with an imitation salute aimed firmly at Ben.

'Now, where was I?' she asked, and paused to collect her thoughts before carrying on. 'We couldn't find the link between King and the Devlin boy. We worked a lot of leads for the next month or so because O'Keeffe was scared the press might make a connection, and when that didn't happen, resources were very quickly taken away. We had no clear suspects, no clear motive and no influential relatives banging down the door demanding action. We didn't even have any D.N.A. to match against a suspect if we did find them. I was pulled from it to work another case six weeks after the second murder, and fairly soon after that the case was put to one side, considered unsolvable.'

'Which takes us right up to yesterday when the body of Connor Maguire was found in thirty-one Buckstone Avenue,' Ben said, taking the floor from Wayne.

He had a quick glance around the room, hoping to find a sympathetic face to direct his words at. His eyes met Peachy's, and the younger man immediately rolled them upwards. Undeterred, he shifted his gaze to a community policing poster at the back of the room, took a couple of deep breaths, and continued.

'He was strangled to death and then stabbed and defiled anally, post mortem. Also, like previous victims, a number of pages from the Bhagavad Gita were found at the scene, although interestingly, these were placed in a circle round the body. I did a bit of online research last night and the circle is one of the most widely used multi-faith symbols. It can be taken to represent the cycle of life. It is also a recognised symbol for infinity. In Dante's poem, *Inferno*, she speaks about the nine circles of hell. Perhaps our killer is using circles in a similar way.'

Ben's voice could not be heard above the laughter. Wayne was drawing circles with her finger around the side of her head making a *crazy* gesture.

'Inspector Wayne, do you have something you want to share with the group?' He was aiming for angry headmaster voice, but wound up sounding more wounded lover.

'No, I'm good. I'm trying to get my head round all the possibilities. You keep talking, boss.' Wayne made a huge circle with her hands. More laughter erupted.

Ben quietened everyone down. It was as if he was in the wrong changing rooms at the swimming pool.

The rest of the meeting passed in relative calm as Ben talked everyone through the third crime scene. He was very factual and direct, carefully editing his notes as he spoke. Later that day, back home, he'd curse himself for not sticking to his script, but right now he was relieved it was over.

If the incident room was an indication of the public face of Withering police station, then Dr Jackson's office was the blueprint for the private one. Sandwiched between the boiler room and the cold case evidence store in the windowless basement, it was more of a cupboard than an office.

There were four fifties-style filing cabinets taking up over half of the room, leaving no space for average office accessories. Instead there were two folding deck chairs and a couple of boxes from the evidence room to make a table.

Dr Jackson sat silently on one of the chairs, his French manicured hands resting on his leg, right above his knee-length pencil skirt.

Wayne sat opposite him, her bulky frame squeezing into the sides of the deck-chair. She stared at him for as long as she could hold it, and then quickly averted her eyes to his shapely ankles. A thinly-veiled leer spread across her mouth.

Dr Jackson was playing some kind of waiting game and he'd picked the wrong opponent. Years of interrogating arrogant perverts had left Wayne with a considerable advantage and ten minutes of the session had passed before Dr Jackson finally broke the silence.

'So, you've finally made it, this is the fourth session we've booked and the first one you've actually attended. Why do you think that is?'

Wayne shrugged her shoulders like a belligerent teenager.

'You're the shrink, why don't you tell me?'

'Okay,' Dr Jackson said, keeping his voice slow and even, 'I think you're very resistant to the process, Jane. Can I call you Jane?'

'You can call me anything you want, sugar, with a voice that husky.'

'Do you find you do that a lot?'

'What's that now?'

'Make inappropriate sexual comments at men you might otherwise be intimidated by?' Dr Jackson kept his eyes focused on Wayne as he spoke.

'If that's what you're going to write in your report I might as well leave now.' Wayne got up from her seat.

'Let's cut to the chase, Jane. You can't leave. You're not here voluntarily.'

Wayne wavered, trying to decide what to do. She began walking towards the door, but paused as she reached it, turned around and sat back down. She stared at the floor.

'Right, let's start again, shall we? Why don't you tell me a bit about yourself?' He spoke in that low, patronising way psychologists speak.

'You've read my file. Why don't you tell me?' Wayne retorted.

'Do you find you do that a lot?'

'What's that now?'

'Answer straightforward questions sarcastically?'

'Who's being sarcastic? That's your job, isn't it? To form an opinion on my mental capacity. And I'm guessing, a flick through my personnel file and you're half way there.'

'I've never looked at your file.' Dr Jackson's tone was confident.

'You expect me to swallow that?'

'I'm completely indifferent to whether you believe me or not, but I'm telling you the truth.'

'What, so personnel sucked up and you haven't actually got it yet?' Wayne grinned.

'No, I've got it. It's in my bag. But I haven't read it yet. It's how I work. I don't want to come to these sessions with a prejudicial view of a client.'

'So, what? You'll base your findings on what I tell you here?'

'Not quite. It's more about how I interpret what you tell me.'

Wayne nodded, then leaned back in the make-shift chair and gave the doctor a warm smile.

'So why don't you tell me something about yourself, Jane?' Dr Jackson asked.

'I'm a police officer.'

'Okay, that's a start.'

'I don't like talking about my feelings and shit. It's invasive, it's undignified, and it's unhealthy.' Wayne volunteered.

'So what do you like?'

'That's easy, adult porn sites. Straight porn, obviously. And Glenfiddich.' Wayne watched for a reaction from the doctor.

'Ah… I see. You're doing it again. Why do you think you do that, bring the conversation back round to sex? Is it because I'm a man and you think it will embarrass me or make me uncomfortable, thereby helping you regain the power you've lost through having to be here?' Dr Jackson held Wayne's gaze as she spoke, but the barely perceivable deepening of his cheek colour told her she was getting to him.

'Nope. I just like porn and whisky,' Wayne delivered another killer smile.

'Anything else?'

'Catching bad girls. I like making the streets safer.'

'Making the streets safer. Is that what you do?'

'Suck it! I know you've read my file. What does it say? That I'm a danger to my team?' Once again, Wayne was on her feet pacing the tiny patch that lay between her chair and the door.

'Are you? Why would you think it might say that?'

'Look, doll, I've been suspended five times. The only reason I still have a job is because I know more about O'Keeffe than her own father. My personnel file isn't going to be a screaming endorsement of my police methods, is it?'

'Does it bother you, that lack of validation?'

Wayne stopped pacing, and turned to face the doctor. 'My job is validated every time I take some dangerous bitch out of circulation for a while. Of course, then it's up to the Crown Prosecution to do their jobs and they're a bunch of half-wits, but I keep up my end of the bargain. I catch criminals. What some dusty file in a cabinet says about how I catch them, I couldn't care less.' She gave him a sly smile, as she returned to her seat.

'You don't worry that it will ruin your chances of promotion and see you tied to a desk job?'

'What have you heard? What do you know?' Wayne jumped up again.

'Oh for goodness' sake sit down, you're giving me a headache,' Dr Jackson snapped and reluctantly Wayne slid back into her seat. 'Jane, I keep telling you I don't know anything, except what you tell me. Think of me as a mirror that is reflecting your thoughts back to you.'

'What the suck is that supposed to mean?'

'I think you know exactly what I mean, Jane. Let's talk some more about the job. Does it satisfy you?'

'Compared to what? Sitting behind a desk sucking with people's heads? Yeah, I'd say my job's more satisfying than yours.'

'Do you like your colleagues?'

'What kind of dumb question is that? They're cops, for Christ's sake! Who the suck likes cops?' Wayne chuckled.

'Do you find you do that a lot?'

'Do what now?'

'Mask your resentments in humour.'

'I didn't know I did. I thought I was funny,' Wayne explained, laughing some more.

'Do you think you're funny?'

'Well, obviously, you don't!'

'We're not talking about me, Jane. If I met you in the pub, I'm sure you'd make me laugh, but here, in a session, it would be inappropriate for me to do so. Do you understand appropriate behaviour Jane, or do you struggle to find the boundaries?'

'Well, the boundaries are constantly shifting, aren't they, pet?' Wayne leaned in as she spoke, her right-hand hovering above the doctor's exposed knee. 'I mean, what is acceptable now? Is calling you "pet"? Is opening a door for you, you know, if we are leaving at the same time? Is telling you that you have a great pair of legs? You do have a great pair of legs, by the way.' To emphasise her point, she gave them a long, hard stare.

'No, yes and no. Why did you feel the need to comment on my legs?' Dr Jackson's voice did not betray any discomfort he might have felt.

'Why did you feel the need to shave them? For some poor bitch like me to comment on them, so you could tell them that they behaved inappropriately and secretly get off on it?'

'Is that why you think I shave my legs, to generate sexual comments and then to use those comments against the observer to boost my own sexual identity?' Dr Jackson asked.

'Well, you put it better than me, but yeah, else why would you shave?'

'Did you ever consider, Jane, that I might like my legs smooth?'

Big Mamma's was a nasty eyesore of a strip joint on the corner of Withering Main Street, right beside a new branch of the Fair Money Company. Its bright blue walls were peeling and only one of three, neon four-foot, plastic penises in the windows worked, but Big Mamma's clientele didn't come for the decor. At 3p.m. on a weekday, it was more than half full.

Ben suppressed the urge to gag as the overwhelming aroma of sex, sweat and booze filled his nostrils. He surveyed the room and noted the many ages and walks of life represented in the customer base. There were some builders at the bar, still in their work gear, slurping pints and daring each other to approach the strippers. There were a couple of tables of suits next to the main stage, clean-cut banking and lawyer types, one hand on an iPhone, the other rotating between their cunt and their beer bottles. The stage was a half-dozen empty crates in the centre of the room where the waxed, peeled, preened pricks swayed on and off, one at a time, occasionally lingering together during a crossover for a punter-pleasing grope.

'Get your dick out! Get your dick out! Get your dick out for the girls!' chanted a very drunk student. She was sitting with seven equally as drunk class mates, slamming shots of watered-down tequila. The slim, brunette, teenage boy gyrating in front of her unclasped his pra and threw it at the inebriated heckler. She immediately lurched at him, missed her step and fell over. Before she hit the ground a pair of burly bouncers had grabbed either arm and dragged her out of a side door.

'Get your sucking hands off me, you dangerous bitches!' she shouted, as the door swung shut behind them muffling her cries until they eventually fell silent.

'Another day in paradise,' Wayne smiled, hailing the bar boy. 'I'll take a pint of lager and a scotch on the rocks, gorgeous.'

'What do you think you're doing? Is that your pint? You can't drink that on duty,' Ben said.

'You're right,' Wayne agreed, 'Forget this pint, doll. Make it a double scotch. Don't want to be pissing all day, eh?'

Before Ben had a chance to respond, the front door swung open and in walked Harriet Hagan, flanked on either side by two security women. Ben recognised her from the photo. She was bigger in real life, not physically, but the camera couldn't capture her aura or recreate the fear that manifested in her presence. Her strongly defined features suggested she had been a good-looking woman once, but her nose had been broken too often and her face slashed too many times, for her still to be considered handsome. She had straight, silver hair that fell onto the shoulders of her turquoise suede suit. She headed for Ben and Wayne, and he could feel his heart beat accelerate with every step she took. Wayne leaned over and whispered, 'Don't forget, she's a professional thug.'

'Inspector Wayne, we meet again,' said Hagan, smiling.

Ben was taken aback by a set of brand new, gleaming white teeth, completely at odds with her scar-ridden face.

'And who is this lovely ladee?' Hagan continued, running her fingers down the back of Ben's spine.

Wayne leapt from her bar stool, grabbed Hagan's hand and twisted it round her back. At once, her security team pounced. Hagan whistled and they retreated. Wayne continued to keep a firm grip of Hagan's hand.

'Touch one of my team again and I'll break both your hands, got it?' barked Wayne.

'Let her go, Wayne,' Ben ordered.

'I'd listen to him if I were you,' hissed Hagan.

Hagan's breathing was becoming laboured. Wayne released her grip and Hagan spun round, punching her full force in the stomach. Ben jumped forward and Wayne raised her hand quickly.

'It's alright, doll! We're just messing around.' She took two steps back and so did Hagan.

'We need to ask you some questions, Ms Hagan,' Ben said.

'Ask nicely and I might even answer them, but not here, in my office.'

Hagan led them through the bar, past the kitchen and down a flight of stairs. At the bottom, there was a steel door which a security guard unlocked, and they all walked through. Heavy velvet curtains lined the back wall and all light came from a free-standing lampshade beside a woodlice-ridden desk. Hagan took the only seat in the room behind the desk. She stared at Ben, then flashed him her twenty-grand smile.

'That beard you've got there, that's real, eh? There's a niche market in male facial hair. The gals love to piss on it.' She threw back her head and laughed. Ben ignored her and carried on regardless.

'Where were you on Monday morning between the hours of two and four a.m.?' Ben asked.

Hagan shrugged her shoulders and glanced at the door. Ben turned around to see a young, sharply dressed woman enter. She caught his eye and smiled. 'Not started without me, I hope.' She came round the back of Hagan and whispered something.

'Was wondering how long it would take you to raise your sleazy head,' Wayne addressed the newcomer.

'D.C.I. Wayne, we meet again, or should I say D.I.? Sorry to hear about your demotion. Allow me introduce myself,' she turned her attention to Ben, 'I'm Gertrude Green, partner at Grisly, Glass and Green, and Ms Hagan's solicitor.' She extended a long, lean hand and Ben admired her recently manicured fingernails. 'I'll be here for the duration of this interview.'

'No need,' Wayne said, 'It's pretty informal, we're here trying to figure out why boys who work for this cunt licker keep winding up dead.'

'Was there a question in there?' asked Green.

'Where were you Monday morning between two am and four am?' Ben repeated his earlier question.

'You don't have to answer that,' declared Green. Hagan didn't look as if she needed convincing and stayed mute.

'True,' Wayne agreed. 'You don't have to answer anything here, Hagan. We could always go back to the station and…'

'I was here all evening,' Hagan replied.

'Can anyone verify that?' Ben asked.

'Half the staff, I should think. I was out front most of the evening. Dennis wasn't well and someone has to keep the boys' asses moving.'

'What's this about, Inspector?' Green directed her question at Ben. He produced a photograph of Connor from his pocket, and showed it to her.

'Do you know this boy?'

Green handed the photo to Hagan, who shrugged her shoulders. 'How the suck should I know? When you've seen one whore...'

'Does that answer your question, Inspector?' Green smiled.

'No, it doesn't,' Ben replied. 'Once again, I'm asking your client if she knows this boy. His address is listed as a property your client owns.'

'Miss Hagen owns hundreds of properties in this town; she can't be expected to personally know every tenant she rents to.'

'We're not interested in every tenant, just the ones who wind up dead.' Wayne walked slowly over to Hagan's desk and stood behind her. She leaned down and whispered something in her ear.

'Get me Dennis!' Hagan shouted and immediately a security guard exited the room.

She returned with the front of house manager, Dennis De Vell, whose tenuous claims to fame included being runner up in a Master Withering contest. Now, a decade later, he was ageing fast, as the lines around his heavily made-up face conveyed. A fringe hung over his eyelashes in a bid to distract from his forehead. His slim figure clung to a strapless, backless, black mini dress, which barely covered his fishnet suspenders. Years of wearing low pulls had permanently reshaped the heels of his feet, and raw, red blisters were visible through the holes in his stockings. Despite this decay, he was still a beauty and shoulders pulled down, head low, he slinked past the detectives and up behind Hagan. He began stroking the back of her head lightly.

'Hey baby, what can I do for you?'

'Answer these arseholes' questions, so they'll get the suck out of my club.' She pushed Dennis's hand away and stood up. 'I'm done,' she declared. 'Anything you need to know, ask Dennis.' Walking past Ben, she stopped and smiled. 'If you ever tire of the day job, you give me a call, beard boy.'

Dennis sat down on his boss's seat and gave Wayne his brightest smile. Wayne grinned back and handed him the photo of the victim. She watched the smile fade and the colour drain from his cheeks. 'That's Connor. What's happened to him?'

'He was strangled.'

Wayne had not expected her words to have such a crushing effect. Dennis's carefully plastered veneer cracked and he began pounding his fists on the desk. 'Not Connor! Please, not Connor.'

Wayne reached into her pocket and produced a hip flask. She opened it and placed in on the desk. 'Drink it,' she ordered.

He did, in one mouthful, and Wayne was sure he was going to throw the lot right back up, but it stayed down. 'Connor was only a kid, a sucking kid! He wanted out, and he would have done it too. He had a game plan. He wasn't going to get trapped in Hagan's glass bubble. Jess! Connor looks so sucking scared. What did the bitch do to him?'

Dennis fought back tears.

'That's interesting,' Ben said, 'Why do you presume a woman is responsible?'

'Is he for real?' Dennis asked Wayne.

'New, from the city,' Wayne explained. 'Connor was strangled, stabbed, mutilated anally…'

The graphic details proved too much for Dennis, who spewed a bellyful of whisky all over the desk. 'I can't do this right now,' he said, covering his mouth with his hand.

'No,' Wayne agreed. 'Why don't you clean yourself up? Sort yourself out and come down to the station tomorrow morning.'

'Not the station. Are you serious?' Dennis retorted.

'Fair point. There's a café two shops down, called Kenny's, see you there, say nine a.m.?'

Dennis nodded.

'Excuse me,' Ben interrupted. 'But I'm the senior investigating officer on this case. I'll decide where and when we question Master De Vell.'

'Absolutely, boss.'

'That's it for now,' Ben turned to Dennis. 'We'll see you at nine a.m. tomorrow at Kenny's café, down from the station.'

Ben sat in Wayne's office and sipped the tepid, bitter liquid that passed for the station's coffee. He had offered his eldest son, Simon, twenty pounds and a pair of new trainers, in return for a night off from feeding and watching the younger two. Ben wanted to be prepared for the following day. He scanned Baker's report for any detail that might prove helpful. The victim had died relatively quickly. *That was something*, he thought. There was evidence to suggest sexual activity before death, but nothing to indicate it was forced. Ben marvelled at the gynocentric analysis. *So what? This boy had made some kind of informed consent to at least some of the trauma he'd endured.* There was bruising around his hands and ankles, consistent with being tied up for a short period, probably under an hour. The stomach contents were the same as the others, oysters and wine, eaten over two hours before death. There was no trace of vaginal fluid, no flesh or skin under his nails, no body hair at all—either his or belonging to a third party. Frustrated with the lack of leads, he tossed it to one side and began reading Orlando King's Mother's arrest report.

He looked up when he heard a knock on the office window. Gertrude Green was outside. He waved her in and his face flushed as she smiled at him. She was dressed more casually now, than this afternoon. She'd swapped her pinstripe jacket for a navy wool jumper which fitted snugly over her work shirt, her gold cufflinks gleaming against her tanned skin. The tighter clothes accentuated her sculpted frame. She reached into her pockets, found a memory stick and placed it on the desk.

'Sorry to disturb you, Inspector, but I've CCTV footage from Big Mamma's last night. Thought it might help eliminate my client from your inquiries.'

'That's very helpful, Ms Green. But you could have just emailed any information you're willing to share.'

'Please, call me Gertrude, and yes, I could have.' Green grinned at Ben.

Ben took the memory stick and stuck it into the side of his laptop. He was conscious that Green had not left.

'Anything else?'

'Can I buy you a drink?'

Ben flushed a deeper red, 'I don't think that would be

appropriate.'

Green leaned over the desk so that her face was almost touching his. 'Perhaps not,' she whispered. 'But it might be fun.' She stroked the back of Ben's hand and winked.

After she'd left, Ben sat there smirking, drinking in the lingering smell of her expensive cologne. The stench of freshly smoked tobacco brought him back to the present.

'She's using you to get closer to the case.' Wayne had pulled up a folding chair and was straddling it back to front.

'Haven't you heard of knocking?' Ben asked.

'Sorry boss, force of habit. Anyway, like I said, she'll be using you, she'll know that you're…' Wayne paused.

'That I'm what, Wayne?' Ben snapped, gripping the edge of the desk.

'That you're new and she'll think that makes you an easy target.'

'Like you do?' Ben replied.

THREE

WEDNESDAY

She leaned back in her chair and closed her eyes, massaging her forehead slowly. Standing up and walking to the door of her study she opened it slightly and stood listening for signs of life outside. Satisfied she was alone, she locked the door from the inside and double bolted it. Coming back round behind her desk, she groped beneath it for her laptop, which was strapped under a drawer. She took it out and turned it on. Waiting for it to connect, she stroked the family portrait that sat facing her. She stared hard at the young girl in the centre, searching for any traces of her old self that might remain; there were none. Good. She turned her attention back to her computer. The heavily encrypted command was routed through eleven random servers scattered across the world, before connecting her to her account. Clicking her mouse over the username, she typed the letter W.

Wayne stood under the café's canopy and finished her spliff. She checked her phone. It was nine-twenty. The boys were both late, but that was men for you. She went in, grateful to have found a refuge from the downpour that had started.

Kenny's café had been a mainstay in her life as long as she'd been with the force. It was as rundown and haggard as she felt most mornings, and she found this comforting. She squeezed herself into her usual booth next to the kitchen.

'Here, Kenny, are these tables getting smaller?' she

asked as the owner glided by, carrying three big breakfasts to table four.

'What do expect? We're in a recession,' Kenny laughed swirling past, picking up two more plates from the kitchen and depositing them with the others.

Within seconds he was back, standing over Wayne, his carefully made-up brow barely breaking sweat. He beamed at her. 'The usual?'

'Yeah, and a big pot of tea. Bring two extra mugs.' Kenny scrawled the order in his book, shouted it into kitchen and scuttled off to make the tea, almost crashing into a barely recognisable Dennis. Stripped of the war paint, his hair pulled into a ponytail, and his desirable frame covered in a velour tracksuit. He looked pretty much like the boy next door, although sadly, not next door to any house Wayne had ever lived in.

'Sorry I'm late,' he panted.

'A man's prerogative,' Wayne smiled. 'Tea?'

Dennis nodded and took a seat beside her.

'It's a shit day, eh?'

Dennis nodded again.

'You're not from round here,' Wayne continued, 'The accent?'

'Devon,' said Dennis.

'Devon. You know, I've always fancied a holiday in Devon, as near as you can be to France without ever leaving the Motherland. Did you like it there?'

'Not especially.' A lock of hair had fallen from Dennis's ponytail and he twirled it around his finger.

Kenny had returned with Wayne's usual, the big brunch: as much meat as could be respectably eaten at either breakfast or lunch merged into one carni-feast. Wayne sniffed the bacon and ran her knife down the seven-inch rib-eye steak that sat between two fried eggs and three pork sausages. Two slices of fried tomato rested on two bands of black pudding and Wayne tossed them to the side before devouring both pudding pieces in a couple of mouthfuls.

She looked up, her mouth still chewing, and caught a look of disgust on Dennis's face. Wayne closed her mouth and swallowed before speaking.

'Sorry, I haven't eaten since yesterday afternoon. Are you hungry?'

Dennis shook his head. Wayne continued to wolf down her food like it was her last meal, and Dennis stirred his tea between sips.

'So, how did you end up living in Withering then? A woman, I suppose?'

'Isn't it always?' Dennis gave her a wry smile.

'But you're not with her now?'

'I wasn't even with her then,' Dennis replied, 'I got here and realised she was married and wanted me to stay in her sister's attic so she could suck me at weekends.'

'Why not get the next bus home?' Wayne asked.

'I only had enough for a one-way ticket. Look, what's with all the questions about my past? Am I a suspect or something?'

'Just making conversation.' Wayne shoved the last bit of steak into her mouth and washed it down with a mouthful of tea.

Dennis eyed Wayne up and down. 'Yeah, well, I'm not here on a social call. Don't you want to ask me about Connor or Hagan or something?'

'Would you tell me the truth if I did?'

Dennis thought for a moment before delivering a one

word reply 'No.'

Ben checked under the two cubicle doors to ensure he was alone in the station's toilets. He leaned his head against the wall and wept like a child. He'd had another showdown with Val at the school gates, only this time it was longer and messier. When she'd finally realised her dad was leaving without her, she threw her morning milk over his trousers. He'd returned home to change, but he hadn't showered again and he felt sticky and smelly. He also felt completely useless. Ben was so shit at this single parenting.

He wondered if he should give the school a call, but he didn't want to come across as one of those neurotic dads. Val's teacher had already got a dig in about the hours he was working, and how that might impact on his daughter's state of mind. Ben would be willing to bet he'd never say that to one of the mums. He splashed some water on his face and liberally sprayed deodorant under his arms and down his pants. He was even stickier now.

Ben stole a quick glance in the mirror and satisfied himself that he didn't look as crazy as he felt. With a shrug, he pulled himself up, took a couple of deep breaths and went in search of Wayne.

He didn't have far to look. She was sitting in her office, which was of course actually his office, scrolling through the horse racing pages of the *Withering Chronicle*.

'Find anything interesting?' he asked her, his voice thick with sarcasm.

'I've got a tip. Blue Monday, running at 3.30,' Wayne replied. 'It's a long shot, but my source seems fairly certain Will I put you down for a fiver?'

Ben ignored the suggestion. 'I'd like my seat back, please,' he said and waited whilst Wayne hauled herself off it.

'Where were you? I went to Kenny's café.' Ben turned the chair back round before sitting in it.

'We'd finished up, so I let the lad go, that was after ten o'clock. I couldn't expect him to hang around all morning, could I?'

'No, I suppose not.' Ben conceded.

'The kids hold you up?' Wayne asked him.

'My kids are none of your business,' Ben snapped. 'I was actually giving O'Keeffe a progress report, if you must know.'

'On the golf course? You made it back in good time then. Usually takes a couple of hours to get from there to here, and that's not counting morning traffic.'

Ben could feel his cheeks burn and quickly changed the subject. 'What did Dennis De Vell have to say for himself?'

'He actually prefers it here to Devon, can you believe that?'

'About the case, Wayne,' Ben struggled to keep his patience.

'Not a lot,' Wayne replied. 'Look, Campbell, these boys never talk, and if they do, it's never the truth.'

'I see,' Ben said. 'So why did you meet him again?'

'Because he's a real looker and it's not often I get to have breakfast with someone that gorgeous,' she grinned. Ben threw Wayne the look he usually reserved for the kids when they swore. 'What about King?' he asked.

'She's been in the cells overnight. I'll get Peachy to bring her up,' Wayne replied.

Walking into the windowless interrogation room, Wayne

was hit by the stench of stale vomit and bad personal hygiene. The small, square space had only a tiny vent beside the skirting board through which fresh air could circulate. King was slumped forward on the table, but sat up immediately when Wayne entered the room.

'I need a drink,' she croaked.

'Don't we all?' Wayne replied. 'But this isn't a bar, it's a police station.'

'I've got to have a drink, please,' King begged, her shaky hand tugging at Wayne's arm.

Wayne turned to Peachy and instructed him to get them both coffees. When she was sure they were alone, she pulled a hip flask from the inside pocket of her trench coat and handed it to a grateful King. She had just retrieved it when Ben walked in, laden down with files. He was followed by Peachy, carrying two plastic cups of lukewarm station coffee, who placed one in front of Wayne, and the other in front of the suspect. King's Dutch courage had kicked in and she knocked the cup on the floor and began shouting.

'This is bullshit- police harassment and bullshit. I'm the sucking victim here! I lost my child, my boy, and this is how you treat me.' Anger flashed in her blood shot eyes.

'Okay, Nancy, take it easy and sit back down there. Let's have less of the sad stories or I'll have to hire a violinist,' Wayne cut in. 'This isn't police harassment, this is protocol. You, Nancy King, have a history of violence against men, especially family members. Your son was the victim of a violent death. We would be remiss in our duty if we weren't treating you as a suspect.'

'Look, I might have been a bit handy with my fists with Orlando's dad, but you didn't know him. He was a whore to live with, drove me crazier by the hour.'

Wayne nodded.

'That's why I left,' King continued. 'Because if I'd stayed, I would have killed the cock.' She looked pleadingly at Wayne.

'Interesting choice of words,' Ben spoke for the first time.

'Ah, look,' King said. 'I didn't mean it like that, I'd never have killed him. I couldn't kill anyone, I'm not that sort.'

'But you're the sort to beat up a man,' Ben said, staring at King's lengthy charge sheet.

'Where were you on Monday morning between two and four a.m.?' Wayne interrupted, anxious to move the conversation on.

King shrugged her shoulders.

'What day is it?' she asked.

'It's Wednesday,' Wayne replied.

King nodded but didn't speak.

'How about the days before June 18th when your son's body was discovered. Do you remember where you were then? Wayne asked her.

'I'll have told you all this at the time. I was pissed, wasn't I? I'm a pisshead not a murderer.' King licked her dry lips.

'How about April 4th this year, where were you then?' Wayne continued.

King moaned before slumping back down on the table and closing her eyes. Suddenly, she jerked her head back up. 'This Sunday night?' she asked Wayne. 'The one that's just gone by?'

Wayne nodded.

'I was in here,' she smirked. 'Got into a bit of trouble at The Ferrywoman Inn and your girls picked me up before closing. They wouldn't let me out till the next day.'

Wayne's eyes followed the charge sheet to the last entry, which confirmed King's story. She was so happy she could have kissed the drunken fool. Wayne could get out of this stinking pit, have a smoke, and move on to real suspects. 'Right, you can go,' she told her.

'Thanks,' smiled King. 'Thank you, ma'am, thank you, sir, you won't regret it. I'm not the one you're looking for; you're wasting your time with me.'

'Not so fast,' Ben said. He tapped the door and waited for Peachy to come in. 'Take her back to holding. We'll speak to her again later,' he instructed the junior officer.

'What?' howled King. 'This is bullshit! Absolute bullshit! Tell him, Wayne, he can't do this to me, I've got rights! Tell him, Wayne.'

'You can't hold her indefinitely on account of her hitting her old man,' Wayne said when Peachy had dragged King away.

'More's the pity,' Ben replied.

Ben turned left into Hovenbath, the sprawling council estate that Connor McGuire had called home. It was one of three high-rise flats, built within a stone's throw of each other on the outskirts of the town. At its peak occupancy, it had housed over a thousand people in under thirty-thousand square metres. These days, there were several derelict flats, boarded up, and the top ten floors of Marriot Court had been evacuated for health and safety, but it was still home to hundreds of tenants. They stood at the entrance to Winifred View. The metal door was open, the security lock no longer working. Wayne lit a cigarette as they entered the draughty corridor.

'You can't smoke inside,' Ben frowned.

Wayne laughed and inhaled. *All pigs are scum* read the graffiti beside the lift. Ben pressed the button and they waited. After five minutes, it became clear that the lift wasn't coming. The twelve-storey stair climb really took it out of Wayne. As Ben hopped sprightly from floor to floor, she dragged herself heaving behind. By the time they reached the last floor, she was sweating and shaking. She coughed for a full two minutes and filled her hanky with mucus and phlegm.

'You alright?' Ben asked.

'Never better,' Wayne replied, before being seized by another fit of coughing. They stood outside 12/4 and knocked hard several times. The music blaring inside was turned down, but nobody answered.

'I can kick it in,' suggested Wayne. Ben looked at his overweight partner, still panting. He slid to the ground and began shouting through the letterbox.

'We know there's someone in there. We're officers investigating the death of your flatmate, Connor. We're not here to arrest you and we're not interested in any crimes you've committed. We're here to find whoever hurt Connor and stop them from hurting another boy.'

Ben could hear footsteps along the hall and the chains being undone. The door was opened by a dark-skinned beauty. His messy brunette mop framed his fresh, young face as he smiled nervously at his visitors. *Even plastered in make-up this kid wouldn't look legal*, Ben thought. *That was probably the point.* He was wearing a red woolly top that stopped at his midriff and a pair of praless, sheer black, see through knickers, which left nothing to the imagination.

'Come in,' he said, leading them through to a dingy living room, where the only furniture was a tattered second-hand sofa and a table littered with empty cans of cheap lager and half-eaten takeaways. The carpet seemed to serve as one big ashtray and the place stank like a nightclub toilet on a Saturday night.

'Have a seat,' he offered, kicking some cans and a pizza box off the couch.

'We're good standing,' replied Ben. 'We'll wait here if you want to go upstairs and change.'

'I'm fine, thanks.'

Wayne grinned at him. 'So, what do they call you?'

The boy stared at his feet as he answered, 'Jeff Stone.'

'Have you heard what happened to Connor?' Ben asked.

Jeff looked at Ben and nodded slowly, his terrified face betraying his attempt to act cool. 'Hagan came round and told us.'

'Did she indeed? And did she warn you off speaking to us?'

Jeff focused on the floor.

'Tell us about him, Jeff. What kind of flat mate was he? Did you like him?' The questions came from Wayne.

'He was cool. He was kind. Yeah, I liked him. He wasn't really like the others. He had a plan, you know. He was saving money to get back to London, to get a house, and get his kid back. Social took his kid, and the only thing he cared about was getting her back. Amy, that's what he'd called her.'

'So he had money saved? Where did he keep it? Who besides you knew about it?' Ben spoke so fast the questions ran into each other. He could feel Wayne's eyes boring into him.

'Don't worry about the money, doll, that's not important. Why don't you tell us some more about Connor?' Wayne cut in. 'Did he have any friends? A girlfriend?'

Jeff hesitated and Wayne seized upon it, grabbing him by the shoulders. 'Who was she, Jeff? You don't want us to start asking you about the money again, do you?'

Jeff pulled away from her before replying. 'Look, woman, I don't know who she was, he wouldn't tell me. She was older, eh? Had her own house and that. Connor didn't say much, but you could tell he was into her. He had this stupid grin on his face all the time and he'd spend hours practising his make-up and planning what he'd wear when they eventually met up. I told him he was a fool. "*The bitch is married,*" I said. "*That's why she's dating you on Skylark.*" But he just laughed at me. He said she wasn't his girlfriend and he didn't care if she was married. It was all front though, the boy had it bad. There was no use talking to him.'

'Was there anything else he told you? Can you remember a name? An address? A place they used to meet?' Ben asked.

Jeff thought for a minute then shook his head. 'They didn't ever meet, I don't think, just online, and he definitely never told me her name. I asked a few times and he told me to mind my own.'

Ben stood outside the flats looking at his partner. Wayne was clutching her chest; the twelve flight descent having taken its toll.

'How the hell did you ever pass a fitness test?'

'I know Kelly,' Wayne wheezed. 'The examiner.'

'We'll need to get the tech team onto Skylark.'

'What the suck is that?' Wayne demanded.

'Skylark's a social media site for teenagers. My two are on it.'

'And a tech team, what's that?'

'You're joking, right?' Ben paled.

'We don't get much call for technical knowhow in these parts. Florence from the fraud squad has some kind of computing degree; we normally ask her if we need a bit of extra help.'

Ben opened his mouth to reply, but found himself lost for words.

Ben reread the letter in his handbag and took a few deep breaths. He was sitting in the car park of Withering High. This was the second time in three days that his home life had invaded work time, *hardly a great start!* Ben had left Wayne back at the station and mumbled something about needing air, before racing across town in lunch-time traffic. He stepped out of the car and walked towards the school's front door. Ben announced himself and was sent to a classroom on the second floor. He knocked and was instructed to wait outside. His heart skipped at the sternness of the order and he retreated to the opposite wall, as if he was a school child again.

He hated these talks. There had been so many in recent years. Different schools, same conversation. *"I'm concerned your children don't have enough female influence in their lives."* Ben had heard variations of this theme half a dozen times. He'd never quite got the logic behind it. Surely, it was excessive female influence that was causing all the problems? If he hadn't conspired for years to lie to his children about what their mother was actually like, then the shock when they found out wouldn't have sent them crash landing straight into denial. *Our good mother, the one you've built up all these years, rationalising her selfishness and minimising her faults, she would never voluntarily leave us. Therefore, father, it is you who made her go. It is your fault, present parent.*

'Mister Campbell, please do come in.'

Sara Singh was a short, wiry, middle-aged woman with bad skin and hideous clothes. She was wearing a multi-coloured shirt under a hand-knitted beige cardigan, which had pockets filled to overflowing with used tissues. Her once black trousers had faded to a dirty grey and were too short for her. Ben did a double take when he clocked the mismatched socks—one navy, one black—bulging out of a pair of Jess sandals. She ushered him into her classroom and closed the door quietly. Singh's habitat was in keeping with her scatty appearance. She indicated to Ben to have a seat opposite her, seemingly unaware that it was stacked high with year 10's projects.

'Sorry,' she said, as Ben continued to stand. She removed the papers and piled them unevenly next to the desk. 'Thanks for coming in, Mister Campbell. I'm Sara Singh, Simon and Drea's Guidance teacher. I've asked you here today to have a little chat about Simon. How does that feel to us? Are we okay with that?'

'Yes,' Ben replied, scanning the room to see who else she might be talking to. 'I'm actually quite busy, so can I ask what the problem is?'

'We don't like to use the word "problem" at Withering High, Mister Campbell. We prefer the word "opportunity".'

'Right,' he sighed.

'This is a great *opportunity* for us to consider where Simon is, ask how he got there, and see how we might get him back on track.' Singh employed sign language to emphasise her verbs. Her finishing gesture was to swoop her two hands inwards, join them and then bring them to rest on her table. 'How do we feel about that, Mister Campbell?'

Ben had no idea how "we" should respond, so he didn't.

'Simon wrote an assessment paper last week that

seemed, to me, to be a cry for help.' As she spoke Singh brought her hand to her eye as if to wipe away a tear, and Ben felt an overwhelming urge to punch her in the face. The aforementioned paper was produced and Ben carefully read the highlighted text.

Where I will be in five years by Simon Campbell
Damaged.
Depressed.
Dealing.
Dead.
Don't know...

Ben resisted the urge to laugh. He looked up to see Singh staring at him intently, an expression of disproportionate concern on her face. 'What do we think, Mister Campbell?' 'Well, he's a teenage boy, prone to acts of rebellion, isn't he? When I was his age I was smoking round the bike sheds, sneaking mascara into schools...' Ben's voice trailed off as he felt the weight of Singh's disapproving stare. 'What I mean, Ms Singh, is that it doesn't strike me as that serious.'

'Ah, doesn't it?' Singh asked, shaking her head.

'I'll look into it, Ms Singh. Thank you for bringing it to my attention. I'll deal with it, severely, I assure you.'

Wayne was in her office on the phone. She motioned Ben to come in. She was scrawling frantically on her notepad.

Ben coughed loudly. 'Have you forgotten this is my office now?'

'Sorry, boss,' Wayne said, putting her hand over the receiver. 'I won't be much longer. Right, so that's a blue 2007 Fiesta reg no TE 49 63. Cheers, Brian. I appreciate it.'

'A fresh lead?' Ben asked.

'What? No. It's a car I want for my Aunt Stella. Brian runs the police auction. I just wanted to make sure I got first dibs.'

'So, you're trying to manipulate what should be a transparent public service, in order to secure a cheap car?' Ben threw his eyes up to heaven.

'You should have a look at their website,' Wayne suggested. 'They've got all kinds of shit you wouldn't believe. They've got clothes, jewellery, interior furnishings, garden stuff. They even had a plane once. A sucking plane! Can you imagine that at a police auction?'

'Have you actually done any work since you got back? Where are we on the rented properties?' Ben asked.

'It's Rita Ryan's agency that deals with it, the same as the last two.'

'Right, let's go and talk to her.'

'She's ninety-seven, boss. I'm not sure she'll be of much help to us.' Wayne replied.

'So who's running the agency then?'

'Her two sons, Ronnie and Reggie. Well, Ronnie mostly, Reggie's a bit... Look, they're both nearly pensioners themselves. I don't see them being tied up in this.'

'Well they are, Wayne,' Ben said. 'Whether you see it or not, people keep getting killed in their properties.'

A new message popped up on the screen and she smiled. That was three he'd sent in as many minutes. He was becoming keener with every communication. Another one flashed and she started to laugh. This was too easy. She changed her status to "off screen" and imagined his cheaply made-up face crumpling with disappointment. She laughed some more. She checked her watch; dinner would be served in minutes. She quickly logged out and put her computer away safely. She was still laughing as she turned off the light and locked her door from the outside.

The Ryans lived in a converted town house over their estate agency on Duchess Street. Despite owning several coveted properties in Withering and beyond, the simple two bed-room flat best suited their needs. It allowed Ronnie, the only fully functioning family member, to run the business and keep an eye on the household. Wayne sat on the edge of the table in their cramped living room, having surrendered the only vacant seat to Ben. She looked from the elderly lady to her two sons and tried to imagine a trio of people less likely to be involved in violent crime.

Reggie sat opposite her, in an armchair next to his mother, his ample frame spilling out over the sides. Wayne didn't know what the politically correct term for someone like Reggie was, but he was definitely not the full shilling. He was dressed in grey tracksuit pants and an oversized T-shirt, which was probably white when he'd put it on, but now it carried the yellow of his breakfast egg and the presumption that his lunch had been tomato-based. He had several cheap costume bangles on either arm and he seemed content just staring at them. Ronnie, in contrast, was tall and elegant, even at seventy he cut an impressive figure, dressed immaculately in a pale pink dress and a snug fitting lilac jacket. His only jewellery was a sapphire brooch in the shape of a rose. He floated seamlessly around the tiny space, handing his guests delicate china cups of tea, then passing them a plate laden with chocolate digestives and Mrs Kipling's fondant fancies.

'We would have got something in, if we knew you were coming,' he said.

'There's plenty here,' Wayne assured him, helping herself to a Jammie Dodger.

'So what's all this about?' The question came from Rita Ryan, who was sitting in her wheelchair. Her frail body was held together by two patterned throws, so that only a shrinking head attached to a scrawny neck was visible. Despite almost being a centenarian, Rita Ryan's mind was still sound. Wayne had realised as much when she'd called to see the family after the first murder. On that visit, she had addressed her questions to Ronnie and felt the sharp end of the old woman's tongue for not including her.

'There's been another murder, Ms Ryan,' Wayne raised her voice as she spoke.

'Another? Father of God, how many is that now?'

'That's three, Mum,' Ronnie said, positioning himself behind her chair and patting her head gently.

'Stop fussing man!' Ryan snapped at her son before turning her attention back to Wayne. 'Why are they using our properties?'

'That's what we'd like to ask you,' Ben said.

'You can't think we have anything to do with these...' Ronnie paused before finishing, 'murders.'

'Of course we don't, Ronnie. We just have to cover all bases.' Wayne resisted the urge to laugh.

'Who holds the keys for your properties?' Ben asked.

'Well, I do, of course,' Ronnie replied.

'And who else? What about work-women? Other staff?' Ben continued. 'Your Mother?'

Ronnie looked from his frail mother to Ben and back again. He made no attempt to hide his distain. 'We have a boy that helps me run the shop, Billy Hart, but he deals with walk-in customers and telephone enquiries. I hold all the keys and I conduct all the viewings. When we need work done, I hire the staff. We normally use the same people, and I let them in to a property and lock up when they leave. I am the only key holder.' Ronnie placed great emphasis on the last sentence, as if to dare anyone in the room to suggest he had played any part in these heinous crimes.

'We're going to need a list of all the people you use and we're going to need to talk to Billy Hart,' Ben said.

'I've already got that list, boss, and a statement from Billy,' Wayne addressed Ben whilst giving Ronnie a reassuring look. He was really quite fit for his age, and if he wasn't part of the enquiry, she would have been tempted to slip him her number.

'We'll need another one now, in light of the latest murder. Don't you think?' Ben spoke like he was addressing a young child.

No! Wayne didn't think there was anything to be gained from talking to Billy again. He'd been overweight and overwrought during the previous interview and unless he'd spent the last six months at Weight Watchers, she could see no purpose in having another conversation. 'I'll get right on it,' she told Ben.

'Billy's not in today, Inspector,' Ronnie said. 'He works Monday, Tuesday and a half-day Friday. I'll get you his home address, if you like.'

After the stifling heat of the Ryan's flat, it was a relief to step out into the fresh air. The heavy rain from earlier had trailed off to a light drizzle. Turning her face upwards, Wayne basked in the cool flecks of water.

'I told you the Ryan's had nothing to do with this.' She

gave Ben a smug look as she spoke.

'Maybe not,' Ben conceded.

The temperature had dropped considerably by the time Wayne returned to Hovenbath, later that evening. She'd almost passed out from the exertion of a second stair climb and had taken a ten-minute rest when she got to the top. Now, as her heartbeat returned to normal, she became aware of the cold night air and pulled her trench coat around her shoulders, as she pressed the front doorbell. She kept her finger on it until she heard movement inside.

'What the suck?' A bleary-eyed Jeff pulled the door open and looked at her. He had just woken up and was wearing a lacy red G-string and a scowl. Wayne grinned at him.

'Can I come in?' She asked, wedging her foot in the door.

'Do I have a choice?'

'Good boy,' Wayne said strolling past him and into the living room. There was a half-smoked joint in the ashtray. Wayne picked it up and sniffed it. 'Who owns this?'

Jeff shrugged his shoulders.

'Then you won't mind if I smoke it, will you?' Wayne lit the spliff and inhaled deeply. A fit of coughing ensued. 'Sucking soap bar!' she spluttered. 'It should be illegal to sell shit like this.'

'It already is,' said Jeff, laughing. 'Anyway, if you don't want it, give it here.'

'Not so fast.' She took another couple of hard draws and handed the joint to the teenager. Jeff stroked Wayne's fingers lightly as he accepted the smoke. Wayne acted like she hadn't noticed. She reached into her pocket and took out a bundle of neatly folded twenty-pound notes, freshly drawn from a bank machine, and handed them to Jeff. He grabbed them and began counting them furiously. There were fifteen notes in total making three hundred pounds. His eyes lit up as he zipped it in the inside pocket of his handbag. He smiled at Wayne and pressed his tight young limbs against the ageing inspector's torso.

'What do you want for it?' he asked, stroking Wayne's inner thigh.

'No!' said Wayne, pushing Jeff off quickly, trying to silence her first groans of arousal.

'So, what are you after?' Jeff asked. 'Everyone wants something.'

Wayne smiled. 'You're right, they do. I want you on the first bus back to London.'

'Why?'

'Look, kid, there's a bad bitch out there killing prostitutes—and you're a prostitute.'

'I'm a dancer.'

'Course you are, doll,' agreed Wayne. 'So, there's a bad bitch out there killing dancers, maybe now's as good a time as any to head back to the big city and see if Daddy hasn't been missing you.'

'That doped-out suck won't even have noticed I was gone.'

'What about friends? You must have some friends you could stay with?' Wayne asked.

Jeff gave her a cynical smile. 'You've never lived in London, have you?'

'No,' admitted Wayne. 'I planned to, but the best-laid plans of mice and women... What about other relatives? You must know someone else there?'

'Uncle Tim. He used to take me whenever Dad would get arrested for shoplifting. But they fell out over Dad's girlfriend, Lisa. She was one violent bitch and I haven't seen my Uncle Tim in years. Don't even know where he stays now.'

Wayne handed him her notepad. 'Give me his surname and his last known address and I'll have one of the girls check it out for you.'

'He's got three kids of his own. He's not going to have space for me.'

'Well, why don't we start by finding out where your uncle is now, and then we can take it from there?'

'Why are you doing this?'

'Why does anyone do anything in this life?' Wayne asked.

'Because they want sex or money.' Jeff's face was deadpan.

'Or atonement,' added Wayne.

She stepped out of the shower and shook herself like a dog, spraying water all over the white marble tiles. She lathered her wet body in a layer of shaving gel and ran a steel razor from her toes to her neck in focused, deft movements. Satisfied that she was hairless, she began cutting her toe nails and then her fingernails down to stumps. Watching the clippings slip down the plughole, she stepped back into the streaming water and washed all the gel and hair away. Grabbing an Egyptian-cotton towel from the rack she rubbed herself down, before wrapping herself in a silk bathrobe. Her feet sank into the deep pile of her bedroom carpet.

Although she'd locked the door before heading into her en-suite, she checked it was still locked. She opened her walk-in wardrobe and felt for a panel at the back. Carefully, she lifted it off and took out a black rucksack, emptying its contents onto her bed. She stroked the bound book and ran her fingers over the duct tape, the knife, and the cheap crucifix. Closing

*her eyes, she anticipated her next kill. She groaned to herself
and her hand fell involuntarily to her hairless cunt.*

Ben sprinkled the last of the cheese over the cooked pasta
and placed it in the middle shelf of the oven. Almost
immediately the fire alarm went off. He waved the tea towel
frantically over the white box in an unsuccessful attempt to
stop the beeping.

'Here, let me!' Drea swung the sweeping brush into the
alarm, sending it straight to the floor, where it narrowly
missed hitting Simon on the head.

'What the hell, Drea? Those things cost money,' Ben
snapped.

'It was doing my head in!' Drea stormed out of the
kitchen and upstairs, banging every door along the way.

'Where are you going?' he shouted after her. 'I'm making
macaroni cheese for tea.'

'Are you going to let her knock the house down because
she's having her period? There's no way I'd get away with
that if I had a period,' said Simon.

'I know, son. If men had periods, we'd have to apologise
for them.'

Simon opened the fridge door and began browsing
the shelves. Ben looked at the outline of his only son. His
tight white shirt and navy school skirt accentuated his
blooming hips and shoulders. He was tall like Ben, but
he'd perfected the hunchback look, it took two inches off
him, and that was without low pulls, which Ben flat out
refused to buy him. His long dark hair was piled high in a
loose bun, allowing his pretty face to be fully seen. Simon
closed the fridge door empty-handed and pouted at his
dad.

'Why do we never have any decent food in this house?'

'Why have you been writing rebellious poetry in your careers class?' Ben countered.

'So, Singh phoned you. She said she would. You've met her, Dad. Would you take advice from her?'

'It's Ms Singh, Simon and don't be cheeky! It's a valid question, where do you see yourself in five years' time?'

'Maybe I could be a writer.' Simon hesitated. 'Like Mum?'

'I see, so of all the individuals and life paths you might emulate, your preferred one is to follow in the steps of an infantile, manising, child-deserting, cowardly loser like your mother!'

Simon's face fell and his big brown eyes blinked back tears. He retreated from the kitchen, banging the doors harder than Drea had.

'Suck you, Dad!'

'Simon, I'm sorry!' Ben called after him. 'I'm an idiot, please come back. I've made macaroni cheese for tea.'

Ben sighed and went in search of his remaining child. He found her curled up on the sofa under two big cushions.

'Hi, Val.' He kissed her gently on the forehead and noticed she felt a bit hot.

'I don't feel well,' she said.

'No? But I've made your favourite: macaroni cheese.'

Val shook her head. Ben felt her face again. He stripped her to her pants and went in search of a thermometer and some junior paracetamol. But by the time he returned, she was sleeping. He closed the curtains and opened a window, then plated up pasta for one and hit the remote.

The end strains of *Celebrity Pet Swap* woke him up. Instinctively, he reached over to Val, and jumped up like he'd been bitten when he felt the heat from her body. Jess Christ, she was on fire! He groped around his pockets for his phone. It wasn't there. The sofa. He pulled up the cushion and thrust his hand down the back, locating it wedged into a corner.

'Val!' he shouted, whilst punching in three digits. He shook her, and pulled her face up and shook her again. He picked her up and held her tight.

'Emergency services. How can we direct your call?'

He couldn't speak. He had his child in his arms and she wouldn't wake up. He didn't hear Drea enter the room. She looked from her father to her sister and held out her hand. 'Dad, give me the phone!'

The ambulance drive to the hospital was like an out-of-body experience. Ben sat clutching Val as paramedics worked around them. Someone stuck a drip on to the back of her hand and someone else wrapped her body in a thermal blanket. They were shouting orders between them in a language Ben no longer spoke. He could only see the vastness of their hands against her tiny frame and the mania of their movements as she lay so still.

'What's her blood type, sir?' the paramedic repeated.

Ben registered the question and shook his head.

'I don't know.' *What kind of father doesn't know his own kid's blood type?* He could feel their eyes bore into him.

'Sir, you're going to have to let her go now. We're going to have to get her inside.'

Ben was vaguely aware that the ambulance had stopped moving. The doors opened as the panic mounted. There was a loud bang as the trolley hit the ground.

'Be sucking careful with her!'

He felt an arm around his shoulder. It was Simon.

'How the hell did you get here?'

'We got a taxi.' He handed his dad his handbag.

'It's okay, Dad. Let's just all get inside.' Drea came around his other side and the family followed the paramedics down the winding hospital corridors.

FOUR

TWO WEEKS LATER

MONDAY

'Thirty, thirty-one, thirty-two...' Leo counted to himself, bringing his chin to his knees and allowing his tight, taut buttock muscles to relax.

Staring into his wardrobe's full length mirror he pinched the flesh of his flat stomach between with his thumb and forefinger and swore. He was still a fat pig. Maybe he should try it again, only he couldn't be sucked, and besides, it would take a lot more than another thirty sit ups to shift the mountain of lard where his waist should be.

He lay on the floor and stared at the mural on his ceiling. There was a sprawling grey castle on one side, and a beautiful prince with long flowing locks, and a much neater waist than his, running happily through lush grass and brightly coloured flowers, spread across the other. He was too old for it now, but he kept finding excuses so his folks didn't paint over it.

He was so tired he could have done with a sleep, but there was no time for that. He leapt up and hastily threw his overnight things together, before squeezing them into his school rucksack. He touched up his face, ran a brush through his hair, then grabbed his stuff.

Downstairs, his stepmum was juggling feeding a baby and frying mince. His dad was back teaching two evenings a week, leaving her in charge of domesticity. He slipped out of his bedroom door and snuck on to the landing, watching the hapless Rachel burn tea, again. When her back was turned, he made a dash for the front door and would have exited unheard, had baby Kelly not thrown her bowl of mashed banana across the kitchen floor, into the hall where he stood.

'For crying out loud, Kells!' his stepmum snapped, retrieving the bowl. She jumped when she noticed Leo. 'What the hell are you doing now? I thought you were upstairs doing an online tutorial.'

'I need help, so I'm going round to Victor's.'

Rachael Stern eyed her stepson up and down. He was wearing a pair of black, plastic boots that pulled two inches off his height and the knee-length green coat that had been his main Christmas present. He had more make-up on than the promotions boy at Shoes the chemist.

'There's no way you're planning to study anything dressed like that Leo. I think you should go back upstairs and see what your dad says when he gets home.'

'No can do,' Leo replied 'I need to go now.'

'Leo, you're not listening, I forbid you to leave this house.'

Leo turned the lock on the door and walked out. He was still laughing as he reached the end of his street and crossed the road to the bus stop.

George hovered on the doorstep, fixing his wig and brushing the stray hairs off his coat. He pressed the bell then brought his hands back to his short, brown, perfectly straight bob and began smoothing it down some more. Ben answered the door with a phone in one hand and a wooden spoon in the other. He motioned the older man to come inside. Val screamed as she ducked past Ben and ran into the living room, closely followed by Simon who was chasing her.

'Welcome to the mad house,' Ben smiled. 'I have to take this. It's the telephone company; there's been a mistake with the bill.'

George nodded, and removed the spoon from Ben's hand. He placed it in the pot on the hob and stirred the bubbling stew before turning the heat down. He looked around for a lid and secured it on the simmering dish. George took off his black, fur-trimmed coat and set it down on a chair in the living room. He found an apron in the kitchen, hanging from a hook on the back of the door, and tied it around his small waist.

By the time Ben got off the phone, George had mashed the potatoes, boiled some frozen vegetables and set the table. Ben watched aghast as all three of his children sat quietly eating. George, meanwhile, had decanted the remaining stew into some plastic dishes and was washing the pot at the sink. On noticing Ben, he removed his hands from the soapy water and rubbed them against the apron to dry them.

'I'm sorry, I got carried away. It's just you were on the phone and I thought the tea might burn.'

'No need to apologise; you clearly know your way around a kitchen.'

Ben was admiring his shiny work surfaces. He noted the floor had been given a sweep as well, because the flour Val had spilled earlier was nowhere to be seen. George had managed to achieve more calm and order in fifteen minutes than Ben had in a day. He just wasn't cut out for this house-husband scene. How the hell had he managed for so long?

'Can I get you a coffee, George?' he asked.

'I'd rather have herbal tea, if there's any?' George replied.

Ben made a hurried search of his top cupboard, sure he'd bought a box of mixed fruit teas at some point. But three-for-two coffee jars lined his shelves. Maybe one of them was accidentally de-caff.

'You know, water's fine,' George said.

Ben poured him a glass from the sink and led him into the living room where the usually blaring T.V. was silent. He looked at the old-fashioned man sitting on his sofa. He has awful taste in clothes, Ben thought, taking in George's sensible black flats and thick winter tights, under a pleated A-line checked skirt, which was a bad match for his checked blouse. George had kind eyes though, and Ben focused on these and his warm smile.

'You're a Libra, aren't you?' George asked.

Ben nodded, surprised.

'I thought so. I overheard you on the phone, all that politeness and tact—typical Libra. It's probably good in the workplace, but they won't be reconnecting the internet anytime soon, I'm guessing.'

'Next week,' Ben admitted.

'I'm a Sagittarius,' George continued warming to his theme. 'We're the opposite, straight shooters, we tell it like we see it. If you like, I can give them another call later and they'll be sending an engineer round this evening, let me tell you!'

'Would you? I mean, assuming you stay, that you want the job. I'm not even sure what the hours are yet… Or when I start back; there are details to consider but…'

'I'd love to be your manny, duck,' George interrupted. 'But don't you want to read my C.V. and my references first?'

'Of course,' nodded Ben.

Had this been a work interview, he would have put so much stock in experience, and the opinions of others, but a manny wasn't like a secretary or a public relations consultant. This was somebody Ben was leaving his kids with and such a decision was informed more by the heart, than by paperwork. They sat on the sofa, chatting away like long-lost friends. Ben told him about Anna, and how she'd left him alone with the kids the decision to relocate to Withering, Simon's problems in school and George listened, nodding in all the right places.

'So, the little one's alright now?' he enquired. 'Still, it must have been a huge scare.'

'It was the most terrified I've ever been.' Ben's eyes darkened as he remembered the night she'd collapsed. 'The on-call consultant was sharp, he could tell it was meningitis straight away, which probably saved her life, but just watching her lying there, attached to drips and wires and monitoring machines. It was horrible, I really thought she might...' Tears welled in his eyes and he felt George place a comforting hand on his.

'I finished all my tea, Dad. Can I have an ice cream now?' Val yelled, from the kitchen.

'She sounds like she's back to herself now, eh? I'll get it for her, if you want to start getting ready. What time are you meeting Jane?'

Ben glanced at his watch. 'Shit! Ten minutes ago! Wayne's gonna go nuts!'

He set about finding his keys and his handbag without much success. He swore again. George rummaged briskly through the hooks behind the kitchen door.

'Is this it?' he asked, showing Ben a black leather shoulder bag that had seen better days.

Ben grinned and Simon ran in with a set of car keys. 'They were in the ignition, as usual.'

He checked the time again. 'I'll still be half an hour late, Wayne will have a field day.'

'She's a heart of gold you know, has Jane,' George reassured him. 'All that sexist bullshit and femo-bravado that she shows the world, that's all an act.'

'Really?' Ben replied. 'It's a damn convincing one.'

Leo stood on the doorstep and rang the bell for the third time. He was freezing. He'd missed the five-past bus, on account of his idiotic stepmum, and he had to wait half an hour for the next one. Finally, he heard the sound of footsteps approaching and the door opened. She wasn't as tall as he thought she'd be and he automatically hunched down a bit. She wasn't as handsome as her profile page either, or as young. In fact, she didn't look anything like her photo.

'You're late.' She spoke in a quiet tone, but he could hear the anger in her voice. She'd been much nicer on Skylark.

'I'm sorry,' Leo said, fighting back tears. He didn't want to start the evening on the wrong foot.

'You're always sorry.'

Leo thought that was a bit unfair. This was the first time they'd met.

'I'm here now.' He flashed his brightest smile.

She opened the door fully and he sashayed into the dimly-lit hall, determined to lighten the mood.

'Where do I put this old thing?' he purred, unfastening the top button of his coat.

She stood behind him and the coat fell into her arms, revealing an almost naked Leo underneath. He heard her inhale and felt her cold, clammy hands traced the outline of his bum. She stopped just above his black lace knickers and held her hands either side of his waist. He didn't like it, or her getting so close. He was here for a photo shoot, not a groping session, but he didn't want to antagonise her. At least not till she'd done his pictures. He gently pushed her hands away and turned to face her.

'Okay, work first, play later,' his croaky voice belied the confidence he was desperate to project. She placed her hands back exactly where they had been, leaned her face into his and whispered.

'I'm the one in charge here.'

Wayne patted her hair down self-consciously as she watched Campbell walk through the main entrance. She had made a real effort for tonight. She had put on her good suit, shined her shoes and even found a tie. It had a fajita stain right down the centre, but it was still a tie. She had even used some of the aftershave that George had got her last Christmas.

Campbell, by contrast, had dressed down, which was an exaggerated form of his usual style. *He could be going out for a burger*, she thought, as she watched him stroll to the table and all the eyes in the room follow him. He looked even taller than the last time she saw him. Withering wasn't ready for a man like him. Wayne stood up as he approached the table and clumsily pulled his chair out.

'My work clothes are all in the laundry so I had to come in my Sunday best,' she explained.

The curry house was full, even though it was a Monday night, and it took ten minutes for someone to take a drinks order. The table they shared was one of ten, neatly packed together at the back of the restaurant. The simple decor, the subtle music and the mouthwatering smells made for a relaxed atmosphere and Ben's muscles began to loosen as he sipped a cool Indian beer.

'This place is all right, Wayne.'

'Of course it's alright, it's my local. I wouldn't have suggested it otherwise. So, are you going to hire George?' she asked.

'I already have.'

'Seriously? That's great, he's a fantastic little worker, you won't regret it.' Wayne grinned from ear to ear.

'Are you ready to order yet Ms Wayne?' the waitress interrupted.

'Ready?' Wayne replied 'I've been ready the last half hour. We'll have the set meal for two. Tell Pavi it's for me.' The waitress scrawled the order on her pad, took Ben's menu from him, and headed off in the direction of the kitchen, pausing to pick up some empty plates from the next table.

'She always throws in an extra naan,' Wayne explained. Ben stared back at her, without replying and Wayne knew instantly she'd done something wrong. She had no idea what, but she'd seen that same look of disbelief on many a man's face over the years. It was always a precursor to some kind of argument about her lack of sensitivity.

'What did I do, Campbell?' she asked him.

'What do you think you did?' was Campbell's unhelpful response.

'If I knew, I wouldn't have to ask,' Wayne took a healthy gulp of her beer.

'You ordered for me—without even asking me what I liked. You have no idea if I'm vegetarian or...'

'Are you vegetarian?' she cut in.

'No, but that's not the point. You can't just go ordering a meal for someone. Who does that?'

'Look, I should have said before, I'm paying. Does that help?'

The look on his face told her it didn't. She finished her beer in one mouthful and, waving her hand till she caught the waitress's eye, asked for two more.

'Now you're ordering my drinks,' Ben snapped.

'Don't panic, pet.' Wayne grinned at him 'If you don't want it, I'll have them both.'

The waitress placed two fresh beers on the table and Ben grabbed one. Wayne waited till he'd drunk close to half of it before speaking.

'Now that you have George, when do you think you'll be back?'

'Why the sudden interest in my domestic arrangements?'

'You need to come back, Campbell. You're sorely missed at the station.'

Ben gave her a look of incredulity.

'Okay, so you're not the most popular lead investigator we've ever had, but we've grown kind of used to you.'

'I was only working for three days.'

'Yeah, but you made a big impression in that time.' Wayne flashed him her trademark grin.

'Right, I'm going to stop you now, Wayne,' Ben said. 'I've got three kids; I know a tall tale when I hear it. Why are you so desperate to have me back?'

'Because O'Keeffe won't replace you; she's so paranoid about the press that she won't allow anyone else in the loop.'

The waitress had arrived with their starters. She put a bowl of mixed samosas and pakoras between them, then edging Wayne's beer to one side, she put a plate stacked with poppadums and a trio of dips next to them. They waited until she was gone to continue talking.

'But surely that means that you're running things in my absence?'

'Well, no. O'Keeffe's equally as paranoid that I'll suck up, and that will end up in the papers so she's heading the team herself.'

Ben started to chuckle. 'No wonder you're singing my praises. Bet I'm way more competent than she is.'

'Peachy is more competent than she is. How the suck she climbed to the top of the greasy pole beats me. So, what do you say? You coming back?' Wayne gave him a jovial punch and her most hopeful glare.

'I don't know. Val nearly died, Wayne. I don't feel right just leaving her.'

'But you're not just leaving her. That's why I sent you George. He used to be a nurse, you know; she's probably safer with him than you.' As soon as the words were out she regretted saying them. She turned her focus to the food.

'Here, have a samosa—have two,' she told him. She then piled her own plate high and wolfed down a chicken pakora, followed by a mushroom one, and washed it down with some beer. 'Are you coming back, or what?' she asked again, before shoving a samosa into her mouth.

'I told you already, I don't know. Can we change the subject? How's the case going? You've made the papers every day, but there's not much in the way of substance.'

'Or truth,' Wayne said. 'I guess even the dim-witted hacks that wind up in Withering were bound to join the dots when there was a third murder. I never thought I'd say this, but it's a good thing; it keeps O'Keeffe focused. There's no way she'll pull the rug on us this time.'

'Have you traced Connor's family?'

'What do the papers say?'

'That he doesn't have one, he's a care home kid.'

'Who knew? Even *The Shade* gets the odd fact right.'

'It makes sense, I suppose.' Ben paused to take a sip from the third beer a waiter had put in front of him.

'How do you figure that?' Wayne asked, chewing down on a poppadum and spraying flakes of it all over the white tablecloth.

'Well, kids from stable homes don't end up working for bitches like Hagan, do they?'

'You keep telling yourself that, Campbell,' Wayne replied.

Leo had been sitting on the sofa for what seemed like an age. He could hear her clattering about in another room and he wondered what she was up to. If she'd been a bit friendlier when he'd answered the door, like she'd been online, then he would have felt okay about going to find her. He wanted to check his phone, but she'd made him switch it off, something about the signal interfering with her cameras. It didn't really make sense to him, but then again what the suck did he know about photography? He glanced round the sparsely decorated room, desperate for a distraction. There was a large book lying flat on the shelf. He walked over to it and ran his fingers along the cover. It had a picture of a woman on a chariot, being pulled along by several horses. It looked like the sort of historical romance horseshit his dad read. *Still, it's better than staring at the walls*, he thought, picking up the Bhagavad Gita and turning to page one.

As their starters were cleared away, Ben patted his stomach.

He'd been absolutely famished and had eaten far too quickly. He consoled himself that, compared to Wayne, he'd been restrained. He took another sip of his beer and made a mental note to himself to slow down the drinking. As if reading his mind, Wayne waved her hand in the air and ordered another round.

'How do you know George?' Ben asked. The question had been nagging him for hours.

'We used to be an item.' Wayne's mouth broke into a leer. 'In fact, George was very close to becoming the first Mister Wayne. Well, I say close, but the truth is we only went out together for about a year. Still, that's a record for me.'

Ben almost choked on his beer. 'You and George. Seriously? I can't imagine it.'

'And why would you say that?' Wayne asked, her tone was sharp, but she had a glint in her eye.

Ben shrugged his shoulders, 'I wouldn't have thought he was your type. Too...'

'Too what? Clever? Cultured?'

'Old,' Ben replied, alcohol loosening his normally diplomatic tongue.

'Old? George is two years younger than me.'

'Exactly,' Ben said. 'I would have expected you to be seeing some dumb twenty-five-year-old with platinum blond hair and enough plastic in his penis to make a gimp suit.'

'That's 'cos you don't know me,' Wayne replied. 'You think I'm some kind of middle-aged perv who needs some immature eye candy to prop up my tiny ego.'

'That's exactly what I think,' Ben agreed.

'The thing is, George and I really worked. We liked the same music—he's a huge country fan—we supported the same football team, we ate the same food—as in anything he cooked. He's outstanding in the kitchen, as you'll figure out. We were just on the same wavelength. I'd go around to his, after a tough day, and he'd let me sit on his porch and get stoned and just be, you know. None of this, *"How was your day, dear?"* bullshit.

He figured if I wanted to talk, I would. You know, I'm not the world's biggest talker, especially not about work. And he got that. If a case was really getting me down, I'd keep to myself for a few days, and he got that too. None of this texting you eight times a day, just to see if you're okay. He was classier than that, was George.'

Wayne looked almost misty-eyed and Ben chastised himself for rushing to judgement.

'Course, he was also great with the old tongue,' she continued, sticking hers out and waving it up and down to illustrate her point.

Ben grimaced. 'So, what happened?'

'Work,' Wayne replied.

'But I thought you said he understood the pressures of the job?'

'There was some other stuff. Anyway, how are you for a drink, shall I get us another two?'

Wayne waved at one of the passing waiters.

'I've barely touched this one,' Ben protested. 'What other stuff? Come on, Wayne. You can't just tell me half a story.'

'It didn't work out; can't we leave it at that?'

Ben groped on the floor for his handbag, and retrieved his mobile. His fingers slid though his contacts till he found George's number and he started to compose a text.

'What are you doing?' Wayne asked.

'If you won't tell me, George will.'

Wayne snatched the phone out of his hand. 'It was a twenty-five-year-old,' she said. 'With platinum blond hair and a very plastic penis.'

Leo's heart was beating so loudly that he was grateful for the music to drown it out, even though it was shit. He was sitting at a dining table in the open plan front room of her studio, pushing some cold oysters round his plate.

The evening wasn't turning out like he'd imagined it would. The place was nothing like he'd expected. It was just a sucking ordinary house and a dull looking one at that. There were no pictures on the walls, no photographs. What kind of photographer doesn't hang photos of her work? She'd been the biggest disappointment of all.

On Skylark she sounded so cool, but in the flesh she was about as hip as his stepmum. They still weren't any closer to doing the actual shoot and now he had to eat this shit.

'Don't you like them? You have had them before?' she asked.

'Yeah. All the time,' Leo replied. He stared at the shellfish before prising one open with a knife, like he had seen her do. Jess! It wasn't as easy as she made it look. He lifted the shell to his quivering mouth and felt the slime of the oyster as it slid down his throat. He coughed so hard it almost came straight back up. She laughed.

'So, do your parents know where you are?' she asked.

'No, you said not to tell anyone. And anyway, I'm old enough to do what I want.'

'Of course you are. It's just they might worry. Don't you think?'

'Why should they worry?'

'Why indeed?'

'And they're not expecting you back tonight?'

Leo threw his hands back in frustration. 'Jess! How many times? I'm an independent man. I can do what I want. You're starting to sound like my sucking father!'

She got up from her seat and stood in front of him. Raising her right hand, she brought it crashing down on his cheek, turning it a deep red. Leo jumped back in shock.

'Don't ever speak of your father like that again, do you hear me?'

Leo rubbed his stinging face. 'Yes,' he whispered. He was proper scared now. This bitch isn't a modelling scout; she's a psycho! Why the suck hadn't he told anyone where he was going? Maybe he could just leave.

'I need the toilet,' he told her.

'First door on your left, down the hall, where we came in. Shall I show you?'

'No thanks.'

He found his boots beside the radiator and his coat on the stand. *I can dress when I get outside,* he thought, as he tiptoed towards the exit. He turned the latch as softly as he could and pulled the door. It didn't budge. Leo tried again, pulling harder this time. The door remained tightly shut. He looked down and saw it was locked. He scanned the wall for a hanging key. There was jangling behind him. He turned to see her dangling a chain of keys, as large as any locksmith's.

'Leaving so soon?' she asked, smiling.

'Look, don't shoot the messenger!' Wayne exclaimed. 'I'm not saying you shouldn't be a meninist, in your free time, I'm just saying, a meninist group in Withering police station, is probably not a good idea. Let's be honest, most of our boys couldn't even spell meninist!'

'Because we're men and we're too stupid, yeah? I get it. But it's 2017. The argument that men are naturally stupid, their brain size being inversely proportionate to their intellect, has been completely disproven,' Ben replied.

'See, that's exactly what I'm talking about, all that pseudo intellectual crap. I'm telling you, Campbell, cops aren't big thinkers. You know Peachy still hasn't finished that copy of *Fifty Shades of Pink* I bought him, says he's seen the movie now, so there's no point.'

Wayne wiped her masala gravy in some naan bread and swallowed it whole, groaning with pleasure. She glanced at the dishes filling their small table and decided on the prawn balti, heaping four spoonfuls on to her plate, then added some rice. Ben tucked into the lamb jalfrezi between gulps of beer, loosening his shirt as the heat of the dish kicked in.

Wayne finished the balti and then searched in her pockets for her wallet. She retrieved a small white card from her pocket and handed it to her colleague. The words *S.W.P. Membership Card* were printed on it. Wayne's name was handwritten underneath.

'There, look! Do I tell everyone in work about this? Do I suck? Because it's not relevant to how I police and because it sucks both my workmates, and the public, off! Why would I do that?'

'It's not the same thing,' Ben replied.

'Why not? Everybody hates socialists. Everybody hates menenists. If you ask me, I've found the perfect comparison.'

'And how about I ask you this, why are you a socialist?'

'I've always been a socialist. My mother was a socialist. My mother's mother was a socialist. My Grandma was one of the founding members of the miners' union in this country. It's in my blood.'

'So, you don't actually know why you're a socialist, do you? If your mother had been a catholic you'd be showing me a crucifix instead. Why don't you ask me why I'm a menenist?'

'Because I don't care why you're a menenist. You should keep that sort of thing to yourself.'

'My dad certainly wasn't a meninist, that's for sure. Dad was a broken man, right from the day my mum walked out on us. I don't think I ever saw him smile after that, like really smile. I don't think I ever heard him laugh. I hated him drinking, but I understood why he did. It was the only time he ever looked alright, not happy or anything, but okay. The rest of the time, he was trapped in this god-awful place in his mind.' Ben paused and took a gulp of his drink. 'He saw so many different doctors, and was in and out of the local institution so often, he had his own bed, but nothing ever seemed to help. Every new pill he took just deadened his eyes a little more. He'd swallow a month's supply about twice a year, and we would have this mad dash to hospital and he'd have his stomach pumped and his bed made up for a few nights. Eventually, he beat the surveillance team that was me and my two sisters, and the ambulance team that actually knew us by name.' Ben blinked back a tear. 'He was pronounced dead as we turned into the hospital car park.'

'Shit happens,' said Wayne, moving uncomfortably in her seat.

'Yeah, that's what I thought at the time, and for the next ten years. That was until my old girl walked out on me—then I finally understood the root of my dad's problems. Sucking women! My dad didn't just wake up crazy one day. He was driven there, because he couldn't cope with the stigma and shame, not to mention the reality of single parenthood. He couldn't understand why my mother had left him, left us all. The poor bastard didn't know what he'd done wrong, but he figured it must have been something big. He had no idea that women behave the way they do because they can. Thousands of years of matriarchal rule had left the world in a state of complete imbalance. He probably didn't even know what a matriarchy was, which is ironic, when you think it killed him.'

'Did it though?' asked Wayne. 'Couldn't we look at it from a purely Darwinian angle? Your dad just couldn't hack it?'

'Okay, let's look at it from Darwin's perspective, remembering first that Charlotte Darwin was a woman. All her theories were based upon the observations of humans within a matriarchy.'

'You're losing me here. Science is science. Facts: plain and simple.'

'Is it though? Science, philosophy, medicine, theology, psychiatry, psychology, and of course art, all disciplines created and maintained almost exclusively by women, until about a hundred years ago. How much truth can any of these teachings hold if they were the preserve of only one gender? And how about the questions we asked, the answers we sought, the language we sought them in? All feminine. Yet females make up half, in fact a little less than half, of the population. What about the second half? Us? Or the *Other*, as we came to be known?'

'Look, you can't argue that. It doesn't matter which of us heats water, it will still boil at 100 degrees.'

'But why did we choose to heat water? Because some woman decided it was worth trying. And how did we end up walking on the moon, because some woman was feeling stir crazy. And why did we build nuclear bombs? Because some girl wanted to see if she could wipe us off the face of the planet. Of course, the other girls thought it sounded cool, so they signed off on her right to do it. Do you get me now, Wayne?'

'Nope, science is science, and politics is politics. Look, all I'm saying is you're a bright boy, Campbell, and you're educated; Withering is crying out for a sophisticated male presence to hide behind. You could go the whole way, if you just worked a bit harder on your physical appearance and worked a little less hard on your politics.'

'Shave, get myself a hair implant, and leave the meninist books at home. That's your advice?'

'And don't forget the walk,' Wayne added. 'You'll go a lot further if you learn to stoop a bit.'

Leo lay in the darkened room, exhausted. His hands and feet were tied and masking tape covered his mouth. He'd struggled for the best part of an hour and his limbs ached. She was moving down the hall, but the sounds were too muffled to make any sense.

He tried to scream again and it proved the same futile exercise as the other forty times he'd tried. Leo focused all his energy on trying to move his wrists, even slightly. It was no use. She'd pulled the ropes so tight that his hands were white. He tried wriggling his feet free again, but he could not move them. The only thing he could do was close his eyes. He searched his mind for his father's face.

The handle turned and the door opened wide. Her shadow fell across the bed. He closed his eyes tighter. Her hand stroked his face and then he felt warm liquid running down his leg. She sniffed. 'You filthy whore!' She moved her fingers to his head and pulled his hair sharply. 'Do you expect me to clean that up?'

Wayne had wanted to loosen him up, but she hadn't planned to get Campbell quite as rat-arsed. They were the only two people left in the restaurant and Campbell was showing no signs of moving. Waiters bustled around them, pulling cloths off the tables and putting chairs on them. Sanvi, the owner, caught Wayne's eye and gave her a disapproving look.

'Shall we call you a taxi then?' she shouted across to them.

Ben's eyes were closed and he responded with a slight snore. Wayne placed her hand in the jug of water on the table, and then flicked her wet fist in his face. He jolted upright, his eyes darting around the table before finding his beer and taking a healthy gulp. He reached out, grabbed Wayne's coat collar and pulled her down to his level.

'Never have kids,' he slurred. 'They suck up your social life.' He fell forward on Wayne's shoulder and began to snore again.

There was something precious and uplifting about a human's final gasps of life. There was something powerfully life-affirming in the action of stopping someone else's breathing, of controlling their destiny. She was completely and utterly exhilarated. She was lying on a cold plastic sheet, half naked, beside a fresh corpse having masturbated into a frenzy. She felt absolutely satiated and at one with herself and the universe. She wished she had realised at a younger age how much joy and righteousness there was to be gained from taking life. She'd been fighting the urge to do so for most of her adulthood. Now that she'd stopped fighting it, she knew for certain it was her calling. It was what God had put her on this earth to do.

FIVE

TUESDAY

Ben stirred the sugar-heavy coffee and willed himself to drink it. As the lukewarm liquid slid down his throat, he thought he was going to gag. *Just keep drinking,* he told himself. He was behind the desk in Wayne's office, half-sitting, half-lying on a chair. He was still trying to figure out how he'd wound up back in work so quickly. One minute, he and Wayne were discussing the possibility of his return, the next, Wayne was texting George and O'Keeffe confirming his eight-a.m. start.

Ben stared at the stacks of paperwork in front of him. O'Keeffe hadn't opened as much as one letter in his absence. She'd scrawled a note on a Post-it and stuck it on the top of the bundle. Ben tried to make out her handwriting, but it was impossible. Was that "n", or "m", or could it be an "h" maybe?

'Here, let me,' Wayne said grabbing the note from him. Ben hadn't heard her come in. He looked up to see her grinning over at him, between bites of what smelled like burnt beef and onions in a white bun. He put his hand over his mouth and tried to suppress his gag reflex as he pointed to the door.

'Can you get that out of my office now?'

He was shouting and he didn't care. Wayne retreated quickly, but the waft of her breakfast lingered, forcing Ben to cover his nose with a handkerchief. His head thumped and he shoved his coffee to one side, spilling it on the desk.

Ben closed his eyes and convinced himself a five-minute power nap would sort everything.

A tap on the desk brought him back to consciousness and Wayne was once again in front of him, this time mercifully, without food. She was still in last night's clothes and he wondered if she'd slept in them. Wayne straddled one of the folding chairs and gave him a sympathetic look.

'Feeling a bit hungover, sir?' she kept her voice low.

'I'm fine,' Ben lied. 'Right, we've a lot to get through this morning. I'm calling in an expert on comparative religions, Professor Lottie McEwan, I found her online. And, even better, she's Withering based.'

'A professor? Why do we need one of those?'

'I would have thought it was obvious, the religious theme.'

'You don't want to pay that too much attention, boss. It's smoke and mirrors. Imagine if she'd put right angle rulers up their arses, we wouldn't go looking for advice from a mathematician, would we?'

Ben knocked back the rest of his coffee in one go and assured himself it was going to stay down before replying.

'It's not just the crucifixes though, it's the pages from the Gita and the circle she arranged them in last time. Come on Wayne, even you must concede religion is playing a part in these murders.'

Wayne pushed her chair back and began pacing the office. 'Piano wire is playing a bigger part. I'm telling you, Campbell, if we go down the religious alley we'll just get sidelined. Let's focus on real leads and key suspects.'

'There are no suspects, that's the point. We don't know who is killing these boys, and we don't know why. Professor

McEwan is going to help us with the why.'

'You want to know why? That's easy, because she's a sucking nutter!' Wayne was pacing so much it was making Ben dizzy. He needed more caffeine and maybe some food. But at the thought of food, his stomach lurched... maybe not.

'I'm taking a ten-minute break,' he told Wayne. He dashed out of the office, desperate to keep the coffee in his belly, at least until he reached the toilets.

Wayne waited until Ben was out of sight before swapping seats. She leaned back in her chair and smiled. She missed her office. She missed being in charge. Glancing at the Post-it O'Keeffe had stuck on top of a fortnight's worth of paperwork, she struggled to decipher any letters. *How had someone so illiterate got so far?* She skimmed through the files, hoping that something might jump out at her, providing an opportunity to get out of the office, before the religious know-it-all arrived.

Peachy knocked on the window and she beckoned him in. He was wearing an Alex band in his hair, taking years off his already youthful appearance. The sight of him made Wayne question, as she frequently did, how someone as hot as Peachy wound up in the force.

'Ma'am, there's a Master Ryan here to see you. He seems very distressed, insists on seeing you, and only you.'

'And who could blame him?' Wayne replied. 'Well, you better bring him through.'

As soon as Peachy had left, Wayne grabbed a comb from her trench coat pocket and pulled it through her unruly mane. She glanced down at the outfit she'd slept in and made an unsuccessful attempt to even out the creases with her hands. She was trying to shove her shirt into her already bulging trousers, when Peachy returned, guiding a decidedly disturbed Ronnie Ryan into the office.

'Get Master Ryan a cup of tea, pet,' she instructed Peachy. 'Lots of sugar.' She helped Ronnie into a chair and pulled her own up alongside him.

All previous images of the ageing letting agent as a sexually vibrant human being faded, as Wayne stared at his disheveled face. He looks his age and then some, she observed, as tears and snot fell into Ronnie's embroidered hanky.

'What must you think of me, Inspector?' Ronnie said, before being gripped by another wave of emotion.

'I think you're very upset,' Wayne replied. 'Why don't you take a few deep breaths and tell me what's happened?'

Ronnie did as he was told and, as his composure returned, so did Peachy with the tea. He sipped it gratefully, took another deep breath and began to recall the events that had led him to seek her out.

'It was just a standard inspection, nothing out of the ordinary. Maintenance regulations require all our properties to have annual safety checks and I take those obligations very seriously, Inspector,' he said.

'I'm sure you do,' Wayne assured him.

'Plumbing,' he continued, 'And boiler upkeep. We use the same woman for both jobs. She's fully qualified and very reliable, and she's worked for us for almost ten years. Julia Owen, she's called. I have her card in here somewhere.'

Ronnie opened his handbag and Wayne placed her hand gently over it.

'You can give me that after. Why don't you finish what you're saying first?'

Ronnie nodded, 'Of course, I'm sorry, Inspector. I've never done anything like this before. I've never even been to a police station. We're law abiding citizens. I've never been in trouble in my life...'

'What's going on?' Ben asked, walking in on the informal interview.

'Ronnie here has witnessed something very distressing,' Wayne told him. She motioned for him to sit beside Peachy, and turned her attention back to the old man. 'Go on, you were saying,' she spoke softly.

'It's happened again. There's another body,' Ronnie blurted out. 'Only I saw it this time. I actually saw it! Julia went in first and she tried to warn me. But she wasn't making much sense, so I decided to see for myself and I did. Father of God, I've never seen anything like it. There was blood everywhere and that poor boy, that poor, poor boy. What kind of sick monster would do that to a child?' He was crying again now and shaking, all attempts to keep it together abandoned.

Wayne placed her hand on his and tried to still his shaking. 'It's okay, Ronnie, you've had an awful shock and you need to see a doctor. All I want from you right now is the address. We can get everything else when you're feeling better.'

'109 Eastbrook Gardens,' Ronnie whispered.

Scrawling it on a notepad, Wayne grinned from ear-to-ear.

'What's so funny?' Ben whispered to Peachy.

'It's where O'Keeffe lives,' Peachy whispered back.

Ben slowed down to try to find a parking space in Eastbrook Gardens and whistled softly. There were twenty detached four and five bedroom houses lining both sides of the street. He could smell the affluence and entitlement, from the individually designed bungalows to the lavish two story villas, all set in perfectly landscaped gardens. There were already a couple of patrol cars in the drive and an ambulance, so he pulled in across the street.

'How the hell can O'Keeffe live here on a Super's salary?' he asked Wayne.

'His Mister has the money; the mother was in arms I think, or maybe pharmaceuticals, something sleazy.'

They passed a few uniforms at the entrance. The sign on the front lawn was for Ryan's Rentals. Ben wondered what a place like this went for, as he walked into the busy hallway, closely followed by Wayne. The number of officers from various units already on site indicated how serious O'Keeffe now took the Wringer.

'It's a great day to commit a crime in Withering; do we work any other cases now?' Wayne said.

'No,' barked a voice from behind. It was O'Keeffe. Ben did a double take. Her appearance was almost unkempt, if judged by her usual grooming standards. The shadow under her chin said she hadn't yet shaved, and her hair hadn't seen a comb. She looked like she'd just jumped out of bed. 'Nothing, do you hear me, nothing else gets attention in Withering till we get this bitch. She's making us look like complete cuntheads!' O'Keeffe was shouting.

'Hardly a difficult job,' muttered Ben.

'Don't try and be clever, Campbell. Upstairs never promote the clever ones. Just tell me you've got something and we're going to get the bitch!'

'We're following a number of leads; we're expecting a break any day,' Ben replied.

'So, you've still got nothing?'

'We couldn't have less, but in fairness, we only arrived five minutes ago,' Wayne informed her boss.

'What the suck?' 'O'Keeffe screamed. 'The bitch has killed four times! This is the second this month. Somewhere in all that carnage she's got to have left us something. Find it!' O'Keeffe turned on her heels and marched out of the house flanked by two anxious looking uniforms.

'Thanks for backing me up there.'

'You were backing yourself into a corner, Campbell. She's left hasn't she? Think about it. She would have stayed all day if she thought we had something.'

Ben scowled and took a few cautious steps into the open-plan kitchen and living space. A camera flashed repeatedly as a police photographer gathered evidence. The body was in the centre of the room bound to a wooden cross. He could see stab wounds all over the victim's back and on his exposed buttocks. His neck had the same deep red gash as previous victims, bloodied piano wire enmeshed in his skin.

The room had been trashed, the kitchen table turned over, dinner plates and half-eaten food crushed beneath it. The wooden shelves had been pulled from the walls. A lamp shade had been thrown across the room and tiny specks of a broken light bulb were scattered everywhere. There were pages of text all over the floor that had been laid down after she'd torn up the place, as they were free from glass and debris. Ben reached down and picked one up.

'This is new' he said, handing it to Wayne.

She glanced at it. 'Reads like the same shit to me.'

'That's because you're a heathen. This isn't just the Gita. There's another text here, Jewish, I think. I studied this way back, when I was in school. Professor McEwan will know.'

'You're wasting your time, Campbell. Hindu this, Kabbalah that. A psycho's a psycho, whatever their faith.'

Wayne stood outside the front door and leaned against the wall. She fiddled in her pocket among last night's loose change and found a half-smoked cigarette. She lit it and inhaled furiously, allowing her nostrils to draw up the smoke. The stench of death and the depth of Campbell's naivety were really getting to her. She stamped out the butt with her boots and looked up.

Baker was bustling up the path, her medical bag in one hand, a cream cake in the other. The old girl was getting heavier every time she saw her. She stopped to bid Wayne good morning. Sweat made her face glisten as she gobbled down her snack. Finishing, Baker took a tissue from her top pocket and wiped her hands meticulously. She then used another few tissues to soak up all the excess water on her face.

'No rest for the wicked. You coming, Wayne?' Baker asked her.

'Nah, I'll hang about here for a bit.'

She cadged a cigarette from one of the girls on the gate and found a seat on the wall outside. Across the street, the first of the news crews had started to arrive. They got out of their vans and hovered together on the pavement. One of them spotted her and shoved a microphone in her face.

'Inspector Wayne, can you tell us anything about this latest killing?'

'No comment.'

Is it the Wringer?'

'No comment.'

'Is it true she hacks off their penises and keeps them as trophies?'

'Yeah, that's her trademark,' Wayne replied. She flicked her butt in the direction of the hack and strolled back up the path. As she approached the house, she saw Baker stagger out. She didn't look so good and she was clutching her shirt, pulling at her tie.

'Martha, are you okay? Martha?' Wayne put a steadying hand around the back of Baker's ample frame as she wheezed and coughed. She didn't like the look of Baker's face; she was as white as cocaine, except for the red of her eyes.

She scanned the drive. The ambulance was still there. Where the suck were the paramedics? She steered Baker in the direction of one of the patrol cars and leaned her against the bonnet.

'I'll go and get some help.' Wayne pulled away slowly.

Baker grabbed her arm and held it in a vice-like grip.

'Don't leave me, Jane.' Then suddenly, she bent over almost in two, and began to groan. She continued to hold steadfast to Wayne before hurling her recently ingested snack all over her friend's boots and trousers.

'For suck's sake, Martha, I only just got these trousers back from the laundry!'

Baker was standing upright again, wiping herself down. She was shaking. 'I'm sorry. Shit. I'm so sorry. I'll pay to have them cleaned.'

'You sucking scared the shit out of me. I thought you were having a heart attack, not an out-of-date cream cake.'

'It's not the cake,' Baker said. 'I know him.'

'Who? The dead kid? You dirty old tramp. I thought you gave all that up when you got sober?'

'No, not like that! I mean I know him; I know his family.'

'Seriously,' said Wayne. 'So, what, he's not on the game?'

'Jess Christ! Of course he's not on the game! What kind of sick question is that?'

Ben sat opposite Professor McEwan as she leafed through the crime scene photos. She was a good-looking woman for her age, which was probably around fifty. Her C.V. was scant on personal details, but filled with the quality of professional credentials that only a Cambridge graduate could hope to achieve. If she was alarmed by the gruesome images, she didn't show it. She simply fixed her pale blue eyes on page after page, nodding occasionally.

There was a knock on the window and Peachy entered, carrying a tray with coffee and biscuits. He put it down on the desk and McEwan smiled at him, revealing a set of even, well cared for teeth. She didn't touch her coffee until she'd seen the last photo.

'There's a lot of material here,' she said, stirring a splash of milk into her cup, before taking a hearty gulp. Ben handed her a thick black folder.

'This is a record of every text she's left so far.'

'And you're sure you're looking for a woman?' McEwan asked.

'The level of violence we're seeing would suggest so,' explained Ben. Did it though? He wondered, and then cast a sideward glance at the blood-spattered body of the latest victim, a piece of cheap metal protruding from his bruised anus. He flinched. It so did.

'From a brief flick through, we're dealing with at least three religions, but I'd like more time. Can I take these with me?'

'Unfortunately not, the huge media interest in the case is making Upstairs jumpy. But I could get you the use of a desk in the main office.'

Ben stood up and walked McEwan through to the bigger office. There were twelve work stations in three rows. The first eight were assigned to particular officers for set shifts. They had files strewn carelessly across them and photographs of loved ones, pets and holiday locations as screen savers on their PCs. The third row had four desks which were assigned to daily staff on a first come, first served basis.

'Take any desk here, except for the last one.'

Wayne had set up home in the corner space, marking her territory with all the subtly of an Amazonian primate. Half-drunk tea cups and the crumbs from rolls and pastries littered the main surface area. There were some rolled up pieces of paper and a collection of coins in the top of the in-tray. Mail and files were stacked to the side of the desk, like incidentals. Ben picked up an empty cheese sandwich packet and dropped it in to the overflowing bin.

'I don't come into your office and mess with your stuff,' Wayne eased herself up behind him and spoke directly in his ear. He jumped. She laughed.

'Look, doll, if you want to clean up my shit, go for it. You missing your house duties?'

Ben felt himself turn crimson. He wondered if McEwan had heard. She'd settled in the next desk up.

'Don't call me doll,' he hissed at her, then clearing his throat he added. 'Inspector Wayne, come and meet Professor McEwan, she'll be working with us on the Wringer case'.

McEwan stood up and held out her hand to Wayne. She ignored it and addressed Ben.

'We've got an I.D., boss, when you've finished flirting with college girl here. We should probably go tell Mum and Dad that their kid's never coming home.'

'Who the hell do you think you are, Wayne?' Ben demanded. They were driving across town to an address Baker had given Wayne, and they were the first words he'd spoke since they left the office. Wayne seemed surprised.

'Look, if your testosterone levels need checked, we can pull in to a chemist on the way.'

'You are the most arrogant, ignorant, offensive, sexist, vile woman I've ever met. And let me tell you, there's stiff competition.'

'That's kind of you to say, sugar, but really, you hardly know me.'

'I'm just a joke to you, aren't I?'

Wayne laughed. The remainder of the journey was spent in silence. They pulled in along the pavement outside Bellview Place. Ben turned off the engine and turned to Wayne. 'This one's not like the others, he's a schoolkid. Why the change?'

Wayne shrugged her shoulders. 'How the hell should I know? Maybe she got tired of hookers and fancied something a bit more upmarket?'

Ben breathed in and out deeply, 'I've never done this before,' he whispered.

'You'll be okay, Campbell, just avoid their eyes.'

'Easy as that?'

'Didn't say it was easy. Of course eventually, you'll have to avoid your own as well, but let's leave that for another day.' Her voice sounded sad, but her eyes twinkled and Ben was torn between an urge to hug her and a desire to hit her. He let her take the lead as they walked up the drive. The closer they got to the house, the slower both their steps became.

'Remember the eyes,' Wayne whispered, gently rocking the brass knocker against the door.

A pretty man, with auburn curls and rosy cheeks answered. As soon as he saw their I.D. his colour faded. 'How can I help?'

'Can we come in Mister Stern?' Wayne asked. She slowly eased the front door open, making it clear it was a rhetorical question. Just then, a woman appeared from the kitchen, with a phone in her hand. She stared at the unexpected visitors.

'It's the police, love,' her husband explained.

'I have to go.' She spoke into the phone, before placing it on the console table. 'You're plain clothes, and there are two of you. Something really bad must've happened.' Her eyes darted nervously from Ben to Wayne. 'It's Leo, isn't it? What's he gone and done now?'

Mister Stern grabbed hold of his wife's hand and squeezed it hard.

'Maybe we better go through to the living room,' Ben suggested.

'For the love of God, just tell me,' Mister Stern demanded.

'We found the body of a young man in a house in Eastbrooke Gardens this morning.' Wayne kept her voice soft and even and her eyes focused on the floor. 'We have reason to believe it's your son, Leo.' Her words could barely be heard over the ear bursting cries from Leo's father. He fell to his knees like he'd been shot, and clutched his heart. 'No, not Leo,' he howled. 'Not my child!'

Ben dropped to the ground beside him, and placed his

hands on the grief-stricken dad. 'I'm so, so, sorry.' For a moment, the cries subsided, and Mister Stern raised his head until they were eye to eye. Ben held his gaze, and realised there was no trace left of the man who had opened the door to them.

The drive back was right in the middle of rush hour. Wayne huffed and sighed and kept her finger on the window button, pressing it up and down, like a monkey on steroids. Eventually, Ben put his hand over the button.

'You know, spend a few years in London and this won't even seem like traffic,' he said.

'You know, spend a few years in London and this won't even seem like traffic,' Wayne repeated in a whiny voice.

'Very mature, Wayne,' Ben replied, keeping his hand firmly in charge of the windows. 'Baker cleared off quick today. One minute she was leaning over the body, the next, she had run straight out of the house.'

'You're observant.'

'Why was that?' Ben asked.

'Maybe she's had her fill of mutilated corpses. I know I have.'

They stopped at traffic lights and Wayne noticed someone going into a shop. She yanked the door open, as the lights turned green.

'What the hell?' Ben demanded.

'See you tomorrow,' Wayne yelled at him. She slammed the door shut and sped across the street, ignoring the bleating horns and angry shouts of drivers. Wayne grabbed a basket at the door of Poundworld, and darted from aisle to aisle in search of Jeff Stone. She found him fingering the blushers in the make-up section and stood directly behind him before he'd clocked her. Fear flashed in his eyes and she could see him planning an escape.

'I've got two officers at the door,' she lied. 'I wouldn't move if I were you.' Jeff remained rooted to the spot. This was the first time Wayne had seen him fully clothed and fresh-faced. He barely looked old enough to be out alone. 'Thought you were going back to London to stay with Uncle Tim?' Wayne's tone softened.

Peachy had tracked down Jeff's uncle to a borough in south London and Wayne had spoken to the man herself. Uncle Tim sounded genuinely delighted to learn of his nephew's whereabouts, and very willing to have him come back and live with him and his family. Wayne sent Peachy to tell Jeff, and when he'd packed his bags and said his goodbyes, Peachy had driven him to the station, and waved the train away, as per Wayne's instructions. *So, what the suck was he doing back in Withering in under a week?*

'Too crowded down there; and too many rules,' Jeff explained.

'And what? Hagan doesn't have any rules?' Wayne tried to sound casual.

'Look, I know you mean well, but where I live is none of your business,' Jeff retorted.

'You're right, kid, it isn't.'

'I suppose you'll want your money back. It'll take a while.' The boy's voice had lost its defensive edge.

'Nah, you hang onto it,' Wayne replied, as she shoved two bars of soap in her basket and nudged past Jeff towards the tills.

Wayne rested her head against the wall outside the back door of Baker's house. She'd tried the front door bell with no success and when she turned into her back garden she realised why. Donald Parton was blaring from the kitchen radio, competing for airtime with Baker. That could mean only one thing. She braced herself and banged hard on the window. There was no response.

'If you don't let me in, I'll break the door down,' she shouted. There was still no response. 'I'm warning you Baker, I'm counting to three. One, two, three...' Wayne swore under her breath as the door remained closed. She took a deep breath, walked back a few paces and ran full force at the door, crash landing in the hall as Baker opened it.

'For suck's sake, Baker!' she cried. Baker didn't reply as she staggered back into her kitchen. Wayne flinched as she pulled herself up and followed. The music was so loud that it deafened all thought. She unplugged the radio at the wall.

'I was listening to that,' Baker protested. She'd returned to her seat at the table and clutched the remains of her bottle of whisky. She poured a generous measure into her glass. 'You want one?' she asked Wayne.

'Best not.'

'Why? You afraid you'll encourage me?'

Wayne walked to the cupboard and took out a clean tumbler. She filled it with the last of the whisky and downed it in one. She banged her empty glass on the table. 'What's going on, Martha?'

'I fancied a drink. It's no big deal.'

Wayne looked at her plastered friend. Her eyes were bloodshot, but the rest of her face was drained of colour. Her shirt was covered in dried puke and clung to her sweat-soaked skin. Baker's fleshy hands shook, as she raised the glass to her mouth.

'Martha! What's going on?' Wayne repeated. She had straddled one of the kitchen chairs and sat facing her.

'I'm tired of being sober. I'm tired of chasing sugar highs. And I wanted something that actually took the pain away, you know a drug that actually works."

'But it doesn't work for you, does it, Martha?'

'It's working right now.' Baker got up and stumbled across the room to her fridge freezer. She took out two bags of ice and put them on the counter. Retrieving the bottle of whisky behind them, she replaced the bags and shut the door. Wayne groaned.

'Don't you think you've had enough?'

Baker was back in her seat, her tremoring fingers defying her desperate attempts to unscrew the whisky lid. 'What do you mean? I'm still conscious.'

SIX

WEDNESDAY

Wayne's bones ached. She was too old to be sleeping on couches. She took some painkillers from her top pocket and swallowed four. She sniffed her armpit. She could do with a wash, but she was already late.

She searched the shelves in Baker's fridge for a cool drink. There was nothing. If she had wanted salad dressing she'd have been good, or double cream, but there was no trace of any other liquid.

She picked up the whisky on the counter, filled a mug a third of the way up and knocked it back. She poured the remainder down the sink. It wasn't worth a quick search in the kitchen cupboards for more of the stash. The spacious kitchen was one of four rooms on this floor alone. An entire team could turn over the place and not find anything. She shut the door beneath the sink and strolled through to the living room.

Passed out on her armchair, Baker's snores were loud and uneven. Wayne put her hand on her forehead, it was cold and clammy. She placed a throw over her. Gazing down at her friend, she fingered her handcuffs and toyed with the idea of cuffing Baker to the chair.

She groped down either side of Baker and found her mobile. Wayne tried to recall the name of Baker's A.A. sponsor, whom she had met once at a very dull Christmas party. Sarah, Susan...? She opened Baker's phone to search her contacts, but instead found a link to an online photo site.

Wayne clicked one of the pictures and a naked boy appeared on the screen. He was kneeling with his arse to the camera, arms outstretched and each of his hands bound to a headboard. He had turned his head to face the camera and stuck out his tongue. She studied the photo for a minute and realised that it was taken in Baker's bedroom. The dirty bitch! She tossed the phone back on the couch. Wayne found her beige trench coat on the floor, dusted some ash off it, and slipped out of the house.

'WRINGER COLLECTS WHORES' WILLIES' read the headline on the front page of *The Shade*.

There were over five hundred copies of the offending newspaper stacked up beside the desk in Wayne's office, and more deliveries were expected. Ben cast a sidelong glance at the growing pile and quickly turned his eyes back to O'Keeffe.

'I won't have it,' she was screaming. 'Do you hear me, Campbell? I won't have that senile bitch suck up the most important case of my career.' Her face was so red that Ben thought she might burst a blood vessel. She was sitting opposite him, her manicured finger tracing a paragraph in page two.

"The Shade has learned that the notorious serial killer, The Withering Wringer, hacks off the penises of her victims and keeps them in a chilled cabinet beside her bed. An anonymous source close to the centre of the investigation revealed to this paper that the Wringer keeps the sex organs as trophies from each victim. When pressed by our reporter, at the scene of the latest killing, D.I. Jane Wayne, a senior investigating officer on the Wringer case, confirmed our source's story."

O'Keeffe stopped reading and kept her finger pointed at

Wayne's name. 'I warned her about this. I told her, but she doesn't listen. Do you know why? Because she doesn't care. Do you know why? Because she's no reason to care. She's got nothing to lose—she's living on borrowed time and she knows it. And what does that mean for me, if I can't exercise any authority over her?'

O'Keeffe paused for so long that Ben wondered if he should answer, but what could he say?

'It means,' she eventually continued after a long sigh, 'That I have to find someone else to blame.' O'Keefe leaned in as she spoke the last sentence, her cold eyes cutting through Ben. 'That's you, Campbell! If she sucks up one more time, I'm taking you off the case. Tell her that, for me.'

O'Keeffe picked up the newspaper and threw it across the floor. She then replaced her hat and left the room, banging the door just hard enough to avoid breaking it.

Ben stood up and watched her leave the main office. When she was out of earshot, he opened the door that divided the two spaces and shouted.

'You can come out now. She's gone.' He heard the scraping of a chair and Wayne crawled out from under her desk, still in the creased suit that she had been wearing since Monday. She made a half-hearted attempt to pat herself down and grinned at Ben.

'You stink!' Ben said. 'Both literally and at this job. Why would you talk to the papers?'

'It's actually an unfortunate misunderstanding...'

Ben put his hand up to silence her. 'I don't want to hear it, Wayne. I've just spent the last twenty minutes watching O'Keeffe in meltdown. Why don't you tell me some good news, like where are we on the computer expert?'

'Not far. Actually, we haven't made any progress. Florence

from the Fraud Squad, she's off duty, not back in till Friday.'

'Well, can't you call her at home? This is urgent.'

'I could do, normally, but she'll be in Leeds. She's got some bit on the side up there. And she never takes her mobile so the mister can't harass her.'

'Right, Friday it will have to be then,' Ben said. Anxious to conceal his contempt for the faithless Florence, he focused his attention on the mountain of newspapers that had taken over the office. 'Let's get this lot shifted and down to the shredder before the second editions arrive.'

The task was interrupted by Peachy, knocking on the office window.

'Excuse me, boss,' Peachy said, turning his head from side-to-side, clearly confused as to which one he should address.

'What is it?' Ben demanded.

'Rachel Stern's here. She's just identified the body and she wants to speak to someone.'

What a difference a day makes, Ben thought, staring through the glass at Rachel Stern. The woman that looked back at him had aged a decade since yesterday. Her handsome face had collapsed into a web of creased lines. Her body sat hunched on the plastic chair, and her eyes searched the room relentlessly, like a wounded animal waiting for the end. Ben took a deep breath and he and Wayne entered the room. The grieving mother didn't look up. Ben placed a cup of coffee in front of her.

'If you'd feel more comfortable in your own home, Ms Stern, we can always go back there to have a chat.'

'I had to get out of the house,' Stern replied. 'The mister hasn't stopped crying since he heard, hasn't drawn breath; I needed space. His father's there now and his brother. I told him I'd identify the body, seemed like the least I could do. I've never seen a dead child before. I saw my mother and she looked peaceful, but not Leo. He looks frozen, as if I poured some water on him, he might wake up.' Her eyes glazed over and Ben left it a minute before speaking.

'Whenever you're ready, Ms Stern, you could start by telling us when you last saw Leo?'

'Monday evening, six o'clock,' she sounded certain. 'I was making tea with the radio on. The news had just started.'

'So, you were both at home?'

'Yeah, I was downstairs, cooking and feeding the baby. Leo was supposed to be upstairs studying. But I caught him sneaking out the front door.'

'Sneaking out to where?'

She shook her head. 'I don't know. He said he was going round to his pal Victor's to study, but he wasn't dressed for a night of exam revision. And of course, when he didn't come home, Victor's was the first number we called. There'd been no study plan.'

'Can you remember what he was wearing?'

'Low pulls, knee high ones, they were black and tarty and his good coat. It was new. Green. He only got it last Christmas. Cost a small fortune. He loved it though, that's why he'd never have worn it just to study at Victor's.'

'And did you confront him about where he was actually going?'

Stern looked at him, her eyes filled with remorse and guilt. 'I've never been much good at confrontation. I think that's why Tom married me. His last wife, Leo's mother, had been a thug, and a wimp like me must've seemed much safer.' She dropped her face into her hands and wept. Wayne pushed the coffee cup closer.

'Have something to drink,' she said.

Stern composed herself and took a few sips of the coffee. She spat it out at once. 'I'm sorry,' she muttered.

'It's alright,' Wayne replied. 'Your kid's been killed, not your taste buds. I get it.'

Ben kicked Wayne hard under the table, then he turned his attention back to Stern. 'So, you just let him go?'

'I didn't just let him go, I couldn't stop him. I had the baby, what was I supposed to do? Leave her and chase after him? Drag him back? He was sixteen, not six. You don't know what it's been like this past year. He had been drinking, smoking, lying to us, playing truant—he had just been suspended. He was out of control!'

'Suspended? What was that for?' Wayne asked.

Stern blushed and focused her eyes on the floor.

'Look, this is a murder investigation,' Wayne kept her voice low. 'It's all going to come out, and it might as well be you that tells us.'

'He'd been behaving inappropriately with a teacher, making suggestive remarks, dressing seductively for her classes. She became very uncomfortable and eventually reported Leo to the head.'

'Seriously, like she wasn't down on her knees, thanking God herself, that a teenage boy had taken an interest in her? I don't see it. Any red-blooded woman would be dancing a little jig. Your Leo, he was a looker, right?'

'You'll have to forgive my partner,' Ben interjected. 'She's from a different time when sexual harassment wasn't a crime, but something a victim looked forward to.' He'd never have said it out loud, but Ben agreed with Wayne. Sexual harassment of boys and men was a real problem, and one that all the years of men's liberation had barely scratched the surface. But grown women claiming to be victims of sexual harassment by young boys? That was just bullshit and completely missed the point about what sexual harassment really was, and why it existed.

'Leo denied the whole thing. Said Ms Singh was the one doing the harassing. Asking him to stay late, then sitting too close, stroking his leg, brushing up against him, telling him how beautiful he was. His father believed him more than I did. You've got to understand, Leo's been lying to us all the time. Swore blind that he never smoked. He claimed that someone must have planted the cigarettes we found in his bag, but then we walk straight in on him smoking in his room. Over £40 went missing from an emergency pot in the house. Then once again he pleaded complete innocence and yet we found out a week later that he's bought a ticket for a gig we said he couldn't go to. He couldn't offer us a satisfactory explanation about where the money had come from. It reached the point where we, well, I, wouldn't believe a single word he said.' Her voice broke and gave way to loud violent sobs. Wayne put a hand on her shoulder.

'We'll get you a car home, Ms Stern.'

All three of them walked in silence to the front reception where Wayne instructed the desk sergeant to take care of the grief-stricken mother.

'She obviously struggled with her crazy teenage son. Are we treating her as a suspect?' Ben asked once Stern was out of earshot.

'Not unless we're really desperate,' Wayne replied.

As Ben pulled in to the staff car park at Withering High, the bell rang for morning break. Swarms of sweaty teenagers piled out into the tentative winter sunshine, and the detectives struggled to hear their own thoughts amid the shrieks and chatters of the youngsters.

'My kids go here,' Ben said as they were walking towards the main entrance.

Wayne stopped in her tracks and squinted. She was staring across the yard at one of the school cleaners. *How did she know her?*

'Are you listening to me?' Ben snapped.

The cleaner turned the corner and disappeared out of Wayne's sight.

'Yeah, yeah, kids at this school. That's nice.'

Ben knew where they were going and they bypassed the school office and headed straight down the corridor to the career base. Wayne peered in the glass door. Singh was at her desk, barely visible behind a large pile of papers. She knocked and then opened the door, allowing Ben to enter first. Singh looked up, her unruly hair flopping in front of her eyes.

'Mister Campbell, I wasn't expecting you. Do we have an appointment?' Singh asked.

Ben remained standing and produced police I.D. from his pocket. 'I'm not here about Simon, Ms Singh. I'm here in my capacity as a police inspector. This is my colleague, Inspector Wayne. We'd like to talk to you about one of your pupils, Leo Stern.'

'Leo's currently suspended. Any questions you have about him should be directed to Ms Paterson, the headmistress.'

'Only we're not talking to the head, Singh, we're talking to you.' Wayne straddled a classroom chair and shuffled up to Singh's desk until she sat opposite her. Singh pulled her chair back until it hit the wall.

'What's this about?'

'We ask the questions, Singh. Now, why don't you tell us how Leo came to be suspended?' Wayne demanded.

'It's not my decision who is suspended. I merely relayed my concerns about Leo's behaviour to Ms Paterson, as it is my legal and moral obligation to do so.' Singh started to wheeze. She reached into the pocket of her shapeless cardigan for her inhaler. She put it to her lips and took in a few deep blasts.

'No need to be so anxious, pal,' said Wayne. 'I know how boys are, especially a certain kind of boy. Was Leo like that, a bit of a goer?'

Singh's face turned white. 'I'm not sure what you're trying to say Inspector, but I don't like your terms of expression.'

'I get that a lot,' Wayne replied.

'Leo Stern was found dead in suspicious circumstances yesterday,' Ben said.

The last of the colour drained from the teacher's face. 'Dead? Dead how?'

'He was murdered.'

'And what? You think I had something to do with it?'

'We never said that, though now that you mention it, we might as well ask. Did you?' Wayne's eyes mocked the teacher.

Singh drew hard on her inhaler.

'Look, Ms Singh, we're just trying to trace Leo's last movements and get some kind of picture of how things were for him in the past few months. We spoke to his mother and we know he was suspended because of complaints made by a teacher. And we know that teacher was you. We just need to understand exactly what occurred between you and Leo. Take your time.' Ben's voice was soft and calming.

Singh shifted uncomfortably in her chair. 'It started with the odd comment. "*Hot cheeks*" that was the first one I think, or the second.' Singh reddened as she spoke. 'Then Leo started lingering longer than others after class. He'd do ridiculous schoolboy things, you know the way they do, like drop his book and bend over to get it.'

Wayne wasn't buying it. She'd have given a year's wages for a schoolboy to drop and bend deliberately for her. So, would any red-blooded female, including this bumbling fool. Singh had 'pervert' written square on her head.

'Truth is, I probably should have reported Leo's behaviour sooner. I didn't want to create a fuss and I didn't want to adversely affect his career prospects by making a mountain out of a molehill. The turning point was about a month ago.' Singh was sweating heavily and wiped her brow with the sleeve of her cardigan. 'I returned from my lunch hour, well I say hour, I mean fifteen minutes—you can't imagine how long a teachers' hours really are—and he was in here, in my room. He was dressed very... inappropriately, and he was sitting at my desk in a very provocative pose. I kept my distance.'

'I bet you did,' Wayne sneered.

'I assure you, Inspector, that I have no desire to get close to a semi-naked teenage boy, on school premises, during my lunch hour. I can't think of a more stomach churning idea. I'm his teacher for goodness' sake! I know I was remiss in not acting sooner, but I didn't have any idea it would get this out of hand. I've dealt with these schoolboy crushes before. In my experience, the best course of action is to ignore the boy until they develop an attraction on someone more suitable, which never takes long; they're randy little beasts.'

Wayne was staring at her in disbelief. Singh reckoned she had groupies, did she? This bitch was so full of shit! 'So, at that point you reported Leo?'

'I told Leo to get off my seat and he did. But then he stood in front of me and started to gyrate his hips and touch me, actually touch me. He'd left me with no option. I asked the head for leniency. You know, if it wasn't for me, Leo would have been expelled.'

'A fact he's unlikely to give a suck about, now that he's dead,' Wayne countered.

Ben and Wayne walked back across the schoolyard to the car park. The kids were mostly back in class, aside from the odd teenager still soaking up the afternoon sunshine. As they approached the car, Wayne stopped and sniffed. She patted down the pockets of her trench coat.

'Shit! I forgot my phone. Look, you go on, Campbell. I'll pick it up and see you back at the station.' Ben gave her a suspicious look. Wayne grinned at him and headed back towards the school.

When she was certain Ben was gone, she did a U-turn and retraced her steps across the car park, all the while sniffing like a fox outside a chicken coop. Her nostrils flared as she walked through the bicycle sheds, and at the back of them she found her prey. There were three teenagers standing in a circle giggling. A pale-faced, acne-ridden girl saw Wayne first. She was about to inhale another toke from an ambitious looking joint. Her hand froze. Wayne took the joint from her, knocked the burning top off it, and put it carefully into her side pocket. The two teenage boys that were standing either side of Acne Face gave each other a nervous glance.

'Who the suck are you?' asked the girl, sounding a lot braver than the expression on her face.

'I'm a police officer, kid,' Wayne replied flashing her I.D. 'I'll be the one asking questions.'

The girl turned to her friends and mouthed, "shit".

'You better believe it's shit,' Wayne agreed. 'So, hand it over, right now.'

The three kids gawped at each other and back at Wayne. Acne Face reached into the pocket of her trousers and handed her a bag of weed. Wayne lifted it to her face, inhaled and smiled. The blond boy took another bag from his rucksack and handed it to her. Wayne looked at the brunette and he shrugged his shoulders.

'I'll have to take you all back to the station and get the sniffer dogs,' she said. The brunette's eyes bulged. He reached into the front pocket of his school skirt and produced a bag that had been resting between his pra and cock. Wayne held out her hand and he dropped the bag into it. Wayne's eyes lit up and she placed the stash in her back pocket.

'And now the question is, am I taking you all back to the station, or is there a way out of this mess?' Wayne grinned and the two boys flinched at the sight of her tobacco stained teeth. The blond one walked up to her and began fiddling with the zip of her trousers. Wayne pushed his hand away.

'What are you after then?' Blondie asked.

'Some information will do nicely.'

Ben and McEwan were locked deep in conversation when Wayne got back to the station. She thought about turning round and leaving again, but she could feel Campbell's eyes on her.

'Wayne,' he called. 'Come join us. Professor McEwan's

giving me her insights so far.'

'Actually, I was just going to check something at the lab...'

'Later,' Ben insisted. He stood up and pulled a third chair beside McEwan's desk. Wayne shuffled across the room and sat down. She eyeballed McEwan, who smiled at her and moved her lips vaguely in reply, before she focused her attention on Campbell. He was like a star-struck house-husband gazing at a daytime soap star. It was embarrassing. She nudged him with her elbow. Ben turned and gave her a quizzical look.

'Sorry,' she whispered.

'I was just sharing my initial impressions of the crime scenes and the material with your colleague, Inspector Wayne. Will I give you a summary of that?'

'If you must,' she replied.

'Now, I wish to stress that this is just theory; I would need a much larger database of evidence to say anything definitively. But I would say this, in all probability, based on the tiny sample of material provided, that we're looking for an atheist.'

'Well, that narrows it down.' Wayne had taken one of the photocopies from the desk and was busy folding it in to the shape of a paper airplane. Ben placed his hand over it. She tried to pull it from under him, but to no avail.

'And what's led you to that conclusion, professor?' Ben asked.

'Well, each scene so far has the juxtaposition of some of the major world religions, with three in total appearing over four crime scenes. This doesn't suggest a devout follower of any one religion, but a voyeur almost, someone outside the religion looking in: an atheist essentially.'

Ben was scrawling notes as McEwan spoke, his left hand

firmly in charge of the paper plane. Wayne lay back on her chair and closed her eyes. She felt Ben's finger poke her in the stomach. 'Do you have any questions for the professor?'

'How much are we paying you for this shit?'

Wayne was outside Baker's back door trying to work up the courage to go in. Suddenly, she remembered the spliff from earlier and her face broke into a smile. She fished into the depths of her raincoat, pulled it out and stuck it between her lips. Once lit, she took a few deep draws in quick succession. Wayne spluttered then laughed out loud. *This was good weed!* She cursed herself for not finding out who the kid's dealer was.

'Who's there?' She heard Baker's voice through the open window.

'It's Wayne, pal. I'm here to check up on you.'

The back door swung open and Baker stepped outside.

'Well, you better come in then, you won't do much checking up out there!'

Wayne walked slowly to the kitchen, sniffing Baker as she passed her. She smelled of lime and mint shower gel and effective deodorant. She brought her nose to her friend's mouth and Baker breathed out garlic and meatballs. Baker pointed to a pan that was bubbling on the stove.

'Have you eaten?' she asked.

Wayne peered into the saucepan and soaked up the aroma of the tomato and basil sauce. She glanced round the entire kitchen looking for any trace of last night's carnage but all she saw were bleached work surfaces and shiny floors.

'Are you sober now? It's like last night never happened, or was it the start of something? Because I stood by last time round, Martha. I watched you lose Ollie and the kids and every ounce of your dignity. It was me who dried you out, remember? I didn't leave your side for a fortnight, didn't so much as piss, without you there. It was me who pleaded with the tribunal panel, told them you were a great doctor, trapped in a drunk's body. I won't do that shit again, Baker, I can't. I don't have it in me anymore.' Wayne took off her coat, threw it across a chair and sat down at Baker's kitchen table.

Baker meandered across the room, and stood in front of Wayne. 'It was a one-off Wayne, I swear to you. A moment of weakness. I woke up this morning with the taste of whisky on my breath and I knew if I didn't stop there and then... I called Sandy and she came over, helped me clean the house, get rid of all the booze. She only left about an hour ago.'

'And that's it. You're not even going to see a doctor?'

'To be told what?' replied Baker. 'That I'm a fat bitch with no self-control?' She patted her bulging stomach and ambled over to the stove. Wayne watched her as she carefully ladled heaped spoonful after spoonful of meatballs into two ceramic bowls. She sprinkled parmesan generously on both, and then deftly wiped the sides of each bowl, before topping them with a sprig of basil. Wayne smiled and felt her jaw muscles unclench. Baker was back.

Wayne breathed in gulps of night air as she strolled back. It was a good time for a walk. The streets were deserted, and as she headed towards the town centre, she began to sort through the myriad of thoughts in her head. She was relieved that Baker was sober, minding a drunk was like minding a child, with none of the funny stuff that kids sometimes do. Also, it made her reflect on her own drinking patterns and Wayne preferred not having to think of such things. Her mind drifted to Campbell. She'd never admit it, but she was starting to think he was alright. *Once you got past his looks, or lack of them,* she thought, *and once you got past his utter ineptitude and his obsession with experts and by-the-book policing.* Actually, after giving the matter some consideration, she realised Campbell was far from alright. *But he's still a damn sight better than O'Keeffe,* her mind conceded. She checked the time on her phone. It was twenty past midnight, time to wake up the night sergeant and make her work for a change.

P.C. Johnston was asleep behind her desk. Wayne carefully pulled the police log book from beneath her then slammed it down on the counter as hard as she could. The night sergeant jumped up. 'What the suck, Wayne? Are you trying to give me a heart attack?'

'Heart attacks are usually proceeded by some level of exertion, so I reckon you're safe,' Wayne told her and both women laughed.

Johnston and Wayne went way back, having joined the force within a year of each other. Whilst Wayne's career had steadily progressed, Johnston's had never got off the ground, largely because she was completely lacking in ambition.

'I just don't give a shit,' she'd explained to Wayne, after the latter got her first promotion.

Looking at her now, over thirty years on, Wayne reckoned she'd had the right idea.

'I need you to dig out some files for me,' Wayne told her.

'No problem,' Johnston replied. 'Who are you after?'

'Not who - what—and I'm not really sure. Get me a copy of every violent crime that I've worked on in the past ten years, starting with the older cases.'

'Seriously?' Johnston asked her. 'That's a helluva lot of cases, boss!'

'It is,' Wayne agreed. 'You better get cracking.'

Wayne settled herself behind the desk in her office and sped read box after box of files as Johnston hauled them through. When she ran out of space in Wayne's office, Johnston began piling boxes up outside it. Eventually, Johnston had run out of boxes and drenched in sweat, she knocked on the door. 'That's them all, boss,' she told Wayne and quickly retreated.

'Where do you think you're going?' a voice called after her.

'I thought I'd get back to the desk,' she replied.

'You thought you'd get back to sleep is what you mean. Go and get two cups from the kitchen and then get your fat arse back here. We've got lots of reading to do.'

Johnston did as she was told and when she returned, Wayne poured two generous measures from her hip flask into the cups. Johnston grinned as she handed her one. Wayne sat behind the desk, her feet on the table, flicking through file after file.

'I'm sorry to ask again, but what exactly are we looking for?' Johnston repeated.

Wayne didn't look up, her concentration firmly focused on the information in front of her.

'I'll know it when I see it.'

'So where does that leave me?'

'Look, just sort out the boxes. I'm only interested in the sadistic freaks. Weed out arson, armed robbery, husband killers—as long as it's just one victim—thugs ; only the really dark dangerous bitches. How many can there be?'

Johnston nodded, and got to work placing case after case neatly to the side of Wayne's desk for her to check.

Wayne yawned as she flicked through psycho after psycho. She stopped at a photo of a paedophile. A pair of dead eyes bored right through her and vivid memories of a decade old investigation began to surface.

'Tara Donaldson, how could I ever forget you?'

'Is that her?' Johnston hauled herself up to look at the bespectacled woman in the mug shot. 'She hardly looks the type.'

'They never do,' Wayne replied. She remembered the woman she'd seen in the playground earlier. She was older, heavier and her thinning hair was pure grey, but it was Donaldson all right. How the suck did she get work in a school?

'So, who is she then?' Johnston had put her feet up on a box of files and was sipping the remains of her whisky.

'She was one of the main players in that paedo ring we busted in 2006. I did nine months undercover to nail the bitch, remember?'

Johnston shook her head.

'She was a child psychiatrist, used to drug her patients and then film them. She was part of a European-wide ring of similar type professionals, all with easy, regular access to vulnerable, sucked up kids. There was so much shit in her flat, it took us three weeks to process it. As soon as she was sent down, I transferred out of Vice, probably a year too late, all things considered.'

'At least you got her before you left, eh?'

'That's what I told myself at the time, but it was bullshit. You never get the Donaldsons of this world.' Wayne raised her cup to her mouth and felt the blessed burn as it slid down her throat.

SEVEN

THURSDAY

'Simon, get down these stairs now, or I'm going without you!'

'Good.'

Ben groaned. This was the last bloody thing he needed, Simon throwing a hissy fit. George had a dental appointment, and in one morning without him, the house had descended into anarchy. Val wanted to wear a superwoman costume instead of her school uniform, and Drea had left the house without breakfast or her gym kit or her maths homework. Ben dropped his handbag at the bottom of the stairs and climbed them two at a time. He knocked sharply on his son's bedroom door. 'Simon, get a move on, or we'll all be late.'

'Like I give a shit if you're late.'

Ben counted backwards from ten before entering the room. Simon was sitting on his bed, his arms folded, and his mouth forming the perfect pout. Streaks of sunlight danced over his features, reminding Ben what a beautiful child he was. There were faint dabs of blusher around his cheeks and a few coats of sheer mascara clogged his eyelids, in clear breach of the school's no make-up rule, but he decided to let it slide. He sat down on the bed and began stroking his son's hair. Simon pulled away from him.

'What's going on Simon?'

Simon switched his attention to his mobile, scrolling through his messages.

'Please Simon, you have to talk to me. How else will I know what's going on with you?'

'Maybe if you were home a bit more often...' Simon countered.

'What home though? I have to work the hours I do to keep us in this one. And to keep you in clothes and fashion magazines and concert tickets. It all costs. Would you rather we'd stayed in London, moved to some grotty estate, and claimed benefits?'

Simon shrugged his shoulders. 'I hate it here.'

'Me too,' Ben confessed. 'But it's a good job and it's got prospects. I have to think like this now, Simon. There's only me to take care of you and your sisters.'

'Mum would help if you just asked her. Maybe I could go and stay with her?'

'Simon, you know you can't do that. We haven't seen her in years, eh? We don't even know where she is and she's gone to great lengths to keep it that way.'

'It's you that she doesn't want knowing her whereabouts, not us. This is all you. If you'd been less of a nag and given her a bit more space, then she wouldn't have had to run away. Would she?'

'She didn't have to run away, Simon, she chose to, just like she chose not to tell us where. And she chose to clear out our joint account, leaving me with no choices at all.'

Pools of water filled his son's eyes, and his heart ached. He reached into his trouser pocket where he always kept £20 spare for petrol and handed it to Simon. 'Why don't you go round the shops after school?'

Simon's face brightened. 'If I had another ten I could get a maxi dress, everyone's wearing them, Dad.'

'Right, if you're in the car in five minutes, I'll give it

serious consideration.'

Simon jumped off his bed like it was on fire and began throwing books and pencils into his bag. He pulled a comb through his hair, and searched his dressing table for a scrunchie. After checking in the mirror, he straightened his skirt and opened another button on his blouse, before he bounded down the stairs. He grabbed an apple from the fruit bowl in the kitchen and gave himself another quick once-over in the hall mirror. When he heard the front door slam, Ben smiled, grabbed his handbag and joined his waiting family.

Wayne sat opposite Donaldson in interview room number one, wearing a new shirt and trousers set she'd bought in a 24/7 supermarket on her way home the night before. Seeing Donaldson had made her consider her own appearance. *What does that say about me, needing to dress up for a paedo?* Still, at least she could concentrate on the stare-off not feeling her old, tight trousers dig into her flesh.

Peachy stood at the other side of the one-way glass with half a dozen others from uniform. They were yelling at the pane and thumping each other on the back.

'Come on, Wayne, I've backed you the whole way,' hollered Peachy.

'Dirty Donaldson, c'mon you know you can do it!' The P.C. to his right retaliated.

'What the hell is going on here?'

Peachy jumped at the sound of Ben's voice. He turned round quickly and smiled weakly at his boss. 'We're observing the interview. Wayne asked us to keep an eye on things.'

'Who's she?'

'Tara Donaldson. She's a paedophile known to us. Wayne spotted her at Withering High yesterday. She had her brought in first thing this morning.'

'Did she now?' Ben stared at Wayne through the glass. Beads of sweat dripped off her skin as she remained locked in eyeball combat with Donaldson. He took a deep breath and opened the door to the adjoining room.

'Wayne, a minute.'

Wayne blinked and Donaldson's face creased into a smile.

'Shit, boss! What the suck did you do that for? I had her there.'

'Had who, where? Who the hell is this Tara Donaldson and what's she doing in an interrogation room without me having ordered her to be there?'

'Calm down, pet, you'll give yourself high blood pressure. You weren't here. I felt it was important to act fast.'

'Really? So why didn't you act yesterday, when you saw her at Withering High?'

'I didn't recognise her instantly, I knew she was familiar, but I couldn't put a name to her. It's been ten years. She's older, she's fatter, she's greyer. I came back here last night and searched through all my old cases.' Wayne ran her fingers through her unruly mop, scattering dandruff on Ben's shoes. His lip curled involuntarily, as he stared at it. 'I figured if we picked her up this morning, at work, it would make more sense than storming round in the middle of the night. What we didn't want was her deleting her hard drive while we boot her front door down. I would have waited for you. But you're a bit late today. If it's all right to point that out, boss.'

'I had business to attend to,' Ben snapped. 'You should

have called me last night, at home, the minute that you figured out who Donaldson was. I don't want you to keep me in the loop Wayne, I want you to remember I am the loop! Got it?'

'You are the loop, sir!'

Ben blushed. 'Right, now tell me everything you know about Donaldson.'

'I was working Vice in 2006 and we pulled her as part of a European-wide paedophile chain involved in the production and distribution of hardcore child porn. It was a tight operation and a good team, we secured a dozen convictions. Donaldson was sent down for an eight-year stretch and she served most of it. She's been out about three years, but she's kept herself under the radar.'

'What the hell was she doing at Withering High with that record?'

'From what I can tell, she was working there. I've sent two uniforms over to figure out how she got hired as a janitor, although it's safe to assume she used an alias. When we searched her house last time we found ten different passports.'

'Right, so what has she said so far?'

'She wants a cup of tea and some Hobnobs.'

'And the stare-off, what was that all about?'

'That was the look I gave her when she said she wanted Hobnobs. Even O'Keeffe settles for chocolate digestives.'

'Okay, let's resume the interview. This time, I'll take the lead.'

Ben sat opposite Donaldson, who seemed desperate for another stare-off. The young detective met her ice cold eyes for about twenty seconds before blinking furiously.

Donaldson laughed.

'Right, Tara,' Ben began. 'Why don't you start by explaining to us exactly how you've wound up working at Withering High?'

'No comment.'

'You must know it's against the terms of your license to be working in a school?'

'No comment.'

'What name did you use? You'd never have got work as Tara Donaldson.'

'No comment.'

'A bit of a climb down, isn't it, Donaldson? It says here you used to be a respected psychiatrist. Now you're a janitor in a high school.'

'Still, there's all that young, unfettered puppy, that probably takes the edge off the pay cut,' Wayne interjected.

'No comment.'

'Did you know Leo Stern?' Ben continued.

'Sure she did,' said Wayne. 'He was one sexy little tart and he knew it. Strutting around the playground like it's Ringford Street on a Saturday night. That tight, taut ass of his begging to be poked.'

'No comment.'

Ben began to lay out crime scene photos in front of Donaldson and her mouth folded into a sly smile as she lapped up image after image. As he placed the last one in front of her, she brushed her fingers lightly off his. Wayne leapt across the desk and wrestled her to the ground. There was a glint in the paedo's eyes as Wayne pressed her forehead against the hard-tiled floor. She opened her mouth to try and speak.

'Right, that's enough!' Ben placed a restraining hand

on Wayne's shoulder. 'What's the matter, Donaldson? You finally got something to say?'

'Like I said at the start of this interview, I want my lawyer.' As she spoke, blood dribbled from her mouth and tasting it, she started to laugh.

Wayne sat in her office waiting for Campbell. She looked at the clock on the wall and confirmed another minute had passed. She tapped her shoe and fished around her coat pockets searching for her tobacco tin. *Who the suck did City Boy think he was, making her hang around like a naughty schoolgirl?* Yeah, she'd attacked Donaldson, but it was no less than the sick bitch deserved. She hadn't broken any limbs, which was actually a testament to her restraint. But she wouldn't be getting any credit for that. Wayne missed the old days, when suspects were fair game and policewomen were above the law. She eyed the wall clock again. *Suck this!* She got up to leave and collided with Ben at the door.

'Sorry I kept you waiting,' Ben said. 'I was getting a report from the station doctor on Donaldson's injuries, which are negligible, thankfully.'

'Give me another ten minutes with her and you can get an update from the morgue.'

'I see, so not content with assaulting a suspect, you now want an opportunity to kill the same suspect. What century are you living in, Wayne? It's highly possible that, whatever we get on her, we'll have to let her go. Nice work if she turns out to be the Wringer.' Ben sat back in his chair and threw his pen at the door, narrowly missing Wayne.

'She's not the Wringer., These boys, they're fifteen and sixteen, right? They're geriatrics to Donaldson, and besides, it's girls she really likes. And she's never killed before, least not that we know of. I've got in touch with Florence from Fraud. She's on her way back from Leeds. She can have a look at Donaldson's computers and we can take things from there.'

'I thought you said she didn't have a mobile.'

'She doesn't. I had a few of the Leeds girls track her down. She's a bit wasted, but they're plying her with coffee and driving her back. Meanwhile, I think we should take another look at Singh.'

'Based on what, other than the fact that you don't like her?'

'And you do?' she retorted.

'We need more than that, Wayne.'

'I had a chat with a few of the kids when I went back to the school yesterday. Word is she's a real perv, "Sleazebag Singh" they call her, "Here comes Singh, watch your thing". You know what I'm saying?'

'Please tell me you didn't question minors without their parents present?' Ben's words came out clipped and sharp.

'Don't worry about that at all, pet,' Wayne reassured him. 'I caught them smoking weed, they're not going to tell their folks that, are they?'

Ben stared at her and shook his head. 'No more! Don't tell me another word. I don't want to know. And don't call me pet!'

'So, can we go back or what?'

'That bitch teaches two of my kids. You're damn right we're going back!'

This time, they didn't knock as they entered Singh's room. As soon as she saw them, Singh dropped her paperwork.

'What can I do for you, Inspectors? I thought I'd answered all your questions yesterday?' Singh was on her knees picking up year 10's essay questions.

'So did we, but that was before we realised you were a lying piece of shit!' Wayne replied.

Singh started to cough and felt inside the pocket of the same shapeless cardigan she'd worn the day before, for her inhaler. Wayne knocked half a dozen folders off the chair behind Singh's desk and sat down.

'I'd rather you didn't sit there, Inspector,' the teacher's words were barely a whisper as she wheezed while clutching her inhaler.

'And I'd rather you didn't lie to police during a murder inquiry, but what can we do? It's an imperfect world.'

'I've no idea what you're talking about.'

'I'm sure you do.'

Ben wanted to intervene, but he didn't know what to say. He didn't know where Wayne was going with any of this and he didn't trust her sources. A group of stoned teenagers could hardly be described as the most reliable of character witnesses. Still, she'd been a smug, arrogant arsehole when she and Ben had that meeting. Maybe this would teach her a lesson that wasn't on Withering High's curriculum.

'Look, why don't we just continue this down at the station?' Wayne suggested.

Ben's head jerked round and he gave Wayne a filthy look. *What the suck was she doing? There were absolutely no grounds to arrest her. There were no real grounds to even be there. Why the suck was he letting Wayne take charge?*

'Can I speak to you for a minute, Wayne?' he tried to keep the rising panic from his voice.

'Not now, doll. The teacher here has something she wants

to tell the class. Of course, we can always do this down at the clink. Shit! Is that the bell? What do you say, Singh? Do you want to be frog-marched across the playground?'

'Leo and I were lovers,' Singh blurted out. 'I'm a weak and foolish woman and he was a sumptuous, beguiling creature. I tried to stop it from happening...'

'I bet you did,' Wayne sneered. Singh flinched and cast her head downwards.

Ben stared open-mouthed at Singh and then at Wayne. He had so not seen that revelation coming. Wayne was right; he was shit at this job.

'I'm sure I disgust you, Inspector. I disgust myself. I was placed in a position of trust, I should never have done what I did. But he was so persistent and so beautiful. And he's actually sixteen, so what we did wasn't illegal.'

'Of course it's illegal, you arrogant cock He's your pupil.' Ben reached into the covert holster under his shirt and pulled out a pair of steel handcuffs. He was conscious of the excessive pressure he applied to Singh's hands as he imagined Simon and her alone in a room together. He placed his hand on Singh's head and pushed her down the stairs and across the playground. The year elevens had a free period.

'Fashion police finally caught up with you Ms?' shouted a red-headed boy.

Ben and Wayne stared through the one-way glass that separated them from Tara Donaldson and her lawyer.

'You tell that cunt licker if she doesn't get her ass in here right now, I'll have her badge!' Green screamed at Peachy. Being trapped in the interrogation room with the paedo didn't suit her and her carefully constructed pleasant demeanour was fading fast. There were beads of sweat on the collar of her bespoke shirt and her normally perfect hair clung to the sides of her head. Donaldson, in contrast, looked made for confined spaces. She sat serenely in her chair, her eyes flitting between opened and closed.

'It shouldn't be long now, Ms Green. Can I get you a cup of coffee or tea?' Peachy ran his fingers through his hair and smiled shyly at the disgruntled lawyer. Green's face softened and she returned his smile.

'No more tea, love, just your boss now, please.'

Ben entered the room first, weighed down with Donaldson's file. Green jumped to her feet and grabbed the top of the bundle just before it fell. Her fingers lightly grazed Ben's hand. Wayne swung the door open just missing both of them. She looked from one to the other and removed the files from Green's hands. She pulled up the seat beside Ben's, turned it around and straddled it.

'What the hell do you think you're playing at, Wayne? My client's been waiting for three hours,' demanded Green. She lowered her pitch and stared directly at Ben. 'Not that you're not worth waiting for.' Ben's face turned crimson. Wayne snorted.

'We've got a homicidal maniac on the loose. Your name-changing paedo isn't top of our priorities,' Wayne said.

'Ms Donaldson has already served her time for previous convictions and was in fact released early for her exemplary behaviour. Her incarceration gave her the opportunity to consider the gravity of her actions and she assures me she's a thoroughly reformed character.'

Feigning sleep, Donaldson opened her eyelids, grinned, and then lowered them again.

'As Inspector Wayne pointed out, Ms Green, we're in the

middle of a woman hunt. However, I'm very sorry we've taken up so much of your client's time.' Ben kept his voice steady.

'We sure are. Imagine if she hadn't been here, staring at your ugly mug. She could have been out there, raping more children,' Wayne added.

'Right, I'll stop you there, Wayne. Have you any facts with which to back up these allegations?' Green demanded.

'Yeah, it's stamped on her forehead, "*I rape kids*". You can see it in certain lights.'

'And you can't come up with anything more substantial than a metaphysical tattoo?'

'Violation of her parole, let's start with that. Assuming a false identity to gain employment in a school.' Wayne raised her eyebrows. 'Shall I go on?'

Green reached down and sifted through some files in her briefcase before producing one and handing it to Ben. 'That's a bit of a non-starter, I'm afraid.' Green continued with a smug grin. 'Ms Donaldson used her real name. She's not actually employed by the school. She's employed by G4T, a private cleaning company. Ms Donaldson had made her supervisor, Ms Henrietta Weeks, aware of her parole restrictions, and Ms Weeks had given Ms Donaldson the green light to work there, in view of severe staff shortages. Here's a statement from Ms Weeks to that effect. I've spoken with Clare Kendell, Ms Donaldson's parole officer, and she's happy that the terms of my client's parole have not been violated. So, unless there's anything else, you need to release my client.'

Ben and Wayne shared a look.

'She can go,' Ben said quietly.

Alone in the claustrophobic room, Ben stared at the

stack of redundant paperwork, while Wayne rocked back and forth on the legs of her chair. 'What the suck did you do that for?' she asked.

'Because we have nothing, Wayne. Other than the fact that you really dislike her, which is not a criminal offence.'

'What about her computer?'

'Useless. She's not even connected to the internet. The only thing she keeps on it is book downloads, hundreds of pages about antique maintenance and restoration.'

'They'll be encrypted,' Wayne suggested.

'Florence from Fraud says no, and you said she's the computer expert.'

'I said she knows more about them than most of us, but that hardly makes her an expert. Why don't you send it down to London?' Wayne pleaded with him.

'No. I'm in charge here and I'm not squandering precious resources on dead ends. Let it go, Wayne. You said it yourself, she's not a killer.'

'No, I never said that. I said she's never been caught. She's a dangerous, deviant bitch and she should be off the streets.'

'That's not your call to make. Right, I'm done here. I'm going to take off and catch up with my kids. You could probably do with an early one too.'

Ben left the file on the table and Wayne leafed through the top pages. She stopped at the first photograph and stared at the naked girl. She couldn't have been more than six years old. Her blonde hair flopped over the top of her eyes but the camera still captured the pain and fear within them. Wayne snapped the folder shut and with one big push, she threw the entire file onto the floor. Dozens of images of naked children carpeted the room. Their terrified faces were distorted by the mud on Wayne's boots as she walked over them and out the door. She didn't look left or right as she departed the main office and walked to the lift. When she got out at the basement she hesitated for a moment, before marching down to Jackson's office and knocking hard on the door.

'Come in,' a voice said. Dr Jackson sat behind his makeshift desk, sipping an Earl Grey tea and reading a text book so large it hid the top of his perfect frame. He lowered it to reveal a floral pink top that clung seductively to his concave stomach and was a perfect match for his rose lipstick. 'You're late.'

'Yeah, sorry about that. It's been a hectic day. Do you think you could squeeze me in now?'

'You're two days late, Jane. You were supposed to be here on Tuesday. You can't just stroll in and think I'm going to see you whenever you turn up.' Dr Jackson closed the book, and gave Wayne the sort of look a school teacher reserves for a particularly wayward pupil. 'However, my five o'clock cancelled, so I have a bit of time. I will see you this once, but just one time. You need to keep your appointments.'

Dr Jackson removed his reading glasses to reveal warm hazel eyes which he'd accentuated with a dusting of shimmery gold eye shadow. Sitting opposite, Wayne felt hot and sweaty. She pulled her shirt from inside her trousers and began flapping it to cool herself down. When she'd finished, she put her hands on her lap and kept her eyes on the floor. After ten minutes of silence Dr Jackson spoke.

'So how was your day, Jane? You said it was busy?'

'It was shit. All we managed was to keep a sick dangerous bitch off the street for a matter of hours.'

'Do you want to elaborate?'

'We pulled in a paedo this morning, as part of the Wringer inquiry. But we had to release her.'

'So, she's not involved?'

'I never said that. I don't know if she's involved or not. But does it matter? She's a sucking paedo. She belongs in a cage where she can't get at small kids and where other dangerous bitches can poke her instead.' Wayne's face turned red and she spat the words at the doctor.

'And you honestly think that's the answer?'

'I suppose you're one of those liberals who think they should all receive help and therapy?'

'Would it be so bad if I was?'

'Yeah, I know your type, Guardian reading, Lib Dem voting, Oxfam subscribing, recycling, vegan -wine drinking, bleeding heart. You think all bad people are basically misunderstood, don't you? That they're victims of childhood neglect themselves, and with enough talk therapy and the odd yoga class you can make them whole again.' Wayne's face turned bright red as anger coursed through her. 'Well, let me tell you something, Mister do good-er. Some people are just evil bastards and it doesn't matter how many hours you spend talking to them or how many elastic bands you give them or how many victim impact statements you read them, they'll still be evil bastards afterwards, it's just how some people are.'

'You favour nature over nurture, the more biblical approach, essentially?'

'Is it? I wouldn't know anything about that. I'll tell you what I do know. Today, we just released a known violent predator. Suck, we probably even gave her a lift home. That same home, where tonight or tomorrow or next week, she'll lure some unsuspecting vulnerable kid. It's where she'll beat them and rape them and insert multiple objects into any hole she can find. She'll then sell images of this depravity to every pervert contact she's ever made, either inside prison or out. That's what I know. And somehow, all of this is made possible by ignorant, well-meaning people like you who have an obsession with prisoners' rights. Suck this, you and your kind make me sick!' Wayne threw back her chair and stood up.

Dr Jackson remained seated and calm. 'Is that us for this week, Jane? Next time, we'll try and keep the focus a bit more on you,' he smiled.

Kai pricked his finger and swore. That was the third time he'd done so in an hour. He looked at his patchwork apron with dismay. He looked at the clock on the wall. It was almost five. Shit! He was meeting her in an hour and he hadn't even started getting ready. He'd wanted to get his apron finished so he could slip in and out of needlework class without being noticed, but there seemed little chance of that now. Suck it! He'd have to skip the class altogether and take the flak from Mother Maria tomorrow. Kai's mobile beeped and he smiled. She was checking he hadn't forgotten about tonight, like he was going to forget about the biggest night of his life! He dropped the apron on the floor and began tossing clothes and make-up on his bed.

Ben was at home with Val for bath time and she was thrilled. *God, it was good to be home before she was in bed!* He patted his young daughter dry and Val told him excitedly about all her dinosaur figures and what they had been doing that day. Val was dinosaur mad at the moment. Ben laughed out loud. 'You and me both spend our days with dinosaurs!'

Val didn't get it, but laughed hard anyway.

'Dad,' yelled Simon. 'The laptop's on the blink!'

'Coming,' Ben replied. Speed drying Val, he wrapped her in a bathrobe, and carried her downstairs. He walked over to where Simon was sitting, picking up the charger as he went. He handed it to his son. 'How many times, Simon? It's not on the blink, it just has to be charged.'

'Thanks, Dad.'

'Right, mind your sister for a while, and I'll go rustle us all up some tea.' He glanced inside the fridge; it was slim pickings. There were two packets of salami, some out of date fresh pasta, a limp lettuce and a bottle of chardonnay. 'Kids, do you fancy pizza?'

'Yeah,' came the unanimous reply.

He ordered two large pizzas and a portion of fries and cajoled the whole family to the table to play a game of Buckaroo. Val looked like she would burst from excitement.

Once Drea and Simon had got their heads round the fact that the table was a gadget free zone, they both got into it. Val was cautiously placing a shovel on the mule's saddle when the doorbell rang. Ben found his purse and took out a twenty-pound note and some coins for the driver. He was carrying the food in his hands when his mobile beeped. He balanced the pizza boxes on the stairs, reached into his left pocket and glanced at the text. He stared openmouthed at the screen, as the pizza fell to the floor and fries covered his living room carpet.

EIGHT

FRIDAY

'Stop here!' Wayne barked.

The taxi screeched to a stop outside 77 Thornton Place. 'Now, sadly, I seem to have left my wallet on the sideboard— an occupational hazard of the unsocial hours…'

The taxi driver sped off swearing profusely. Wayne glanced at her watch, it was 3.10 a.m. The street was completely silent. She approached the door cautiously and noticed it was slightly ajar. *Suck!* For a moment, Wayne wondered if she should call for back up. She decided against it. This was their first solid lead in four murders; she didn't want anything to suck it up.

'Campbell, you there?' she called cautiously, stepping into the unlit hall.

'In here,' came the faint reply.

Wayne turned into the first room off the hallway. Ben was kneeling over the body of a dead woman, stroking her cheek. Beside them lay another body. It was a boy. He was almost naked, and had suffered the same fate as all the previous Wringer victims. The scene was what she'd come to expect—the floor was strewn with pages and pages of some shit religious book. The evidence would be taken back to the lab and pored over for days. Theories would be thrown around in the desperate hope that the torn pages had any sucking purpose at all, which Wayne frankly doubted. They were just the random quirks of a sick bitch; she might as well have left them pages from *The Shade*. She noticed a lamp in the corner of the room and switched it on. Ben shielded his eyes.

'What the suck are you doing here? Who the suck's she?' Wayne stared from Ben to the corpse.

'She's my wife, Anna. Or she was my wife, till she left us four years ago... She left us with nothing, just walked out.' Ben's voice was unsteady.

Wayne was stunned. She didn't know what to say. Campbell was married... to a woman, and an normal looking one at that. Surely not! She couldn't picture it. Sure, he'd had kids, but she assumed they were the product of some gay surrogacy pact, or other equally modern city set up. But Campbell straight? It sent shivers down her spine.

'What's your ex doing here? What were *you* doing here?'

'I got a text about 8.30 p.m. It was from her, she asked me to meet her here. I couldn't quite get my head round it. Four sucking years without a word and then this casual text with a kiss on the end.'

'Did you call the number?'

'Suck yeah! I spent the next two hours dialing and redialing, probably texted her fifty times. Might as well tell you most of them said "Bitch". A few actually said, "Suck off and die bitch!" And what do you know? For once, the silly cunt actually did what I asked.'

Ben's tears fell fast and unchecked. Wayne stepped over him and reached into the dead woman's pockets. She found keys, a wallet, a till receipt with the address they were in scrawled on it, and a couple of cocaine wraps. But no phone. Wayne put the wraps in her own pocket and everything else back where she'd found it. She carefully patted down the trousers on what felt like an expensive suit, but could feel no bulge that would hide a mobile.

'It's not here. Have you searched the house?'

Ben didn't reply. He was running his fingers over his dead wife's skin, tracing her outline, mouthing the word, "No" over and over. Wayne reached into her trench coat and pulled out her hip flask. Handing it to Ben, she noticed he was wearing lipstick, that was a first. She sniffed, he had perfume on too. She took off her coat and placed it round his shoulders, guiding him gently away from the body at the same time. His blouse and jeans were covered in her blood.

'Right, I'm calling it in. I want you to go home, shower and get your head together. I'll be over in an hour and you can explain to me how your ex-wife wound up on the Wringer's hit list.'

Baker was the first to arrive. She knocked quietly on the living room door. Wayne was surprised to see her. She was sitting on the back of the overturned sofa, taking in the details of the chaotic scene, careful not to disturb anything.

'Should you be here? Don't you think you need a few days off?' Wayne asked.

'I'm going stir-crazy, staring at the walls, counting the hours till the off-license closes and I can say I've done another day sober. It's driving me nuts, Wayne.'

'You've been sober two days, Martha.'

'Exactly, and it seems like years. I need to work, Wayne, please.'

Wayne walked over to her friend and sniffed her breath. She was sober all right. Baker smelled of aftershave and Kola Kube sweets and was her usual well-groomed self. Her navy suit had been freshly pressed and was a perfect match for her pin-striped shirt. It was a mark of her personal hygiene that, when static, she rarely perspired, despite carrying twice what she should in body weight. Wayne looked her in the eye. There was no trace of a glint. The emptiness that had pervaded the other night still lingered.

'I need to get some things clear first. What's your connection to the previous victim Leo Stern?'

'I'd rather not say,' Baker switched her focus to the floor.

'Then you won't be working here tonight,' Wayne replied.

'I know them through A.A.' Baker's voice was a whisper. 'Her Mother Rachel Stern is in the fellowship.'

Wayne nodded. That made sense. 'And the boy?'

'I was his Rachel's sponsor for the first two years, I know her whole family. I need to be part of this, Wayne.'

Wayne drew her gaze away from her friend's begging eyes. 'Okay, the stiffs are yours, but you've got to stay sober, Baker. If you so much as gargle with mouthwash, then you're off the case. I'll make sure of it personally.'

Baker gave Wayne a warm smile. 'Thanks pal, I won't let you down. I promise.'

Wayne withdrew from the murder scene and left her to get on with it. As soon as she stepped outside, she was hit by a blast of cool air. She pulled the collar of her shirt round her neck, taking in a whiff of her armpit as she did so. It wasn't a good smell, but after the stench of the house, it was positively benign. Wayne spotted an empty black cab and whistled for it.

Ben put the kettle on and stared at his reflection in its shiny surface. He looked old. He felt old, ten years older than he did that morning... Jess! Was it only twenty hours since his biggest worry was getting Simon to go to school? And now... *How the hell would Simon take this? How would any of the kids?* He didn't even know how to take it. *Anna dead It didn't make sense.* Anna, who had popped out for some avocados four years earlier, and wound up in San Francisco, only to vanish again by the time Ben had secured a contact number. And there had been nothing since—until the text. He scanned his phone and found it.

How's it going, Babe? It's been a long time. In the area for a few days. Staying at 77 Thornton Gardens. Drop by for old time's sake. Anna x

It was so Anna, the mistress of understatement. Ben had half expected to be seduced by her at the door, or at least charmed into a state of submission. He never thought for a second that she'd be dead. Ben cursed himself for hours of procrastination, as he'd paced the floor reliving all the anger, pain and devastation of her desertion. *What if I'd got there sooner? What was she doing in Withering? It can't have been a coincidence! Did she want to get back together? Was that why she'd texted?*

'Where are you going for that coffee? Brazil?' Wayne shouted from the living room. Ben snapped back into host mode. He put a large cafetiere on a round black tray, and grabbed some clean mugs from the cupboard. He rooted in his biscuit tin for a few stray digestives that the kids hadn't noticed, and arranged them on a side plate. He carried the drinks through, and nearly dropped the tray on the carpet when he saw Wayne skinning up at his living room table, on top of Drea's math's book.

'What the suck do you think you're doing? The kids are upstairs.'

'That's alright, there's plenty to go round,' Wayne smiled

and licked the side of her cigarette before tipping it onto her rolling papers.

'You're a cop, Wayne. I'm a cop!'

'Relax, Campbell. Everyone knows that cops have the best drugs.' Wayne presented the completed spliff to Ben. He stood holding it between his fingers until Wayne removed it and put it in his mouth. She held her lighter to the joint's tip. 'Inhale, for suck's sake, or it'll go out!'

Ben did as he was told, inhaling a bit too deeply, and coughing so hard, phlegm came up. But he went in for another draw anyway and giggled loudly as he exhaled. He passed the smoke to Wayne. 'That's good shit.' As he spoke, he stroked his newly shaven face and Wayne was struck by his beauty. He looked just like Baker had said he would look.

'It suits you, you know, not having all that hair. If that's not a sexist thing to say.'

'If it comes out of your mouth, it's sexist,' Ben replied, then laughed hard. 'Did I actually say that?'

'It's a fair point,' Wayne agreed.

'Anna's blood was all over my beard; I couldn't face washing it. This seemed the easiest option. She had no right showing up like that, no right at all. Stupid bitch!'

'Stupid bitch!' Wayne echoed, handing him back the joint. 'So, what's the deal with you and her? I never even knew you were married.'

'You never asked,' Ben replied. 'Where the hell did you think my kids came from?'

Wayne didn't reply.

'I met her the year I started uni. She was a guest lecturer on my media studies course. She was ten years older and I was pretty much in awe of her from day one. She got pregnant during our first year together. Before I knew what was happening, we were getting married at the local registry office. I dropped out of uni to take care of Simon and I'd planned to return the next year. But then she got pregnant with Drea, and I never made it back. We were happy, I think, for a while. At least I was. But she was always restless, always had one eye on the door, and the other on any pretty boy's cock. She got a job as a foreign correspondent for the London Chronicle, before Drea was out of nappies. After that, she was more like a hip auntie to the kids than a mother. She'd suck off somewhere dangerous for a few months and come back laden with gory tales and grand gifts.'

Ben took another drag of the joint. 'The less present she was, the more the kids revered her, Simon especially. I'd get all his tantrums and all his moods, and then she'd show up with a new Barbie house and some hand-made bangles from the streets of Senegal. As if by magic, he'd morph into the world's easiest going kid. Think he was scared to be anything but perfect round her.' He blinked back tears before continuing. 'Course, then she'd call me neurotic and unhinged when I tried to explain how things really were, and the tragedy is, I'd believe her. She'd have dramatic stories of foreign catastrophes, burning buildings, babies blown to bits before her eyes. My moaning about the mundanity of housework and childcare seemed so petty in comparison.' Ben paused to have another smoke and realised he had finished the entire spliff, himself. 'Sorry,' he mumbled to Wayne, who was already on the case putting another one together.

'But how come you had Val then? Sounds like you already had her number?'

'You'd think, eh?' Ben said. 'It was her idea, we were growing further apart and I'd started to mention separating. I think she panicked. She plied me with flowers and adjectives about how great a dad I was. I guess I was starved of attention and desperate to rekindle what we once had, so I agreed. Looking back, she never wanted Val, she just wasn't ready to lose me. I'd got my degree through the OU by then, and there was a real chance for me to start building my career. And she clearly didn't want that.

She promised things would be different with Val. She quit her job, moved home and went freelance. Only that didn't make her happy either. She'd stay out for days on end, and come back with some absurd tale about a story she was writing. I knew she was sucking around again; I just didn't have the energy to confront her.'

On impulse, Ben began stroking his face. He grimaced as his hand touched smooth skin. 'Val was a difficult baby, and between looking after her and the other two, I was worn out. In a funny way, I was glad when she finally left. I could get on with being a single parent, which I more or less had always been. In fact, if it wasn't for Simon being so fond of her, I'm not even sure I'd have tried looking for Anna.' Ben finished and buried his head in his hands, weeping.

Quickly, Wayne thrust another spliff at him. 'Here, dry your eyes and smoke that,' she told him.

'I don't think I can handle anymore,' Ben replied, but Wayne was having none of it.

Despite his initial reluctance, Ben smoked half the reefer before declaring, 'You're all the same, you know. Women. You're all the sucking same. You. Her. The sucking Wringer. You're all the bloody same.'

'That's a bit harsh,' Wayne replied, taking a long draw

from what remained of the joint. 'I mean, I'm as useless as the next self-satisfied, self-serving, bird—absolutely. But, you know, I don't go round killing young boys and inserting crucifixes in their anuses and nor did your ex… I'm taking a guess here?'

'It's just a question of degrees though, isn't it? Anna spent her whole life chasing cock, like around the next corner was going be it, the puppy that she'd never leave. And why? Because she was constitutionally incapable of seeing beyond the sexual objectification of men. She couldn't see any of us, me, as human beings, and let me tell you, nothing wrecks the sexual objectification of your man like fatherhood. Seeing the love of your life knee deep in shit and vomit, eyes glazed from permanent night feeds, hair greying with no time to fix it… For a man, that's just the process of life, but not for you women.

It's like a death knell on this bigger thing you've been promised, the eternal waiting prick. The pricks you see on TV, in magazines, the rows and rows of nameless cocks you download nightly and stream through your consciousness, that's how life should be. Men shouldn't be people with needs and wants and greying hair and frayed fingernails. To accept this, is to admit you've been cheated. Instead, you get back on the road and seek out the next erect penis that's going to make you feel like you're not past it, and this utterly soulless way of being creates the Wringers of this world. In a world where everyone hates men, and all men are whores and love being humiliated, debased, raped and beaten, is it any wonder that some women go that extra mile and become serial killers? Death and sex are utterly synonymous in our culture. Don't you watch TV? Don't you read? Your casual sexism, Anna's casual sex, the Wringer's casual killing, they're all by-products of that same beast: misandry.'

'The more I get to know you, the more I understand why you're single,' Wayne said, hoping to lighten the mood.

'That's it, laugh it off, because that's what women do when they're uncomfortable, make a joke or make a pass. It doesn't matter how inappropriate either move is, it's just something you do.'

Wayne was beginning to seriously regret giving Campbell a spliff. She made a mental note to never offer him a line of coke. She stared at her feet and lifted her coat to make a move.

'I can see you've had a long night. Why don't we pick this up later?'

'Don't go,' Ben pleaded. 'Don't leave me here alone with my thoughts.'

Wayne allowed her coat to fall back to the floor and reached for her papers in the top pocket. It was going to be a long night...

Baker was sitting at her desk, and about to get her ample mouth around a fruit scone buried beneath a mountain of clotted cream and homemade jam, as Wayne knocked on the door.

'Jess Christ, you look a right state!' Baker said.

'I look exactly how a real detective looks, knee deep in fresh corpses,' Wayne replied. She pulled herself up and puffed herself out as she spoke. The cheap shirt and trousers that she'd bought in haste had not passed the quality control test of a two-day wear. Her beige trench coat had doubled up as a pillow for the twenty minutes she drifted off on Campbell's couch and it stank of tobacco and weed, even more than usual. Flecks of dandruff fell on the floor, as she ran her fingers through her unruly hair.

'If everyone working here looked like me, maybe the case would be solved by now. What have you got?'

Baker had put up a partition between her office space and the two dead bodies and Wayne was grateful for it. Any more blood and guts and she'd struggle to hold down the breakfast she needed to power through the day ahead.

'The same person killed both of them,' Baker said.

'For suck's sake, please tell me you've something more than that.'

'The boy's M.O. is exactly like the others. He was strangled then stabbed and defiled. Our woman was just stabbed once, at close range, through the heart. She was a tall woman and looks fit, so I'm expecting the toxicology report will indicate drugs in her system, or maybe she just didn't see it coming. I've found her I.D. though, Alice Waterstone, she was an insurance saleswoman.' Baker handed Wayne her driving licence.

'Where did you get this? I searched her pockets.'

'Not well enough. She had a secret pocket sewn into the back of her jacket. I only noticed it when I undressed her. There was something else in it too.' Baker handed Wayne a memory stick. 'I've had a quick look and it makes for some interesting viewing.' A leer spread across her friend's face.

'Oh yeah? Should I be taking this home for a private screening?'

'Well, I wouldn't be playing it in the office that's for certain, not with Campbell likely to come in at any second.'

'This has footage of Campbell?'

'All I'll say is it shows Campbell like you've never seen him before, or are ever likely to.' Baker assured her.

Wayne raised her eyebrows, then took the memory stick and shoved it in her trench coat pocket. 'Let's keep this between ourselves for now, until I determine if it's relevant.'

'I also found this note stuffed in the boy's mouth. The Wringer had wrapped it in cellophane to make sure we'd be able to read it.'

Wayne took the bagged note from Baker and unfolded it.

"*Death will find you even if you hide in fortresses built up strong and high.*"

'What the suck is that supposed to mean?'

'Sucked if I know, but I figured you could take it to that Cambridge cock, and see what she makes of it.'

'Or, I could rip it up,' Wayne replied. 'Right, Martha, you look whacked, you should probably go home and get some sleep.'

'Just as soon as I finish up here,' Baker scooped the remains of the jam and cream up in a spoon and swallowed it, smiling.

Wayne was back behind her own desk in her own office and it felt good. She fiddled with the dongle in her pocket, and considered having a quick peek, but decided against it. She spread out the takeaway breakfast she had picked up from Kenny's café and inhaled the smell of the bacon and sausage hungrily. She had just taken her first bite, when a throaty cough made her look up. It was Campbell, still stoned and standing at the side of her chair.

'I didn't think you would be in today,' said Wayne.

'I couldn't stay at home, I'm going nuts. Have you spoken to Baker yet? Do we know anything?'

'Look, Campbell, one of the victims is your ex-wife. I

shouldn't even be talking to you about any of this mess.'

'Shit. Yeah, of course. You're right. Obviously. I'm not thinking. I'll go and explain everything to O'Keeffe; I should have done that first.'

Wayne's eyes widened. 'So, you haven't spoken to O'Keeffe yet?'

'To be honest, I think I'm still wasted,' Ben mumbled. 'What the hell have you done to me?'

Wayne got up from her seat and peered through the window out into the main office. A few of the team were at their computers and everyone seemed occupied. She pulled a second chair round beside her own and motioned for Ben to sit down. Wayne leaned in close, lowered her voice and asked, 'Your old woman was carrying a false I.D., calling herself Alice Waterstone, does that mean anything?'

Ben shrugged his shoulders.

'And you've no idea why she might need an alias?'

'She was a journalist; she did a lot of undercover stuff. But she never really spoke to me about it. I was just the husband, there to clean cook and be sucked—bone dry in the end.'

'Right, let's try not to get distracted by what a cunt your old girl was, and concentrate on the here and now. This wasn't a common alias she used, and other people won't know it?'

'What people? Anna cut all ties when she bailed out. Her mother died last spring and she didn't even turn up for the funeral.'

Wayne leaned in even closer and whispered, 'Okay, this is what we're going to do...'

Withering's Catholic Youth Hostel for Boys was in

desperate need of a makeover. The sign was ancient and so many letters had fallen off that it read, '*Wither cat you tel*'. The reception area was no better. It stank like two-day-old socks. A thick layer of ingrained dirt covered the surface of the main desk, itself barely visible beneath the stacks of out-of-date magazines and other random clutter. Wayne rang the Call Bell, whilst Ben leafed through the visitor's book. A fit young woman in a tank top and cut-off jeans walked down the corridor.

'How can I help? You look a little old for our hostel,' she sniggered.

'Is this the face of a stand-up comedian?' Ben barked flashing his I.D.

The young girl paled. 'Sorry, sir.' Ben noted the details on her name badge and scrawled them quickly in his notebook. Olivia Palmer, Youth Support Worker.

'Does a Kai Munroe stay here?'

'Kai, yes, although he didn't stay last night. He was supposed to be in needlework before tea, but he never showed and he wasn't there for lockdown.'

'The kids are locked in at night?' Ben asked.

'It's for their own safety and its part of the contract we agreed with the council.'

'What time is lockdown?'

'10.30 p.m.'

'And if a kid comes home after that?'

'He doesn't get in. Rules are rules.'

'And they're left to walk the streets? And fall victim to whatever predators they encounter?'

'These are tough boys we're dealing with, Inspector. Most of them are well able to look after themselves.'

'Except when they can't, eh Olivia?' Ben's face was so

close to the youth worker's that they almost touched.

Wayne pulled Ben back from the counter. 'Steady on, duck! It's not her fault your old girl got killed and you can't hold your spliff,' she whispered.

'I think it's Mother Maria you need to speak to, she runs things here.'

Palmer led them down the corridor to the priest's office. It was halfway between two dormitories. She knocked on the door and went in alone. Ben and Wayne hung back until she signaled for them. Mother Maria sat warming herself by an open fire. She was gaunter and more haggard than the last time Wayne had seen her, which was hardly a surprise. Mother Maria must be well past eighty now thought Wayne. She turned around slowly and seeing Wayne, the old priest beckoned her closer.

'Which one of my boys is in trouble this time?'

'We need to ask you some questions about Kai Munroe,' Wayne said.

'Kai, has something happened to dear Kai? Is he okay? He didn't come back last night,' she addressed Wayne.

'I'm sorry to have to tell you Mother, but Kai was strangled last night.'

Mother Maria's face crumbled. She clutched her chest and closed her eyes, mumbling in what sounded like Latin. The shaken priest bent down slowly and picked up her walking stick, using it to lever herself into the standing position. Wayne placed her hand on the ageing priest's free arm and helped her stumble the couple of steps across to her desk, where she lowered herself into another chair. She fiddled with the top drawer until Wayne pulled it open for her and took out a bottle of Irish whisky.

'Can I offer you a drink?'

'No thanks, Mother,' Ben replied. 'We're on duty.'

'Surely a small one wouldn't do any harm?' Wayne said quickly. She ignored Ben's disapproving glance. Mother Maria poured a generous helping for Wayne and another for herself before replacing the lid. She reached out to return the bottle to the drawer.

'Not so fast, Mother,' as Ben spoke, he leaned over and stopped the desk from closing with his hand. 'What's this you've got here?'

He pulled out a plastic bag from Mother Maria's drawer. It contained four silver crucifixes; identical to each other and indistinguishable from those found at the crime scenes. 'What do you have these here for?'

Mother Maria looked bewildered. 'I'm a priest, Inspector, a Catholic priest. Isn't it obvious?'

'But why do you have all these crucifixes? How many crucifixes does one priest need?'

'We always keep a supply here, in this locker. I keep spares if someone loses the crucifix from their Rosary Beads. And I give them to parishioners if they're feeling vulnerable and in need of spiritual guidance. I'll often give them to the boys if they're feeling down. It's good Christian practice, nothing more. But I like to keep a record of my acts of kindness.'

'And what about Kai, did you give him one?'

'I did, as a matter of fact, a few days ago,' as she spoke she searched for an entry in her diary. Under Wednesday morning, she had written, "Kai in spiritual pain, hope and pray the crucifix will help." She closed the book and held Wayne's gaze steady.

'Although our guests are young adults, sometimes they behave more like little boys. I noticed him crying in the corridor yesterday. He was very upset, but he wouldn't tell me what was wrong. It's not my place to force these young men to talk. Instead, I gave him a crucifix and said I hoped it would offer him protection.' The irony was not lost on the small group.

'Did he have any family?' Ben asked.

The priest shook her head sadly.

'Friends? Visitors?'

'That teacher came a few times to see him. She always brought him books and treats.'

Ben cradled his head in his hands. He reached into his handbag and found some paracetamol and his shades. He swallowed two and hid in the darkness of his sunglasses. He was back in Wayne's office, witnessing a showdown between her and Peachy. The latter's bottom lip was quivering and he reckoned there might be tears any second.

'I said I'm sorry, Wayne. But I was following procedure, Singh admitted sex with a minor, was charged, and given a date to appear. Why would we hold her?'

'Because she's a violent sexual predator that teenage boys need protecting from. Isn't that reason enough?'

'Well, if that was the criteria for holding someone, we'd have no free space at all,' reasoned Peachy. He was standing next to the door reaching out for the handle. His hair had been swept back into a ponytail, accentuating his high cheek bones and giving him an air of innocence. He looked like a schoolboy trapped beneath a headmistress's glare. 'We could have Singh picked up now,' he offered.

'If it's not too much trouble, doll.'

Ben could detect a softening in Wayne's tone and

marvelled at the effect a pair of well-toned legs had on the female psyche.

Sarah Singh had not expected to be leaving her house and was wearing a pair of faded track suit bottoms and a once-white T-shirt. Peachy hadn't allowed her to change, and she sat shivering in the airless interrogation room. Her eyes were moist and the strain of a second arrest was showing. She scratched her head and scanned the room repeatedly.

'I've already been charged in connection with Leo. What do you want from me now?'

Wayne flicked over a folder and handed her a photo of Kai Munroe taken at the crime scene. Singh looked like she might gag as she stared at the mutilated corpse. She turned her head away.

'I don't know why you're showing me this.' Her voice was barely a croak. Ben poured water into a glass and handed it to her. She took a few grateful sips and as she put the cup down, Wayne slipped another photo of the victim under her eyes. This time it was a close-up of Kai's face, contorted with fear. Singh put her hands to her mouth and spewed vomit into them. Wayne grabbed the photo and pushed Singh's head to the side. Ben handed her a roll of paper towel and she hastily cleaned up, tossing a wad of stinking tissue into the bin.

'Do you know him?' Wayne had put the photo back directly in front of the school teacher. Singh sat in silence stroking the face in the portrait. When she eventually spoke, she directed her words to Ben.

'Leo introduced us. He thought I might be able to help Kai, be some sort of steadying influence. He had no family here and I think he saw me as some kind of mother figure.'

'Shame he didn't see you for the kiddie fiddling pervert that you are. I suppose he was obsessed with you too?' Wayne leaned in so that she and Singh were head-to-head. She breathed stale tobacco into the teacher's blanched face.

'It wasn't like that at all. I tried to help him. I was the one that recommended he try Mother Maria's to provide security and comfort. I know how it must look to you, but I'm not a bad woman; I'm just a weak one,' Singh began to cry and looked pleadingly at Ben. His expression was deadpan and he looked straight through her.

'You're not the weak one, you're the powerful one. You're the responsible one. You're the adult. The one that's in charge of kids who put their trust in you, and parents who leave their children with you, expecting them to be educated, not raped.' Ben's voice grew louder and louder until suddenly, he hurled himself across the desk, knocking Singh to the floor and landed cat-like on top of her. He raised his fist and was about to pound it into her face when he felt Wayne grab him.

'Steady there, doll. We don't want to lose her on grounds of police brutality.'

Ben came back to his senses and Wayne, feeling his calm return, let his arm go. Trance-like, he released his hold on a shivering Singh and stood up.

'I want a lawyer,' Singh snivelled, having curled herself into a ball on the floor. Wayne walked to the door and shouted on two uniforms to take her back to holding.

'I need some air,' Ben said, grabbing his jacket from the back of the chair and exiting the interrogation room.

Wayne caught up with Ben in the car park. He was leaning on the bonnet of a patrol car with his head cast downwards and his eyes closed.

'You okay, Campbell?' she asked, softly touching his shoulder. She could smell vomit from his breath. Ben shook his head. Wayne reached into her pocket, found her tobacco tin and took out the emergency one-skinner she always kept there. She lit it and handed it to Ben who shook his head again. Wayne shrugged and continued to smoke. 'Go home, Campbell. It's been a long day.'

'I can't do that, there's too much to do. Thornton Place was another of Ryan's rentals, we should get over there.' Ben tried to stand, but his feet were so unsteady he leant back on the car again.

'I'm getting uniform to take you home, and if you argue with me, I'll have you arrested,' Wayne told him, as she pulled him to his feet and guided him slowly back towards the station.

Wayne inhaled deeply and flicked the butt in the ashtray. Okay, she was good and stoned now. She could watch this again. She pressed *play*. There was Campbell, straddling the chair like he had been before she pressed *pause*. Wayne felt embarrassed and wasn't really sure what to do. But she also felt aroused. It was hardly surprising.

Campbell was naked, simulating oral sex with a watermelon, his tongue looking considerably longer than it ever did at work, flicking back and forth over the fruit. It was one of the most erotic scenes Wayne had ever witnessed, and she had seen a *lot* of erotica.

A woman's bare arse obscured the screen, and Campbell and her were laughing and joking. The woman's face came into view and Wayne immediately recognised the runaway wife.

Wayne turned it off. She felt like a pervert watching a

dead bird and her husband suck. Still... the dongle was in Anna Campbell's pocket. It would be remiss of her not to watch it. She dropped her hands to her trousers and unbuckled the belt with speed. She pushed the chair aside and dropped to her knees. Naked from the waist down, she positioned her cunt in front of the table leg and pressed *play*.

NINE

SATURDAY

Ben woke with a start and checked the time on his bedside clock. *Shit! It was 9 a.m.! How had he slept so long? Why hadn't the kids woken him? Val? Was she alright?* He flung off his covers and darted across the hall to her bedroom, which was empty. He could hear the strains of children's TV from downstairs and what smelled like grilled bacon, from the kitchen.

Simon was busy setting the kitchen table where Val was already seated, positioned so that she could view the morning programmes, in the living room. 'Am I in the wrong house?' he asked.

'Morning, Dad,' Simon smiled. 'You've been working so hard lately and I just wanted to give you a break. Come and have breakfast.' Simon pulled out the chair beside Val and Ben sat down.

'What do you want, Simon?' The words were out before he could stop himself and he instantly regretted it.

'That's just typical of you, Dad. Last time I'll do you a favour.' Simon slammed the plate of bacon and eggs onto the table. He marched out of the room, banging the door so hard Val jumped. Ben sighed and wondered if his youngest would notice him slipping back to bed. As if reading his mind, she demanded her breakfast.

'Have mine,' Ben offered. He had no appetite. His mobile beeped and he searched the kitchen trying to locate it. His mind seemed unable to accomplish the simplest of tasks.

Eventually, he made it into a game with Val, who found his phone in under a minute, and claimed her prize of chocolate buttons.

'Can I eat them right now for breakfast?' Val asked. Ben nodded. The message was from Wayne; it was the third she'd sent. Singh's lawyer was at the station demanding an interview. The last text told him not to worry, that Wayne would handle it.

'Like hell you will!' Ben replied.

'You're sucking joking me!' Wayne snapped at Peachy. She had just been told that Green was Singh's lawyer. Wayne stood outside the interview room staring at her through the one-way glass. Green was engaged in a deep conversation with her client, carefully covering her mouth and whispering, so it was impossible to make out her words. Singh listened, her eyes conveying the fear that her lawyer was trying to hide.

'Is there any scum in this town you don't represent?' Wayne asked Green, as she and Peachy entered the room.

'Nope,' replied Green. 'I'm a champion of the underbitch, Wayne; rooting out injustice wherever I find it, more often than not, in your holding cells.'

Even first thing on a Saturday morning, Green was groomed to perfection. Her dark grey suit and matching charcoal shirt in sharp contrast to Singh's vomit-stained clothes. She handed Wayne an A4 sheet.

'My client has prepared a statement that contains everything she knows about the victims. Perhaps reading that would be a good start. It's a handwritten draft but we'll get one typed up and over to you first thing Monday morning.' Green focused on Peachy as she spoke. Wayne glanced at the sheet, then tore it in half and tossed it on the floor.

'This isn't some classroom assignment, Singh. You're our chief suspect in multiple homicides. You're going to have to try a hell of a lot harder than that.'

Singh's hands began to tremor and her breathing became harsher. 'I need a new inhaler,' she gasped.

'And I need a new plug for my bathroom sink,' Wayne replied. 'What's your point?'

'Are you denying my client the urgent medical attention she requires?' Green asked.

'No, she'll receive it in due course. Peachy, take a note, the pervert needs an inhaler. Singh, take a note, I need answers. Like how long had you been doing young Kai Monroe?'

'I'm not sure "doing" is the correct legal term, but if you're trying to establish whether my client was engaged in a sexual relationship with the victim, then I suggest you ask that,' Green said.

'Never. We were just friends. I was trying to help him, like I explained to you yesterday,' Singh interrupted her lawyer.

'Friends?' Wayne replied. 'So, what did you get out of the friendship with the sexually uninhibited, barely legal teenager?'

'You don't have to answer that,' Green counselled. 'Look, Wayne, we've already established that Ms Singh knew the victim, a fact not wholly incompatible with her work as a local school teacher. We also know of her ill-chosen relationship with one of the previous victims, who was, I believe, friends with Kai Munroe. Do you have anything concrete to suggest that their relationship was anything other than platonic?'

Wayne gave the lawyer a look of contempt then returned her stare to Singh. Sweat glistened on her twitching face, as she tried to compete with a stare-off champion. 'Okay, exactly what did you talk about, you and your friend?'

'He needed direction,' Singh replied, her voice barely a whisper. 'He'd fallen in with the wrong crowd, and he wanted help getting his life back on track. It was me who suggested he stay at Mother Maria's, so that he could break free from Big Mamma's.'

'What the suck has Big Mamma's got to do with Kai?'

'He worked there, that's how he met Leo. I assumed you knew. You're the experienced detective.'

By the look on Green's face, it was a surprise to her too.

'Leo worked there too?' Wayne asked. How the hell had they missed this?

Singh nodded.

'And that's how you get them, you pay for it. At least that makes a bit more sense.'

'Was there a question in there, Inspector?' Green asked.

Wayne looked from the lawyer to her client and back again. 'Nope, no more questions for now. Peachy, take her back to holding.'

Singh began to cough and splutter. Green placed a reassuring arm on her shoulder.

'My client's an asthmatic who needs urgent medical attention, compounded I imagine, by the assault she experienced in this very station yesterday evening. Or did you think she'd forgotten about that?'

Wayne gave Peachy a quizzical look. 'Assault of a suspect at Withering police station? That doesn't sound right. Perhaps your client's mistaken?'

'Your psycho partner attacked me here yesterday,' Singh

shouted.

'Partner? Now you're definitely mistaken, I'm single,' Wayne's delivery was deadpan.

'She means your work partner, Wayne, as you very well know. My client alleges that last night, whilst being interrogated, she was the victim of an unprovoked, sustained, physical attack. It was carried out by serving officer Inspector Ben Campbell, who along with yourself was conducting the interview.'

'Then your client's wrong. Inspector Campbell left the office early yesterday afternoon because he wasn't feeling well.'

'That's a lie!' retorted Singh, giving Green a look of desperation. 'She's lying. Campbell led the interview, she pulled him off me!'

'We can clear this up simply, Inspector,' Green said smugly. 'Why don't you provide us with the tape of the interview?'

'Unfortunately, the machine broke; a fact not noted until after the event. What're the chances, eh?' Wayne's voice sounded apologetic.

'This isn't over, Wayne,' Green declared. She stuffed papers in her briefcase and hastily retreated, promising her client that everything would be fine.

Ben sat in Wayne's office and cradled his head in his hands. He had a thumping migraine which 1000mg of paracetamol wasn't touching the surface of. A lie down in a darkened room was the best option, but there was zero chance of that happening. The knock on the door felt like a sharp stab in between his eyes as he lifted them slowly. Wayne swaggered in and he noticed that she'd at least changed her clothes. But her clothes didn't look any cleaner; they were just different than yesterday's shirt and trouser combo. Or were they? He couldn't be sure of anything right now.

'Can I have a word, boss?' Wayne had turned her chair around and was rocking back and forth on it. She looked even shiftier than usual, as she kept her focus to the floor.

'I can't do this, Wayne,' Ben blurted out. 'I can't lie and manipulate information in a major criminal investigation. Apart from moral considerations, there are practical ones. I'm breaking the law, and if I get caught, then what happens to my kids? I say if, but I mean when, Wayne. You honestly can't think we can get away with this?'

Wayne gave him a sly smile. 'All those cop shows and detective series that you've watched far too many of, well, let me tell you something, they do policing a great disservice. They create the impression that police forces are generally competent and that the police are usually intelligent, insightful, resourceful people. Now, in the short time you've worked here, you can't have failed to notice that none of this is true. Your average cop is thick as pig shit, no pun intended. It's what you do when you're too stupid to get a real job. In fact, the only people dumber than police are criminals, which is why we have any success at all in solving crimes. Do you get what I'm saying, Campbell?'

'Even if that's true, and I'm not saying it is, it doesn't change the fact that we are concealing evidence that may help catch this maniac. Not only that, as if that's not enough, but I'm guilty of assaulting a suspect, and after the interview I just witnessed, I'm also now complicit in a cover-up regarding that assault.'

'And they said you'd never make it as a cop!' Wayne let out a throaty laugh.

'It's not funny, Wayne,' Ben fumed. 'The mother of my children is dead and I haven't even told them. What sort of father does that make me?' The conversation was interrupted by a knock on the door.

'Sorry to intrude, but he's here, Wayne. I've put him in the relatives' room,' Peachy said. Wayne nodded and waved him away quickly.

'Who's here?' Ben asked.

'That's what I wanted to talk to you about. Maybe it's best if you see for yourself.'

Wayne's voice was hardly audible as she shuffled off her chair. She ushered Ben across the building, to one of two relatives' rooms adjacent to the morgue.

The room was painted magnolia and was decorated in a bland balance of nature pictures and inoffensive abstracts. There were half a dozen leather seats spread around it and a table in the corner with some mugs, jars of teabags and coffee, and a kettle.

On one of the chairs, sat a pretty brunette, mid-twenties at a stretch. He was trying to wrestle a mug from a toddler.

Ben couldn't take his eyes off the child. She was the image of Drea at the same age. She even had her lopsided grin, just like Anna's. Immediately, his heart began to pound so fiercely that he feared he was having some kind of attack.

He looked again at the young dad, his gaunt, worried face, carefully painted. His clothes were playfully masculine with a slight hippy edge, a denim skirt just above the knee, a faux fur jacket bearing 'Occupy' and 'PETA' badges. It was like looking at a younger version of himself.

'Thanks for coming in, Mister Waterstone This is my colleague, D.I. Campbell,' Wayne said.

Ben stared at the stranger. He opened his mouth to

speak, but he could find no words as the thumping in his head had morphed into a full-scale riot. He needed to get out of this room, and fast. Without explanation, he turned and fled down the corridor.

On reaching the men's toilets, he sprayed the caffeine that had passed for breakfast, all over a cubicle floor. He leaned his body against the unlocked door, allowed his face to fall into his hands, and wept like a child.

Eric stood outside Mother Maria's door. Before knocking, he yanked his mini skirt down, so that it covered his thighs, and fastened two of the buttons on his blouse. When there was no response, he knocked again, much harder. A frail voice from within commanded him to enter. Mother Maria sat behind her desk staring at a ledger. Her shaky hand held a magnifying glass and she peered intensely into it. Eric wondered why priests never retired, like normal people. The old bird was way past running this place; she didn't look like she could run a bath. He waited for what seemed like an age before the priest put down the magnifying glass and gave him a kindly smile.

'How are you finding it here, Eric? Are you settling in well?' she asked.

Eric nodded.

'Mother Jane says you keep yourself to yourself. She tells me that you don't join in any of the groups. Don't you like any of the activities?'

Eric shrugged his shoulders. He flicked his dyed blond hair over his forehead to obscure his face.

'Hostel life is not easy, Eric. Having to share with so many people and having so much of your time accounted for can be difficult. But the daily classes have been carefully devised to build your confidence and skills. They may seem a bit dull and boring, but they actually have purpose.'

'What's the purpose of me knitting a scarf?'

'Knitting's a great life skill to have. Do you know my father was still knitting scarves in his seventies? Glaucoma had stolen his eyesight and his hands were riddled with arthritis, but he kept knitting because it made him feel useful.'

'I think it's a shit way to spend an afternoon!'

'I'll pretend that I didn't hear you use the 's' word and concentrate on what's more important, your welfare. There's lots more to do besides knitting. There's sewing, there's baking and in the interests of being modern, we even have a bicycle mechanics course. Why don't you give that a try?'

'I don't have a bike, Mother,' Eric replied.

'Indeed. Well I'm sorry that none of these pursuits interest you, Eric, because you are going to have to get involved in some of them. That's the condition of you staying here. You do want to continue staying here, don't you, boy?' Her kindly face had been replaced by a harder one.

'Yes, Mother, of course I do. Can I still go to the cinema tonight? Remember, I asked you last night?'

Mother Maria looked confused. 'You said I could go,' he told her, hoping to prod her memory.

'All right then,' she replied. 'But make sure you're back before 10.30, remember you won't get in after that.'

'Thanks, Mother,' Eric sprang from his seat. He bounded out of the door, displaying his first signs of enthusiasm since his arrival a week earlier.

Parked up the street from Big Mamma's, Wayne and Ben sat in the front of Ben's car. Wayne had reclined her seat and had placed a newspaper over her head. But still she tossed and turned, seemingly unable to find a comfortable position. Ben sat upright, unmoving, staring straight ahead.

'This is bullshit,' complained Wayne. 'This is absolute bullshit. Why are we here again?'

'Jess Christ! Wayne, get over it. We're here, because I'm in charge, and I think staking out our main suspect is a worthwhile use of our time and resources. Not that I should need to explain that to you.' Wayne fiddled with the radio in the car. She eventually found a country music channel that was blasting out Donald Pardon and smiled. Ben turned the music off.

'I was listening to that!'

'Not right now, Wayne. I've got a blinding headache.'

'The story of my life, doll,' Wayne chuckled.

'How the hell could Leo work in a lap dancing bar without his parents knowing? Who interviewed his father? Where did he think his kid was every night?' Ben asked.

'Peachy spoke with the dad and he told him that Leo worked part-time in a tanning salon with late opening hours. He hadn't got round to confirming with the salon's owner, what with the pace of events this week.'

'Obviously, it's not Peachy's fault. He's too good looking to be incompetent.' Ben snorted.

'Now, that's where you're wrong. Peachy's good looking enough to be very incompetent and he usually is, only not this time. God, I need a smoke!' Wayne patted down her coat pockets as she spoke.

'Well, you're going to have to wait, aren't you? You can't smoke in this car, and you're not getting out in case you blow our cover.'

'What cover? For suck's sake, Campbell, we're outside a

club owned by Withering's most notorious gangster. And you really think she doesn't know we're here?'

'Someone's coming out. It's Green. Is she ever out of that place?' Ben sat upright and got ready to turn on the ignition.

'Not unless she's at the station. Right, we've seen Green get in her car. Can we go now?'

Ben rolled down his window. 'Smoke,' he commanded. 'For suck's sake smoke, if it will shut you up for five minutes.'

Eric checked the text on his phone to make sure he had the right address. He scrunched his hair to try and give it more body and cursed himself for not breaking in his new shoes before tonight; his feet ached. Feeling flustered, Eric applied a coat of lippy freestyle because he couldn't find a mirror in his bag. He'd have to do. After a deep breath, he rang the doorbell and waited, his heart pounding with excitement.

'You must be Eric,' the woman who answered the door said.

She wasn't at all what Eric had been expecting. She was much older for a start, and her clothes were very ordinary, very dull. He wondered if he'd made a mistake coming. But as she led him through to the kitchen, he noticed a camera on a tripod in one of the rooms off the hall. That must be where she does her shoots. Eric relaxed. Maybe the edgiest photographers looked the most normal? Maybe they got all their edginess out in their photos?

'Shall I take your coat?' she asked him.

Eric took his coat off slowly to reveal the skimpy black lingerie he had been instructed to buy and wear.

'How do I look?' he asked giving her his best pout. Her eyes didn't leave his willy, and instantly he regretted coming.

'Take your cock out!' she ordered him.

Eric had been around enough women to know the ones who mean business, so he complied.

'You look perfect,' she said smiling. 'Like a lamb to the slaughter.'

'For Christ's sake, Wayne. When I said have a smoke, I didn't mean a joint. You're a police officer on duty, you can't just skin up in my car.'

'We're not police officers right now, we're undercover. The weed will make us look more authentic, and besides, I'm bored out of my skull.'

'You have no sense of responsibility at all, do you?'

'That depends on what your definition of responsibility is.'

'What if a school kid walks by and smells it? What are you going to do then?'

'Well, I wouldn't share it with them, if that's what you're getting at. Now that would be irresponsible.' Wayne laughed at her own joke. Ben threw her a filthy look and rolled down his window fully.

'Oh, loosen up will you, Campbell? So what! I smoke dope? So does one third of the population. Your bank teller is probably stoned and your chiropractor. I bet even Mother Maria likes a spliff. It's not a big deal!'

'It's a crime, that's what it is!' retorted Campbell. 'And it's your job to uphold the law, not break it.'

'Strictly speaking, yes. But no, actually. I investigate real crimes. You know? Crimes where there's a victim and a perpetrator and a need for retribution in order to maintain the world order. My job is to keep people feeling safe at night. Please tell me who suffers when I toke up?'

'Your marijuana supply forms part of a chain with lots

of vulnerable people being the links. Like those that work in the growing fields, for very little or no pay, in squalid conditions that are never subject to work protection checks. The mules, often poor, desperate foreigners who, by definition, have no rights, because they're breaking the law. And, of course there are also the addicts that buy it, including the not inconsiderable number who will eventually fall prey to mental health issues as a direct result of their addiction. Let's not forget about those.'

'You know, I've never really been convinced about this alleged link between weed and going nuts. I've been smoking it most of my life and look at me. In any event, none of those statistics count if you're a cop. My weed comes straight from a box that's going to wind up in a furnace. I'm smoking it before it gets smoked. It's actually a type of public service,' Wayne drew hard on her spliff to illustrate the point.

'Jess Christ, Wayne—you smoke seized cannabis!'

'You bet I do! In fact, I actually seize cannabis just to smoke it. When you turn up at someone's door for something unrelated, but you get the smell, what are you going to do? As a policewoman, am I supposed to ignore illegal activity?'

'How do you sleep at night?'

'Better than you, I'd imagine. Actually, the weed helps with that.'

Ben didn't laugh. Instead, he began cleaning the car window with a packet of tissues from his handbag, shoving his nails into the grooves to loosen the dirt.

'So, do you want to talk about what happened this morning?' Wayne asked. 'It's a lot to take in, finding out your old girl married again, had a new family.'

Ben continued to clean furiously, dumping soiled tissues at his feet.

'That's fine with me,' continued Wayne. 'I'm all for passive aggression in place of meaningful conversation. It's what this great country of ours was built on.'

Ben had found a layer of dust beneath the steering wheel. He was desperately trying to remove it, but failing miserably as the paper disintegrated with the force of his efforts. The wad of tissues was tossed on the car floor and he stamped it into the mat. 'I gave that bitch the best years of my life and that's how she repays me. Why couldn't she just walk out, like a normal person? Why did she have to disappear and reinvent herself here, in this hell hole, of all places? Who does that? And why text after all this time? What was she even doing at that house?'

Wayne sighed, 'Ronnie Ryan was supposed to show her round at 8.00 pm. It was decided at the last minute—they'd met by chance at a business lunch. Ronnie's mother took a bad turn, which happens quite frequently, and he didn't want to leave her. He never cancelled because it had all been organised slapdash in the restaurant, and he didn't have your ex's number. I guess the Wringer answered the door to her and improvised.'

'You're telling me that she just happened to be at the wrong place at the wrong time?' Ben's bottom lip began to quiver.

'Or the right place, depending on how you look at it. This is one of Rita's high-end spinster pads. By the sound of things, Lover Girl was obviously planning to rekindle something with you and the kids. If she'd succeeded, and I'm not saying she would have, then you would never have known about her other life. This way, she's gone and you don't have to foot the funeral bill. And the added bonus is that you don't have to face your children's grief for a spineless bitch, who wasn't worthy of any of you to begin with. It's win-win if you ask me.'

Wayne took another draw on her spliff, before tossing the butt out the car window.

The deluded little fool had lost consciousness, which suited her purpose perfectly. She'd just listened to the child prattle on for an hour about how he couldn't wait to be famous.

'I'll make you famous, doll,' she said. 'They'll be reading about you in all the papers.' Sometimes it was too easy, these kids were so gullible. They were all so desperate for their five minutes, so utterly sure, in spite of overwhelming evidence of their ordinariness, that they were special, that they were going to be the next big thing.

She looked at the sleeping boy and could not see one thing about his face, his body, his very being, that was anywhere close to exceptional. He was just another whore the world had never noticed and wouldn't miss. Of course, when you put all these boys together, as the press had taken to doing more and more, then they acquired a bigger persona. The whole being much greater than the sum of its parts. They were interdependent, her and her whores. She was going to make them remembered and they ensured that she would never be forgotten.

She checked her watch. It was almost midnight. She had a lot of work to do in a small amount of time. She opened her rucksack and took out a copy of the Gita.

'Wait up! There's a taxi stopped outside.'

'It's a club, Campbell. It's going to have taxis outside.

Look, there's another!'

'And another!' said Ben. 'What the hell? There are five taxis now.'

Just then Hagan came out of the club. She walked towards a taxi waiting directly outside the door, seemed to change her mind, and walked instead to the taxi in front of it. Again, just before she got in, she appeared to have a change of heart, and crossed the road to another taxi. She opened the door then closed it again and walked back towards the first taxi.

Ben was dizzy just looking at her. She paused outside the first taxi and waved across at Wayne and Ben, before jumping in. The taxi sped away, followed in quick succession by the other four black cabs.

By the time Ben had turned onto Market Street, there were seven identical taxis on the road and Hagan could have been in any one of them.

'See, I told you this was a bullshit waste of time. You can't stake out a major organised criminal. It's insulting their intelligence to even try.'

Ben said nothing. Wayne was right of course, and he felt like a sucking fool. There was no point in continuing to track her, she could be anywhere, but he didn't want to concede defeat.

'I think it's that second cab, there,' Ben said, pointing to a black cab.

'No you don't! You know this is a complete waste of your time and mine, you just want to try and save face. I'm all about face-saving, me. We just go back to the station and tell them Hagan's not left her club for the last twenty-four hours and we've bribed a door woman to tell us when she does. O'Keeffe will see the logic in that, and it's a lot cheaper than a stakeout. Plus, you don't have to spend any more time trapped in a car with me. What do you say to that idea?'

'I say we follow that black cab,' Ben said, driving straight through a red light.

An hour later, she surveyed her scene. It was perfectly chaotic. Any brainless idiot could trash a house. But it took an exceptionally clever person to create such carnage and not leave a shred of evidence behind. She took a piece of paper wrapped in cellophane out of the front pocket of her rucksack and opened his mouth. He spluttered and spat it out. She sighed. He was starting to come round.

'We'll just wait and put that in after, shall we?' She retrieved a length of wire from her rucksack and judged about two feet, cutting it with pliers.

Kneeling behind him, she pulled up his head by his hair and slowly slipped the wire under his neck. He jerked. She found the end of the wire either side and brought them up to meet in the middle. Then she closed her eyes and pulled. He tried to scream, but it's hard to scream when you're being strangled. She pulled with her all her strength and he twitched and gasped and eventually ceased to move. She pulled even tighter, knotting both wires together and she let the wire fall from her hands.

In the moment of absolute clarity that followed, she felt inspired. She quickly took out her hunting knife and began stabbing the corpse viciously. When her frenzy abated, she dipped her gloved finger in a fresh wound and began slowly forming letters in blood on the living room wall.

Ben had given up chasing random black cabs. He and Wayne had followed his hunch about twenty miles out of

Withering, until the cab picked up an elderly couple. Wayne had demanded to be let out, there and then, in the middle of nowhere. He'd tried to reason with her but she'd been livid. He didn't blame her. Ben had been wrong, but that was the problem; his hunches, his ideas were always wrong. Maybe he just wasn't cut out to be a copper? His mind was too ordered, too structured. According to Wayne, good detectives needed to be more chaotic—and they drank a hell of a lot. Maybe he should just drink more or buy some weed?

He banged the door a little too hard on the way in.

'Tough day at the office, dear?' George enquired smiling. He was standing over the hob stirring what smelled like bolognaise, good bolognaise. 'Try some,' he offered, holding out the spoon for Ben.

'It's good, Dad!' enthused Val. 'I helped make it, didn't I, George? Didn't I help make it?'

'You did, pet,' agreed George. 'In fact, you did so much, it was more like I helped you. I'll tell you what Ben, you've got a future Jemima Oliver on your hands.'

Val wouldn't have a clue who Jemima Oliver was, but she beamed at the comparison.

'Thanks again for giving up your Saturday to mind my lot,' Ben said.

'Any time,' George replied. 'It's not like I've anything else on.'

'Where are the others?' Ben scanned the living room, which looked suspiciously empty.

'Simon's in his room being a hormonal teenager. Drea's at karate,' George pointed to the timetable Ben had taped to the fridge. 'Arlene's Mum will drive her home.'

'Jess, how did I survive without you George?'

It was George's turn to beam. 'Get yourself changed and cosy and I'll get tea on the table. But then I'll have to shoot off, I'm afraid. I'm meeting a few of the boys down at the bingo hall.'

Ben wasn't listening to George. He had just opened a letter from Simon's school.

Dear Ms and Mister Campbell,

I am writing to inform you of an incident that occurred in school this week. One of our Year Twelve pupils reported the theft of some money that she kept in her locker. As is standard practice in these situations, we carried out a bag search of all Year Twelves, as only these pupils have access to the lockers.

The money, kept in a very distinctive wallet, was found in Simon's bag. When questioned, Simon could offer no reasonable explanation as to why this might have occurred. Therefore, it is with considerable regret that we have decided to suspend Simon immediately, pending further inquiries. I have arranged for Simon's teachers to prepare work that Simon can do at home, to ensure that he does not fall further behind with his studies. I am available during school hours should you wish to discuss the matter further.

Yours sincerely,
Ms K Patterson
Head Teacher, Withering High School

TEN

SUNDAY

The strains of Tommy Wynette carried into the shower and Wayne sang along loudly as she lathered her whole body in soap. The shower head was temperamental, and when she turned the flow to high, it sprayed water all over her bathroom.

'Shit!' she swore as she tried to locate the *off* button, a task that was made all the more difficult by the suds in her eyes.

Eventually, she found it and the water came to an immediate halt, leaving Wayne covered in soap and shivering as she grabbed a well-worn towel from the radiator. It was Sunday morning and she was taking her Aunt Stella to church. The phone rang and, wrapped in the towel, Wayne rushed to pick up just before the answer machine kicked in.

'Now, calm down, Stella, we won't be late... Oh, it's you, Campbell. Why are you calling on a Sunday? Better not be planning another stake-out...'

'There's been another murder. Meet me at 32 Watson Road as soon as you can.' Ben rushed his words together and hung up.

Wayne cursed and threw the towel to the floor.

Wayne arrived at the scene before Ben. She walked up the drive, past a Ryan Rentals sign and said hello to the two uniformed officers standing at the gate. She headed for the front door, which was slightly ajar. Wayne walked slowly down the hall, following the stench of recent death, and turned into the living room. The victim lay face down, in the centre of the carpet, surrounded by the familiar sight of overturned furniture, broken ornaments and ripped pages from a book—no doubt a religious text. Above the mantelpiece, the Wringer had written a few lines in what looked like blood, and Wayne squinted trying to make out the scrawl.

'That which you have will save you if you bring it forth from yourselves,' a voice interjected, translating the bloody graffiti for Wayne. It was Baker. She didn't look dressed for work; in fact, she barely looked dressed at all. Her jumper was back to front and the space between her trousers and shoes, where her socks should be, displayed her hairy elephant ankles. Suck! Wayne hoped she hadn't fallen off the wagon.

'Why the hell are you here?' asked Wayne.

'I was in the area,' Baker replied.

'You working weekends now? I thought nothing would keep you from your warm bed on a Sunday morning?' Wayne asked.

'Do I have to account for my every move now? Should I get a lawyer?' Baker's face had turned crimson and her hands began to shake violently.

'Jess! Take a chill pill, Martha! I'm not questioning you. I'm just asking, as a friend.'

'There can be no friendship without trust,' Baker snapped and shoved her still trembling hands into her pockets. She stormed out of the crime scene, almost colliding with Ben in the hall.

'What was that all about?' he asked Wayne.

'Something or nothing. She won't have had her full English yet. Forget Baker, we've enough to worry about here.'

'The Wringer's getting worse, isn't she? More garish, more elaborate. I mean, who does this sort of shit?' asked Ben, his eyes glued to the wall. He took out his mobile and dialled a number. He spoke clearly into Professor McEwan's answering machine, leaving some scant details, and stressing the urgency.

'What the suck is urgent about talking to the Cambridge cock?' Wayne asked.

'No rush at all—if you can reference and explain the wall quote?' Ben retorted.

'Nope. But then, I don't care what it says. Not unless one of the letters has some trace D.N.A.'

'We've got to follow every lead we find, and like it or not, this is a lead. Professor McEwan knows her stuff, Wayne. She has a first-class Oxford degree and a Ph.D. from Cambridge. She's one of the country's leading experts on comparative religions.'

'And if we were organising a multi-faith festival, I'd give her a call.'

Ben's phone rang and he stepped into the hall.

Surreptitiously, Wayne slipped on a pair of plastic gloves. She scanned the floor, looking for the victim's handbag for I.D. It was beneath a pile of the torn pages. She should have waited for forensics, but she wanted any kind of jump start she could get on the case. Wayne shook the contents of the clutch-bag into her hand: some loose change and a bank card inside a purse, a cheap make-up set with a compact mirror, a hairbrush, and a scrap of paper with a number written on it. Wayne studied the number. She took out her own phone and searched her contacts. *Shit!* Glancing around, she shoved the piece of paper into her back pocket and replaced the clutch bag where she'd found it. Wayne's stomach lurched and she knew she needed to find a toilet urgently. Keeping her focus on the floor, so as not to disturb the chaos that passed for a crime scene, she stepped carefully back into the hall, locating a bathroom, two doors down.

Locking the door, she slid to the floor and emptied the contents of last night's binge into the porcelain bowl. Feeling lightheaded, she placed her hands either side of her, on the ground. 'What the suck?' she yelled. Looking down, she could see her vomit spreading out over the floor, and feel it's dampness seeping into her Sunday trousers. Jess Christ! In her lifetime as a serving officer this was her first puke on the job, and the bog she'd barfed into wasn't plumbed in.

McEwan seemed lost in thought as she stared at the confusion and disarray that was the hallmark of the Wringer. Her eyes found the quote, which Ben had called her about, and she nodded.

'This is very interesting, but it rather blasts a very big hole in my last theory. This is a quote from one of the Gnostic gospels. Unless I'm wrong, which to be frank, is very rare. I'd need to check the reference to be exactly sure which verse and author.'

'Gnostic gospels? They weren't discovered until last century, were they?' asked Ben.

'1945, in Egypt,' confirmed McEwan. 'They've proved something of a controversial subject among scholars. Some say they strike at the very foundations of Christianity, and others refuse to believe their authenticity.'

'And what's your theory now, professor?'

'This is all very specialist. Gnosticism, though essentially Christian, is hardly a rank and file religion. Similarly, that last quote you sent me, such reading material would only be expected from the most devout Muslim. What would motivate an atheist to acquire such in-depth knowledge of so many religions?'

'What are you saying professor, that we're no longer looking for an atheist?' Ben asked.

'At this point I truly don't know.' McEwan replied.

Wayne had to return home and swap her Sunday best for her least dirty pair of trousers. This meant it had taken her longer to get to Baker's than she'd have liked, and she wasn't at all surprised to find a half-cut Baker answer the door.

Wayne grabbed her by the throat and pinned her up against the wall. 'You lied to me, Martha,' she bellowed. 'And you're sucking me about in the biggest case either of us has ever had. You've got ten seconds to tell me what's going on, or I swear, I will drag you down to the station, right sucking now, and book you as our prime suspect.' Wayne released Baker, who was by this time gasping for breath.

'Get the suck off my property, you crazy bitch,' she croaked, rubbing her throat.

'That's not going to work, Martha. I'm going nowhere.' Wayne tossed a scrap of paper at Baker. 'What the suck is your number doing in our vic's bag? How many other victims do you know?'

'It's not what you think,' she said recovering her voice, and walking slowly down the hall towards her kitchen. Wayne followed leaving the door ajar. Baker picked up the bottle of whisky on the kitchen table and decanted a large measure into the glass beside it. She took a second glass from her top shelf, filled it and handed it to Wayne. 'Slainte,' she said and clinked her tumbler against Wayne's.

Wayne hurled her drink against the kitchen wall and tiny bits of glass splattered all over the white tiled floor.

'For suck's sake, Wayne. That's Waterford crystal!'

'Like I give a shit!' she retorted. 'I don't want your whisky, I want answers. This isn't a social call and I'm not your friend right now.'

'But you are though, that's why you're here on your own, because you don't really think I'm her, do you, Jane? Seriously, do you honestly think I go round torturing and killing young men?' Baker had eased herself into a chair and fingered the side of her glass.

'I don't know what the suck to think. Why don't you help me out? Who's the victim, Martha, and what's he doing with your number in his bag?'

'He's a hooker, one of Hagan's boys. At least he was when I knew him. Star, he called himself.'

'A hooker? He's a sucking child, that's what he is!'

Baker kept her head low and sipped her whisky steadily. 'You're right, Wayne, he is—was—a child. And I was a lonely old woman, desperate to reclaim some of what Ollie took when he walked out.'

'Ollie walked out because you couldn't keep your pants up. Don't go putting this on him.'

'You're right again,' Baker agreed. Her glass was empty and she poured another large measure into it. 'I use hookers, Wayne. Half the station does. Don't stand there in judgement and tell me you never have.'

'I sleep with men, not boys.' Wayne's voice was getting louder again.

'And you've always asked for I.D., have you? Come on,

Wayne, you know what it's like. When the little whores are tarted up and stick their bits out, you can't tell if they're fifteen or twenty-five. And what's more, if you're honest with yourself, you don't actually care.'

Wayne stared at her friend. It was like looking at a stranger. She opened her mouth to protest, then shut it again, completely lost for words. She fumbled in her pockets for her tobacco tin and stumbled out of the house, as if it was her who'd drank the half bottle of whisky.

'We've got an I.D. boss, and an address. Here, check this out,' Peachy sounded very pleased with himself as he placed the sheet on the desk. Ben read it and nodded.

'Has anyone seen Wayne?'

'She called in for one of the patrol cars to take her home about an hour ago,' Peachy replied.

'What? She can't just go home when she feels like it, she's on duty! Who the hell does she think she is?'

Ben fumed to himself for the whole of the journey across town. He'd tried calling Wayne but she wasn't answering. *She'd better answer the door,* he thought, *or I'll knock it down!* What the suck was happening to him? He was thinking more like a woman every day.

He pulled up outside Withering train station and checked his phone for the address Peachy had given him. To the left, he saw Kent street, which was a row of semi-detached two storey houses. He found 5 and 5B easily enough, but he couldn't seem to locate 5A. He was drawn to someone blaring Babs Marley and he followed the music round the back of the house and downstairs. There was no number on the door, but the strong smell of weed wafting from under it told him he was in the right place. He rang a total of six times, each one progressively longer, until Wayne answered. She looked him up and down and then returned to her darkened living room, leaving Ben to follow her.

Wayne's home was like a student flat with sparse mismatched furnishings and a threadbare carpet.. Even the posters on the wall were more in keeping with a hippy hangout than the abode of a senior officer. Not surprisingly it was a complete tip, and Ben felt sure the strong dope was masking more sinister smells. Wayne was sitting on the sofa, the room's only seat, balancing a C.D. on her lap as she carefully skinned up.

'Take a seat,' said Wayne.

Ben ignored the offer and decided to stay standing.

'Right, can you turn the music down, please? I can't hear myself think,' he asked.

'That's the general idea,' explained Wayne.

Ben spotted the remote control on the floor and pressed the 'off' button.

'I'd offer you tea or coffee, only I wasn't expecting company, and I don't want any,' she told Ben.

'I don't want a drink; this is the middle of your shift. Or have you forgotten that you're still on duty?'

Wayne wet the top of the skins with her tongue and neatly finished rolling the fat joint. She scanned the cluttered sofa for some roach material, settling on a bit of cardboard from an empty pizza box. She tapped the final product onto the C.D. case several times, put it in her mouth and lit it. She smiled widely at Ben, as she handed him the spliff.

'Are you trying to be funny?' Ben asked.

'Nope. I'm just trying to be sociable, that's all.'

'You're supposed to be in work right now.'

'No. I'm supposed to be half pissed in my aunt's living

room listening to her tales of when she singlehandedly took out a Korean village.'

'Never mind your auntie's war stories, we got an I.D.'

'Eric Fitzgerald, or as his clients prefer to call him, Star.' Wayne cut in.

'How the hell do you know that?'

'He's a prostitute, one of Hagan's; Baker was one of his clients.'

'Martha Baker, the medical examiner?' Ben's reaction went from disbelief to disgust. 'The dirty old bitch.'

'Less of the old, she's the same age as me, is Martha. We went to school together. I've known her forty years. She's not capable of strangling these kids.'

'You're not capable of making that call. You're too involved, Wayne; this needs a detached view.'

'And all that religious bullshit, that's just not Baker. She's a confirmed atheist. Always has been. That's why she works so happily with the dead, because she doesn't see souls, she sees corpses.'

Ben shot her a look.

'What?' asked Wayne.

'McEwan said we might be looking for an atheist.'

'McEwan Spewin', she'll say anything to justify her bottom line. Has she handed in any invoices yet?'

'Enough about McEwan! You think she's a smart arse who can't help at all? I get it, Wayne. You've made your point loud and clear. But this isn't about McEwan. It's about Baker. We need to bring her in.'

'She's not our woman, Campbell. I'd stake my pension on that.'

'Keep acting like this and there won't be a pension to stake. Right, I'm calling Baker in. You get your shoes on, brush your teeth and try and look a little less like you've been in a car crash. We're going back to the hostel.'

Ben parked the car on the street opposite the hostel. A small group of boys stood outside shivering as they shared a cigarette. Wayne sniffed them suspiciously, as the two officers strolled into the empty corridor of Withering's Catholic Youth Hostel for Boys. Ben pressed the bell at reception, prompting a room at the back of it to open and Palmer, the receptionist, to stroll out, a false smile plastered across her face. 'How can I help?' she asked.

Ben flashed his I.D., 'We need to see Mother Maria. Now.'

'Has something happened? Not another one of those murders?' Palmer sounded scared.

'Just get us the main woman,' Wayne instructed her.

It took a good ten minutes for Mother Maria to get to reception. Palmer held onto her arm and guided her slowly down the corridor. Then she led her and the two police officers into the deserted canteen, where she eased the wheezing priest into a chair. 'If you could make this quick, please,' she asked, 'Mother Maria was just about to have a nap.'

'We won't take long,' Wayne assured her.

The old woman cleared her throat and whispered 'How can I help, have you got an update on Kai?'

'It's not Kai, Mother,' Wayne spoke kindly, 'It's another one of your boys.'

'Eric?' the priest's voice was barely audible 'Father of God, not Eric!' Mother Maria pushed the chair back and dropped to her knees. She found her rosary beads, blessed herself, and began to pray in Latin. Wayne bowed her head and placed her arm on her chest. Ben stared from one woman to the other.

'Right, enough prayers for now, Mother,' he said tapping her on the shoulder. 'Can you sit back down, please? We have questions for you.'

'I'm not sure that's necessarily wise,' Wayne broke in.

'I'm in charge Wayne, I make that call. Right, Mother, we've found another one of your boys, brutally strangled, his dead body placed like Jess on the cross.'

Mother Maria didn't move from her kneeling position. Instead, her praying became louder and her breathing more laboured.

Ben continued, 'Post mortem, he was stabbed over fifty times, before a crucifix, identical to the ones in your desk, was shoved up his anus.'

At that point the priest clutched her heart and let out a desperate groan. She collapsed on the floor and her body began to convulse. Ben's first aid training kicked in and he sprang into action. He yanked her robe off her and pulled open the shirt underneath. She had stopped shaking now and lay perfectly still. Ben checked for a pulse. He couldn't find one. He leaned over her, held her nose closed and shoved all of his breath as far into her mouth as it would go. Nothing happened. He did it again. Mother Maria coughed, spluttered and took a breath for herself. Ben felt his eyes well up.

'I need an ambulance, now!' he shouted at Wayne.

'Already on it, boss,' Wayne replied as she informed the operator of their location.

Suddenly Mother Maria grabbed Ben's shirt and pulled him downwards. She tried to speak but all that came out was spit. Her eyes pleaded with him, desperate to convey what her mouth couldn't. Then, just as suddenly, they closed and she stopped breathing. Ben pulled her hands off him, and opened her mouth to resuscitate her. He felt Wayne's hand restrain him.

'She's gone, Campbell.'

Ben looked from Wayne to the priest and back again. Pools of tears fell unchecked down his face. 'I killed her,' he cried.

'No you didn't,' Wayne replied. 'She was eighty-three. Life killed her. She had a good end, didn't die alone, it was over in minutes. What more might she hope for?'

'Not to draw her last breaths with some lad screaming obscenities in her ear,' Ben said.

'There's many a woman would pay good money for that,' smiled Wayne and she patted the young Inspector on the shoulder.

'Now, get that down you, girl. It's a bit burnt, but it's still fodder. If we got this in the Korean prisoner of war camp I would have thought it was Christmas,' Aunt Stella enthused, placing a meal in front of her niece.

Wayne looked at her plate. She had no idea what the suck it was supposed to be. She consoled herself that it wouldn't have looked or tasted any better if she'd got there nine hours earlier. She moved the food round the plate with her fork. She wasn't hungry and even if this shit was edible, she wouldn't have been inclined to eat. She raised a spoonful to her mouth cautiously. The old girl had taken the trouble to try and cook it. She tried to swallow, but it was no use, she spat it out all over the floor. 'Can't eat, Stella, I've had a shit day, I just want to get drunk. Go on and pour me some of that whisky.'

As she watched Stella hobble across the dimly lit

kitchen, and struggle to open the whisky bottle, Wayne felt a twinge of guilt. Stella was her only living relative. Still, she told herself, the old girl wasn't in that bad nick given her eighty six years of living, most of them hard. She still had her eyesight and she could still hear a bit. She still lived alone and she could still cook for herself and shit for herself and piss for herself. She could clear enough from under her feet to keep things ticking over between visits from a cleaner, that Wayne paid to come twice weekly. All things considered she was in better shape than most of her peers, and what more could Wayne be reasonably expected to do? She wasn't cut out for caring. That's why she'd never married, or had kids, or held down a relationship long enough for either of these eventualities to come into play.

'Get that down you,' Stella commanded, handing her a glass half full of neat whisky to drag her mind back from the morose places days like today took it to. 'Then, you can tell me what's got you so wound up. Is it the job? I've been reading about that mad bitch in the papers all week. She has the whole town up in arms. Is it your case? Are you top bitch?' Aunt Stella was so excited she rushed all her words together.

'Course I'm top bitch,' she lied. 'Who else would they trust to get her?'

'And are you close; do you have any suspects?' Stella helped herself to another whisky and replenished Wayne's glass.

'We have a few, but I don't know, Stella. None of them feel right to me, you know, in here.' She rubbed her expansive belly.

'You've got to go with your gut, Jane. So, who do you have, in the frame, as they say?'

'Well, Harriet Hagan's in the picture.'

'She runs Big Mamma's, doesn't she, and that strip joint down by the quays? So, she's on the suspect list.'

'All of the boys are whores and who owns every whore in the town? She's got solid alibis for the first couple of crimes though, and there's no doubt that we're only dealing with one killer, so I think we have to discount her.'

'So who else? Come on, you've got the pimp and who else?' Aunt Stella demanded after performing the ritual glass filling again.

'There's a schoolteacher called Singh.'

'Is she Indian? It'll be her, surely Wayne, it has to be.'

'She's my current favourite, but I don't see it. She's a weasely, spineless excuse for a woman. She preys on vulnerable teenagers and pays them to suck her. She's in this up to her neck, but she doesn't fit the profile. She's shy and awkward and very nervous all the time. I think our girl's a successful, confident woman-about-town. With every killing, she's got bigger and bolder. I don't think we're looking for a woman with a twitch.'

'Could be an act, though. Barbara Casey comes down to the legion every Friday in her dead husband's wheelchair. The bar staff feel sorry for her and always give her double measures. Truth is, she's fitter than a fiddle and does a three mile round walk every morning to pick up her papers from the town. It's amazing what people will believe, if they have no reason not to.'

'Maybe,' Wayne said.

'Anyone else?'

'Tara Donaldson. She's a paedophile with previous and I caught her working at the same school one of the dead boys went to.'

'Forget the Asian. It'll be the paedo,' Stella declared. 'Of course, it's the paedo—it's always the paedo.'

'The set-up is too flash for her and I don't see what she'd get out of it. She could be uploading it or even streaming it live, I suppose...' Wayne registered the confusion on her aunt's face. 'The internet, Stella,' she explained. 'She could be recording the killings and selling the footage online.'

'Paedos sell that sort of thing on the internet?' Stella's eyes widened.

'There's nothing you can't buy online these days, Stella, not a sucking thing. So maybe that could be it, but I don't see it being Donaldson.'

Stella shuffled back over to her dresser and found an unopened bottle of whisky. She carried it back to the table and topped up the two almost empty glasses. 'So, who is your money on?'

'None of them. And, as of today, there's Baker as well,' Wayne sighed.

'Who's Baker? You haven't told me about her, is she good for them?'

'Sucked if I know, Stella. You know her, Martha Baker.'

'Martha? *Your* Martha?'

'She's hardly mine. But yes, my Martha.'

'Martha Baker as in *Baker the Brave*?'

Baker had earned the nickname four decades earlier because of her refusal to sleep with all the lights off, when the two girls had stayed over at Aunt Stella's.

'That was a long time ago, Stella. But yeah, Baker the Brave.'

'Baker the Brave didn't do this, Jane. Don't talk madness. Sure, Baker the Brave can't get to sleep unless the hall light is on!'

ELEVEN

MONDAY

Simon ducked down behind the bushes in the Simpsons' garden and waited for Ralph's dad to pile the kids in the car and leave for the school run.

When they were out of sight, he went over to the living room window and tapped on it. A grinning Ralph waved at him and beckoned him round to the back door.

Simon shivered. It was dull and freezing in Withering. It was ten times colder than it would be in London at this time of year. Simon missed London. He missed his old school and his old friends and his old haunts. He missed doing stuff with people. There was nothing to do in this shit hole and nobody to do it with. Ralph was his only friend, and he was a bigger freak than Simon. Ralph answered the door, giggling.

'He swallowed it then?' Simon asked.

'Hook, line and sinker! He was so worried, he was going to take the day off work, but I managed to convince him I'd be asleep all day so there was no point.'

'You got any beer?' Simon asked, stepping into the kitchen and leaning on the radiator to thaw out his bones.

'Jess Christ, Simon. It's not even 9 o'clock!' Ralph said. 'Anyway, have you forgotten what happened the last time?'

'Yes,' admitted Simon and they both laughed.

After much persuasion, Ralph had a quick scan of his cupboards and found some cooking sherry. He poured Simon a half cup of the dubious-looking liquid.

'You're not having any?' Simon asked, downing it in one mouthful.

'Better not. Dad went mental the last time.'

'Whatever,' Simon shrugged. He helped himself to some more before Ralph tucked it back behind the self-raising flour.

Simon's phone beeped. It was probably from George. No doubt, he'd have discovered Simon wasn't in his room and he'd be going ape. Suck him! He read the text. It wasn't from George after all. His face broke into a smile. Meanwhile, Ralph placed armfuls of male beauty products on the kitchen counter.

'This is some of Dad's best stuff and I've brought through some of my own as well. Where do you want to start?'

Simon cast an admiring glance over a black velvet bag bursting at the seams with expensive looking make-up. The products were the kind his dad used to wear, when he still dressed like a man. He fingered several two-tone nail varnishes and settled on blue-black. It would give him an edge. 'Let's start with my nails,' he instructed an eager Ralph.

Ralph did as he was told, filing Simon's nails down, pushing back his cuticles, and then coating them in two, thin layers of the varnish.

'Hands done, face next,' he said. Ralph was really good at putting make-up on other people. He placed Simon in front of the kitchen window.

'It's best to work in natural light,' he told Simon, clearly proud of his expertise. He cleansed and toned his friend's face and then applied a layer of moisturiser. Next came a primer. 'This acts as a sort of base for the foundation,' he explained, applying it evenly all over his face. Simon wished he'd just shut up and get on with it, but he didn't say.

After the base coat, Ralph applied concealer beneath his eyes and then he put on a layer of foundation. His face had a look of fixed concentration as he swept Simon's face with two rounds of powder.

'It's all in the strokes of the brush,' he said. 'Up, down, up.'

Moving on to blusher, Ralph looked at the colour Simon had picked and paused.

'Your skin's too dark for pink. Let's go with a more peachy tint. Now, puff your cheeks out, like this, I need to get an even application.'

Ralph took a deep breath and filled his mouth with air and Simon copied him. He didn't dare catch his reflection in the mirror, for fear he might look like a demented hamster. But all this effort would be worth it; for her.

After he'd finishing accentuating his cheek bones, Ralph finger-brushed Simon's eyebrows. 'I'm not liking these stray hairs. When did you last have them waxed?'

'Two weeks ago,' Simon replied. The truth was, he'd never had his eyebrows waxed or threaded. His dad would go nuts at the mention of it. He'd pluck a few stray hairs every now and then, but that was the height of his eyebrow maintenance. And he paid even less attention to his legs; it was highly embarrassing.

Ralph found his dad's tweezers. 'Ideally, we'd steam your face first, 'coz it makes the hair come away quicker, but with all this make-up already on, that's not a good idea.' He tilted Simon's face back and began to pluck. His movements were fast and furious as he yanked hair after hair, ignoring Simon's yelps of agony. 'If it doesn't hurt, you're not doing it right,' he said, sitting back with a satisfied grin.

Simon's eyes were filled with tears as he stroked the stinging skin below his brows.

'Good job!' Ralph enthused. He looked at the eye shadow Simon had chosen and sighed. 'The taupe and khaki will look dull against your skin tone. Let's go for a mauve, with a dash of rose pink, that'll really set your eyes off.' Ralph lightly brushed the two shades over Simon's eyelids.

Simon winced, his skin still inflamed. He winced some more as Ralph followed the eyeshadow with two rows of midnight-blue eyeliner.

'Have you got the eyelashes?' asked Ralph.

Simon reached into his bag and pulled out a set, freshly stolen from the local chemist.

'Great!' Ralph squealed as he set about carefully gluing them onto each of Simon's eyelids.

'Jess! They're heavy,' Simon groaned.

'You never wore them before?' Ralph raised his eyebrows.

'Course I have, just forgot how heavy they are,' Simon lied.

Next, Ralph outlined his lips with a pencil. He filled in the outline with a matching shade of lipstick, *Provocative Plum*. He stood back and admired Simon like a work of art, then he held up a mirror to him.

Though his skin was irritated because of all the make-up layers, and his eyesight was impaired by his false lashes, and his face was throbbing as a result of the plucking, Simon thought he looked sucking amazing.

'You're a genius,' he declared and Ralph glowed with pride.

'So, are you going to tell me what the make-up lesson's for?' Ralph asked.

'Nope,' Simon replied, his face still fixed on the mirror.

Ben sat behind Wayne's desk, a mountain of paperwork obscuring his view. He picked a folder off the top and flicked through witness statements from yesterday's murder investigation.

Every house on the street had received a visit, and every occupant aged over eighteen had been interviewed. The result was hundreds of pages of data that was more than probably useless, but just might contain a nugget of vaguely relevant information.

He pored over every line, growing more despondent with each new interviewee's response. The ringtone of his mobile provided a welcome distraction and he answered it immediately.

'Hello, Inspector. It's Professor Lottie McEwan. Is this a good time?'

'Absolutely, what have you got for me?'

'I'd rather not discuss it on the phone. Can you come over to my place?'

Ben stood up and glanced out into the main office. He couldn't see Wayne anywhere and, much to his surprise, he wanted her with him on this.

'No problem. I'll be round in an about hour,' he told the professor, with a confidence that wasn't justified.

Martha Baker's holding cell stank of B.O. and fear. Wayne's nose wrinkled with disgust as she entered the confined space.

The medical examiner sat shivering in the corner of the bed, her knees pulled up to her double chin, her head bent forward and her eyes closed. She opened them slowly and on seeing Wayne, she reached out and grabbed her arm.

Wayne shook it off.

'You've got to get me out of this, Wayne. I didn't kill those boys, I swear.'

'Swear on what? Your words are aren't worth much at the moment.'

'I'll be straight with you, this time. I should have been from the beginning. I'm sorry.'

'You can start by telling me what Eric was doing with your number in his pocket.'

'Honestly, I don't know. He must have kept it.'

'And why would he do that?' Wayne asked. She was pacing the cell like a caged tiger, not daring to make eye contact with Baker.

'How the hell should I know? Maybe it was because I was kind to him?'

'Kind? Was this before or after you sucked him for money?'

'Give me a break will you? It was right after Ollie left that I started going to Big Mamma's. I was lost without him and the kids. But I was determined not to drink, so I went there instead. It took my mind off what a shit wife and mother I'd turned out to be. Can you blame me?'

'You're going back a few years now. When did you first meet Eric?'

'Must be about six months ago. He was new to the game, you could tell, and he had an innocence about him. But that never lasts long…' Baker's voice trailed off

'That's because of sick perverts like you!' Wayne had stopped pacing and stood over a quivering Baker. 'Where did the kindness come in?'

'I'd buy him dinner and top up his mobile phone, things like that. Over and above what I had to pay him, to be kind,'

Baker explained.

'Well, aren't you the sucking patron saint of hookers? But why did he call you Sunday morning, early hours? What did he say?' Wayne studied Baker's reaction carefully. 'We know about the call, Baker. We're the sucking police, remember. Or did you really think we wouldn't?'

'I don't know why he called me. And I couldn't really hear him. I thought he said something, but it was so muffled. It sounded like "help", but I wasn't sure. I'd just been watching *The Omen* and I thought maybe I was getting a bit jittery. Then he called again about twenty minutes later. This time he definitely whispered "help". I tried to talk to him, ask him questions, find out his address, but he didn't respond at all. Just these intermittent croaks for help and then, after a couple of minutes, the line went dead. I tried to call back, but the phone went straight to his voice mail.'

'And how exactly did you make the jump from taking a call at home to being at the crime scene?'

'I went down to the station. One of the boys owed me a favour and I'd rather not say who.'

'Tough, because I'm asking you. Who?' Wayne brought her face inches from Baker's.

'P.C. Simmons. I asked him to run a trace on the call and he came back with the address. I drove there straight away and found exactly what you found. It was 3.00 a.m. He'd been dead about two hours, which puts his death within minutes of getting off the phone to me. I was the last person he spoke to.' Baker was welling up.

'And whether you were actually the last person to see him, remains in question.'

'Wayne,' pleaded Baker, 'You can't honestly think that of me! We go way back.' She pulled herself out of her slouch and allowed her feet fall to the floor. Wayne took a step back. She searched Baker's face, forcing their eyes to meet.

'Let's talk about Leo,' Wayne held the stare.

'There's nothing to say about Leo. He was the son of a family friend. End of.'

'Which makes you all the more of a sick bitch. Now, what was the story with you and Leo?' Wayne repeated.

Baker's face contorted with pain. She looked away and started to weep again. 'It was him that did all the chasing,' she said.

Wayne's face remained impassive.

'I fought it. God knows I fought it. But you've seen him; he was sex on legs.'

'He was a *child*,' Wayne retorted. 'A sucking child, for Christ's sake!'

'That's debatable. He didn't sound like a child, and he didn't look like a child. And when he set about manipulating me into bed, he certainly didn't act like a child,' Baker's lip had curled into a snarl.

Wayne threw her a look of disgust, but Baker continued.

'Get down off your high horse, Wayne. You'd have hoovered him up like a skanky carpet if it was you he'd taken a shine to!'

'And this is what I got you sober for, is it? To prey on young boys?'

'No, you got me sober to appease your own conscience. And so that you'd have someone to drive you places. And someone to listen when you're so wasted you're incoherent. You used me just as much as I used those boys.'

Wayne stared at Baker looking for a trace of her oldest friend, but all she could see was her anger, masking her fear, masking her guilt, masking her lies. Baker was no different to any number of crooks she'd put away over the years: arrogant, agitated, and above all else, certain of their innocence. She backed away towards the cell exit, her eyes fixed on Baker.

'You can't leave me here, Wayne. I'm your oldest friend in the world.' Baker bawled at her.

'You're no friend of mine.' Her voice was barely above a whisper, as she retreated from the cell.

Wayne leaned against the corridor wall. She could hear Baker's pleas echoing in her ears, and she shut her eyes in the hope it might quieten her mind.

'What are you doing down here?' Campbell's voice invaded her thoughts and her eyes sprung open.

'Have you just been to see Baker? Campbell sounded more schoolteacher than colleague.

'And what if I have?'

'You can't go interviewing suspects alone in their holding cells. This isn't the nineties.' Ben scolded her.

'Of course it's not the sucking nineties. If it was, a jumped-up city tart like you would be making the tea, not second guessing a Senior Police Officer.' Wayne spat out each word.

Simon fiddled with his computer cable to try and get the connection to work. He looked at his watch. It was nearly time and he couldn't get a signal. *This sucking town.* He kicked his bed. *Nothing works in this shithole!* He wondered if he should go downstairs and nick his phone back from George. He'd given him a right earful when he'd got back and then confiscated it. George was a soft touch though; he might even give it back, if Simon sounded apologetic enough.

He found him in the kitchen reading *Man's Weekly*.

George looked up and smiled kindly. 'I hope we're not going to have any more high jinks from you, or else I'll be telling your dad everything.'

'Please don't, George, it will just worry him. I'm sorry and I won't ever sneak out again.' Simon gave him his best begging eyes. 'So, can I have my phone back. Please?'

George raised his eyebrows and gave Simon a long, hard stare. 'You pull another stunt like this morning and you'll never see this again. I'll take it home with me and give it to my nephew for Christmas. You hear me?'

'I hear you, thanks, George. You're a legend.' Simon planted a hurried kiss on his cheek and ran back upstairs.

Ben sat in lunch hour traffic, tapping his fingers lightly against the steering wheel. Wayne sat beside him and played with the belt buckle on her trousers.

'You think we've got her, don't you? You think it's Baker?' Ben said eventually.

'I don't know what I think.'

'Do you think it would be wiser if you stand down?' Ben kept his voice low.

'Stand down? What does that even mean? Where the suck did you do your training? Wayne shook her head. 'Do you mean that I should quit? Why would I do that? Just because I know one of the main suspects? Baker is known to every copper in Withering. She's been the medical examiner for nearly thirty years. Are you going to process this whole case on your own?'

'The entire force doesn't have a friendship with Baker that spans a lifetime. You do, Wayne. You're too close to this. Can't you see you have no objectivity at all?'

'Coming from a man whose wife is a victim, I sure as hell can be as objective as you.'

'Firstly, that fact is not known to anyone but you and me. And secondly, she's my ex-wife, profoundly estranged ex-wife, and the key word in the sentence is victim. My ex-wife isn't our chief suspect, that would be a deal breaker.'

'Deal breaker? For suck's sake, boy, will you speak English for once? Look, here's what's happening, I'm not walking away. So, are you going to make me? Or are we going to see the Cambridge cock?'

Ben pulled off the main road fifteen minutes outside of Withering and he slowly navigated the country lanes that led to McEwan's farmhouse. Sign posts were scarce and faded, and he feared the Sat Nav had got it wrong when he spotted a large house a couple of miles in the distance. Wayne wolf whistled.

'What did McEwan call it again, her rural hideaway? Sucking hell, if it was any bigger, it would be a castle. I told you we were paying her far too much.'

They had reached the end of the drive and the huge house was still well in the distance. Ben presented his I.D. for a security camera and a large black iron gate opened slowly. They drove towards the manor house passing rows of lush grass, where well fed deer roamed freely and probably ate better than most people. 'How the other half lives...' Ben said.

'Not half, Campbell. One percent,' Wayne corrected him.

They parked the car in the court yard, which was subdivided into stables and storage sheds, with a large open space that housed a tractor and a Land Rover.

McEwan stepped out of a feeding room and waved over

at them. She was wearing brown overalls and carrying a pitch fork, which she shoved in a bale of hay, before greeting them. 'Did you find it alright?' she asked.

'It was a challenge,' Wayne said. 'It being so small and all.'

'This way, Inspectors. I'll take you through the trade woman's entrance. McEwan walked them across the yard and through a large black door into a hall, lined either side with wellingtons and riding boots. 'We're just getting the downstairs floors modernised, so if you don't mind, I'll have to ask you to take your shoes off before you go through to the drawing room. My brother Paul will get you a drink, and I'll join you once I've changed.'

'These boots don't come off,' Wayne declared.

'Seriously?' Ben scowled at her.

'Not a problem,' McEwan smiled at them. 'Perhaps you'll be more comfortable sitting in the kitchen, we're more relaxed about footwear in that part of the house. Go on through and I'll shout on Paul.' McEwan pointed to a door to their left.

The door took them through a scullery to a huge open plan kitchen, which was the strangest blend of antique and modern that Wayne had ever seen. There was a table in the centre, which looked like it had been there a few hundred years, along with half a dozen heavy wooden chairs. Surrounding the ancient dining set were glossy kitchen cupboards with gleaming stainless steel worktops. A designer microwave sat next to a shiny four-piece toaster, and a floral china tea set that reminded Wayne of her father's wedding gifts. To the right of the table there was a polished red Aga cooker, wafting the smell of baking scones across the room. Wayne wondered what the brother looked like, because he was obviously handy in the kitchen.

Her curiosity was satiated by the arrival of Paul McEwan and Wayne could see at once why his baking skills needed to be so superior. This was the type of bloke that the term 'dowdy' had been invented for. He was wearing a shapeless black frock that was as out of date as the crockery he was laying on the table. McEwan's brother didn't introduce himself, or speak a word, as he set about making an afternoon tea worthy of competing in any country fete she'd ever been to, which admittedly was only one.

He laid out scones, two types of jam—blackberry and plum—a pound of butter, a dish of cream, and a freshly-baked fruit cake. He filled a china teapot with water from the enamel kettle on the top of the stove. He hovered over the brewing tea for a couple of minutes, before bringing it to the table and pouring them each a cup. Campbell picked up his cup, as McEwan's brother replaced the teapot on the counter and brushed his damp hair back from his blotched face, causing Wayne to wince.

'Can I get you anything else, Inspectors?' He spoke for the first time, fixing his lifeless eyes on Wayne.

She wanted to say 'no' because he had a look of deranged bachelor about him and she didn't want to give him any encouragement. However, her eyes had been drawn to a seventy-year-old malt that stood proudly on the bottom dresser and she felt compelled to taste it. She filled her tea cup to the brim with milk and drank its contents in one gulp.

'Any chance of a small one?' she asked, pointing her cup in the direction of the whisky.

If McEwan's brother understood her, he didn't act on it, choosing instead to wipe a dish cloth over and back across a stretch of counter.

'Are you serious?' Ben asked.

'I imagine she's very serious, Inspector,' the voice came from McEwan, who had entered the room from the other door.

She had changed into a white polo shirt and a pair of beige, corduroy trousers, all previous outdoor smells masked in cologne that was probably more expensive than the whisky Wayne craved. 'Paul, pour our guest a large one, and I'll have one too. Can I tempt you, Inspector Campbell?'

'Best not,' Ben replied.

'Probably wise,' McEwan smiled at him, taking the drinks from her brother and handing one to Wayne.

'I'll go check in on the deer then,' her brother told McEwan, scuttling out of the kitchen.

McEwan took a healthy sip of her whisky, then handed Wayne a clear plastic folder, inside of which was an envelope and a letter. 'I got this, this morning.'

The envelope had the professor's name and address type written on the front, but no postage stamp. The letter was an A4 typed page written in a language Wayne didn't understand. She returned it to McEwan.

'Do you call the cops every time you get one of these?' Wayne asked, her tone conveying her complete lack of interest.

'It's from the Wringer,' McEwan replied.

'Why do you say that, Professor?' The question came from Ben.

'It's the next passage in the Gnostic gospels. It follows on from the quote on the wall.'

Even Wayne looked interested now. 'Who delivered it? What time did it arrive? Did anyone speak to the messenger?' she rushed her words together.

'It was here when my husband came downstairs this morning.'

'How did someone get in the main gate?' she continued.

McEwan shrugged her shoulders. 'They climbed over it, I imagine.'

'And your husband heard nothing?'

McEwan shook her head.

'What about security? You have security? We had to show I.D. on the way in. You must have C.C.T.V. footage?' Wayne asked.

'I don't I'm afraid, Inspector. The camera at the gate is the only security I have. It's not a recording device. You can only get past the gate on foot, and the three mile walk to the house has always proved a sufficient deterrent. The modern burglar is a curiously lazy creature.' McEwan smiled.

'Why the hell didn't you call this in first thing?' Wayne's voice rose.

'I think you'll find I did, Inspector.'

Ben blushed. He put the letter carefully in an evidence bag and labelled it with his pen. 'Have you noticed anything else unusual, Professor?' he asked.

'No. But then I'm an academic, Inspector; I tend to notice very little when I'm immersed in the ancient Vedic texts or trying to translate an early Roman letter.' She laughed, but the joke was lost on Wayne.

'How about your husband?' Wayne asked.

'My husband's not the observant type,' McEwan replied. 'But you're welcome to ask him.'

She excused herself and returned five minutes later with a tall, willowy man, who she introduced as Ivan.

'Ivan a piece of that!' Wayne thought, watching McEwan's

husband glide into the kitchen, like it was a ballroom. No mean feat given the heavy concrete floor.

He was strikingly beautiful. Wayne felt an ache in her loins just looking at him. Even though it was still the afternoon, he was dressed in evening wear. A floor length, lime green, silk dress clung to his curves. His honeycomb blond hair stopped just below his shoulders, and he was wearing a feather fascinator that matched his dress. He smiled at Wayne and she thought her heart might melt, or at the very least, that her cunt might drip all over the concrete floor.

'How can I help, Inspectors?' he played with his hair as he spoke. His nervous quirk highlighted the considerable age difference between him and his wife.

'We need to ask you a few questions about the letter you received.' Wayne was conscious of a sweat breaking out beneath the collar of her shirt. 'Did you see who delivered it?'

'No,' he said immediately.

'Have you noticed anyone unusual hanging about the place? Have you had any unexpected callers? Workwomen perhaps, or someone delivering leaflets? Anything at all?'

'No.' Again his answer was instantaneous.

'Take your time, doll,' Wayne urged him. 'There might have been something or someone you saw, that didn't seem important at the time. Is there a new post woman, perhaps, or window cleaner?'

'My husband is not a doll, Inspector, although admittedly he looks like one. He has answered your questions as fully as he can. I'm truly sorry he can't help. You can go now, darling.' McEwan instructed him.

Mister McEwan exited as gracefully as he had entered,

reminding Wayne of a silent movie star from the twenties.

She was still staring at the last glimpse of his pert buttocks when Ben waved his hand in her face. 'Wayne, we're leaving.' She returned her attention to the present, polished off her whisky in one mouthful and followed him out of the room.

Simon was in bed sulking. George had called him down to eat something, twice. He wasn't hungry. He'd finally got online two minutes after five, but it was too late. She was gone. He was furious with George. It was his fault, George's and his dad's. If his dad had let him stay home alone, instead of hiring George to mind him, like he was a sucking kid, then all of this could have been avoided. He'd be sitting in some fancy apartment talking about his future, instead of lying here, wondering if he hadn't sucked the whole thing up. She could have picked anyone, but she'd picked him and now he'd sucked it up!

'Simon, come have your tea. I'm leaving early tonight and I want everyone fed before I go.' George opened the door to his bedroom and Simon slid under the covers completely.

'I'm not hungry. Leave me alone.'

George wasn't the type to be easily dissuaded. He came over and sat on the teenager's bed. Simon lay perfectly still. 'Can you bring your head to the surface, so I can at least look at you?'

'Leave me alone. I said I'm not hungry. Go away.' Simon shouted, but the words still came out muffled.

'What's going on, Simon? You were fine earlier. Who have you been texting on that phone? Has someone upset you? Maybe I should just take it away again.' George reached for the phone on Simon's beside table, but the boy threw his covers off and grabbed it before George knew what was happening.

'Get your hands off my phone,' he screeched, as the phone beeped. Simon turned his back on George to read it. All at once. his shoulders dropped and relief poured into his body. He hadn't been dumped. Tonight was postponed, but she wanted to reschedule.

Simon turned around and beamed at George. 'Actually, now that I think about it,' he announced. 'I'm starving. What's for tea?'

Wayne and Ben made their way back to the station. They were bumper-to-bumper with Withering's entire workforce, anxious to avoid paying the childminder another hour, or desperate to catch the first soap instalment of the evening.

Wayne placed her hand on Ben's horn and honked it loudly. A few horns honked back as Ben pushed her hand away.

'We just have to wait, like everybody else.' Ben spoke as if Wayne were Val.

She responded by putting her hand back on the horn and honking even louder.

'I would have thought you'd be in better humour, now that Baker is out of the frame,' Campbell shouted over the horn. Wayne removed her hand.

'How do you work that out?'

'Well, she was in the cells last night, wasn't she?'

Wayne nodded. 'Suck! I never even thought of that.' She stared straight ahead, lost in thought. 'Maybe she's got an accomplice?' she eventually suggested.

Ben shook his head. 'I'm not buying it. We've been working on the theory that there is only one killer, where's your evidence there's anyone else involved?'

Wayne shrugged her shoulders.

'This is good news, Wayne. aren't you pleased that your friend's in the clear? And your position on the case isn't compromised. It's a result of sorts, I'd say.'

Wayne gave her partner a non-committal look.

They drove the rest of the journey in silence, punctuated by Wayne's loud sighs.

Turning off the ignition, Ben glanced at the car clock. It was 18.15. 'Shit! Is that the time?' Ben said. 'It's George's big date tonight, and yes, I got it out of him—I know it's with you.' There was a smugness to Ben's tone.

'You'll make a great detective someday, Campbell.'

'You could try sounding a bit happier about it. I told him he was a fool to give you another chance, but he seems fairly smitten.'

'Then he's definitely a fool,' Wayne replied.

Climbing out of the car, she watched Campbell drive away, before strolling slowly round to the back of the station, scanning her route for skiving cops.

Confident that she was alone, she leaned against the front of a patrol car and lit a one-skinner. Immediately, she felt more relaxed as she closed her eyes and tried to assimilate the latest facts into her crowded mind. Baker couldn't have done it, she was innocent, this was good news, surely, only it made no difference, not really. She and Baker would probably never get past the investigation, and she wasn't even sure she wanted to.

She stamped her butt into the ground, fed her I.D. into the back-door entrance, and headed downstairs towards the holding cells.

Peachy sat behind the desk tapping away on his mobile

as usual. He jumped when he saw Wayne, dropping his phone.

'If I see you doing that again, I'll have to give that lovely arse of yours a few slaps,' chided Wayne, bending down to retrieve it for him.

Peachy blushed and stuffed the phone into his pocket.

'Right, open up,' Wayne ordered him. 'Baker's going home.'

George patted his wig down and smoothed out his silky blouse. He could feel beads of sweat forming beneath his freshly shaved arm pits and he wished he'd worn a cotton top.

He sneaked a quick look at his face in his compact mirror and was relieved that his make-up was staying firm. George switched his attention to his skirt and tried in vain to rub away the creases that his seating position had created.

'Another glass of house red, sir.' The pretty waiter smiled and placed the wine in front of George, swiftly removing the empty glass he had drained. George thanked him and started nibbling on a breadstick.

The restaurant door swung open and he looked up expectantly, to see a young couple breeze in. He opened his handbag and checked his phone again. There were no missed calls, no texts.

George hated mobile phones. He was old enough to remember a time before them, when his emotional wellbeing didn't rely on the bleep of a text. He was annoyed with himself for caring so much. The truth was that he wasn't much better than Simon, when it came down to it, just marginally subtler.

He wondered how long was too long to wait? George

knew the answer. But he didn't want to go yet, what if he left and Wayne showed up five minutes later? He was being pathetic and he knew it. There was only one thing for it; he ordered another glass of wine to take the edge off the knowledge.

The cute waiter cleared away the place setting opposite him. He wanted to tell him to leave it, but then he'd feel even more mortified when he walked out alone. After a hefty gulp of wine, he reached for his phone again. He sent a one-worded text, sank back his glass and slunk out the door.

Peachy got to the cell first, as Wayne was moving at a snail's pace. She heard him scream and ran the couple of metres to the holding place where Baker was being kept. Peachy was trying to unlock the cell door, but he was shaking so much he couldn't insert the key. Auto pilot firmly in charge, Wayne grabbed the key from him and opened it. Once inside, she pulled out the insides of her trench coat pockets and amid the debris she found her penknife. She yanked it open and jumped on the soiled mattress, leaning over to access the beam from which Baker was dangling, her entire frame supported by the tie around her neck. Wayne hacked at the tie with her knife, until the silky fabric ripped apart and Baker's body fell to the ground. She knew she was dead but that didn't stop her clawing at Baker's neck like an animal.

'Get an ambulance,' she heard herself scream at Peachy. He didn't respond. She looked up to see him bent in two crying and shaking, fresh vomit spread over his half-inch low pulls.

Wayne removed her hands from Baker's neck and stood

up. 'Pull yourself together, man,' she barked at him. Her reaction only served to make Peachy convulse even more.

'It's my fault,' he wept, snot and puke spoiling his perfectly made up face. 'I should never left her with her tie, I just didn't want to humiliate her any further.' He looked at Wayne, desperate for some form of atonement.

Wayne had averted her gaze to the dead woman at her feet, her overweight body sprawled against the concrete floor. Baker's eyes protruded from her bloated face, her lips blue, a pool of spit having formed in either corner.

Wayne detected the stench of human faeces, and figured she must have shat herself straight afterwards. 'Well, that ship has sailed,' she said. Peachy's sobs and splutters were starting to do her head in. 'Right, doll, I'm going to hit this alarm in ten seconds, and you need to be out of here, before I do.'

'What do you mean?' Peachy demanded, between wails.

'It doesn't take two people to clean up this mess. Sign out, leaving the time slot blank. Do it now.' Wayne's voice was barely audible over the wail of the alarm and as Peachy skulked away from the scene, half a dozen officers ran past him, towards the cells.

Wayne stood outside and watched, like she was an extra in a movie. It's only when cops are covering their backs that they really come into their own, she thought. She stood aside and admired the speed and dexterity with which her colleagues turned over the tiny room, searching meticulously for any slight deviation from standard procedures for which they might be held to account.

Eventually, they turned their attention to her, confident that all blame could be laid at Wayne's door. P.C. Brady, the longest serving officer on the team, made the approach.

'We need to ask you a couple of questions, Ma'am.'

Wayne had been Brady's superior for most of his career and he delivered the request in a low and respectful tone.

Wayne nodded and followed the constable down the corridor to the lift. As they turned into the main office, she mumbled something about needing a piss, and took a detour in the direction of the staff toilets.

Once she was certain that she was out of sight, she slipped out a side door, triggering an alarm and a second flurry of heightened activity in the normally sedate police station.

Wayne strolled nonchalantly across the car park and out the front gates. She didn't stop moving until she reached the nearest off-licence.

TWELVE

A WEEK LATER

MONDAY

Ben pulled the hoover out of the hall cupboard, and swore when he realised the bag had to be changed. He glanced at the clock on the wall. It was almost five, *shit!* He needed to get dinner started.

'Drea, get down here and do the hoovering,' he shouted up the stairs. He grabbed the bulging shopping bags from the hall and dragged them into the kitchen, narrowly avoiding tripping over half a dozen cars that Val had lined up either side of the fridge.

'Val, get down here now and clean up these toys.'

He tipped one of the bags of food onto the counter and found the steak mince. Ben turned the hob on full and emptied the packet of meat into a huge frying pan. As it started to brown, he found the onions, garlic and peppers and began to peel and chop furiously. He added the vegetables to the pan and searched the bags for tins of tomatoes. He poured the tomatoes on top of the mixture, turning the heat down so the sauce could simmer. He washed the basil plant in the sink and ripped the leaves off before tossing them in. The aroma of fresh basil filled his nostrils and triggered memories of his old life which was one long, endless round of home cooking and sauce stirring and soup making. *How the hell had he survived it?*

Now, the ping of the microwave or the delivery woman's knock on the door alerted the kids to the fact that it was tea time. A howl from Val brought him back to the present. She had stood on one of her cars and crashed straight into the fridge.

'Well, if you cleaned your bloody toys up this wouldn't happen!' he snapped at his youngest, instantly regretting it as her cries became more pronounced. He picked her up and tried to comfort her as he dragged the laundry basket into the hall and shoved it into the cupboard.

'Drea, get down here!' he shouted up the stairs. 'I won't tell you again.'

'Why are you always yelling, Dad?' Val asked.

'You'd yell too, if you had three kids, a house to clean, a job to go to, bills to pay, and nobody to help.' Ben became aware he was raising his voice again, as Val pulled away from him.

'George never yells,' she replied.

Simon pulled Ralph inside through his bedroom window and they both fell back on the bed, giggling.

'Shhh!' whispered Simon as he crawled off the bed, across the floor, and opened the bedroom door slightly.

All he could hear was his dad shouting. He smiled, and turned to give Ralph a reassuring look. He was surprised by how happy he was to see Ralph, but put it down to the fact that, due to being grounded, he hadn't left the house for a week.

Ralph had brought magazines and chocolate and was busy laying them out on the bed. He offered Simon a Fudge bar, but he shook his head and patted his concave stomach.

'So, where's your phone?' Simon asked. Ralph threw it

across to him. He grabbed it and began flicking his fingers forwards and backwards across the screen until he found the site he was looking for. She was online and he felt his pulse quicken and his heart pound as he sent her a smiley face.

Ben dragged the lasagne out of the oven with a worn-out tea towel, burning his fingers in the process. 'Shit!' he swore, barely avoiding knocking the hot dish all over the cooker.

The fire alarm and front door bell rang simultaneously, and he rushed to turn one off and answer the other, a trail of smoke and steam following him into the hall.

Wayne had pressed the bell again before he got to it. She was struggling to balance two bottles of wine and a bouquet of depressed-looking flowers. Wayne thrust the bunch into Ben's hand.

'You took your time,' she said.

She walked past Ben into the kitchen and put the wine down on the counter. Her tongue began to salivate at the sight of dinner and her belly began to rumble. 'Sorry,' she mumbled. 'I haven't had much in the way of nutrients this week except vodka and tomato soup, and they probably don't count.'

'They don't,' Ben agreed. 'Red or white?' he asked, locating a cork screw before he noticed they were both screw top.

'I don't care,' Wayne replied. She'd tossed her coat on the back of a chair and sat down expectantly at the table.

Ben poured them both a glass of red and shouted his brood down to the table. When nobody came, he slid into the seat beside Wayne, and they both savoured the first drink of the day.

Simon sat on his bed playing with Ralph's phone. His friend had very reluctantly left it with him, but he was coming back after tea to collect it. Simon sent her a third message, but so far he'd had no replies. He wasn't that surprised. *Someone like her could speak to anyone she wanted, why should she wait a week to talk to him?* He felt tears sting his eyes as his dad's voice called him downstairs for tea. He ignored him and checked his messages again. Her status hadn't changed; she was still online.

'Why are you ignoring me?' he typed and hit 'send', a wave of regret flowing through his retreating fingers. His phone beeped.

'All good things come to those who wait,' the message read. He began to reply when his phone bleeped again.

'Are you alone?'

'Told you I live alone,' Simon typed.

'What are you wearing?'

'What would you like me to wear?'

'Good boy!'

Ben piled a mix of lettuce leaves onto his plate and sat down, content that everyone had a meal in front of them. Drea barely noticed her food, her head buried in her Blackberry. Simon looked almost happy as he passed a bread roll to Wayne. Val was sitting beside her, ignoring her food as she showed off her Spiderwoman card collection.

'Put them away till after we've eaten,' Ben ordered. To his surprise, she did, before sniffing her food suspiciously.

'I don't like this! I wanted macaroni cheese!' she complained.

'There's ice cream for dessert, but only if you clear your plate.'

Val seemed to be considering her options. She tossed the food around her spoon, before wolfing down three big mouthfuls. Ben smiled, and filled his glass before offering Wayne more wine. She knocked back the contents of her glass and held it out.

'You drink a lot of wine,' Val told Wayne.

'We don't comment on how people eat or drink, Val, it's rude,' Ben chastised her.

'It's a fair point, though,' Wayne conceded. 'I drink like a fish.'

Val laughed and began ducking her nose into her glass of water. 'I'm drinking like a fish too,' she squealed, delighted.

'Right that's enough!' Ben snapped 'Val, stop messing, finish your dinner.'

Ten minutes later, only Ben and Wayne remained at the table surrounded by empty plates and Spiderwoman cards. Ben poured the last of the second bottle into his and Wayne's glasses. He smiled as he realised he was probably drunk. 'Everyone at the station misses you,' he told her.

'I doubt it; they just don't like you.'

'You know, I'm only trying to be nice here, you could make an effort too.'

'If you're serious about staying in the force, Campbell, you need to stop being nice.'

Ben ignored her as he piled the empty dishes on top of each other, banging cutlery against plates as he worked. He carried the stack to the kitchen sink and turned the hot water tap on. Wayne remained seated, tapping her cigarette against the side of the packet.

'You're not smoking that in here,' he warned.

'So, are you going to tell me what's going on with the Wringer,' she asked. 'Or do I need to buy us another bottle of wine?'

Ben's face paled at the thought of more alcohol. He filled the kettle, switched it on and then staggered back to the table. 'Florence from fraud has been going through Skylark profiles trying to track her. That's the Wringer's hunting ground, no doubt about it, but she's covered herself completely. Florence has found a dozen profiles that are more than probably her, but they're all being re-routed through foreign IP addresses.'

'In English, please,' Wayne asked.

'We can't get a location for her through Skylark. She could be based anywhere.'

'Anything else?'

'We found trace amounts of vaginal fluid on the carpet. It was a tiny sample, but enough to rule out Singh, Donaldson, Baker and Hagan, so now we don't have any suspects.'

'The Wringer's first cunt-up though, it's the beginning of the end when she starts to get careless. Her subconscious desire to get caught is surfacing, as my shrink might say. It's a good thing, Campbell. Next time, she might be even messier, leave us a thumbprint or something.'

'I don't want a next time,' Ben replied. 'It's our job to stop crimes, not anticipate them.'

'But there will be a next time. Like night follows day, she'll kill again.' Wayne drained her glass and her eyes scanned the room. 'Campbell, where's your drinks cabinet?'

Simon pulled his bedroom curtains closed, turned the lock and hit the volume on his iPad. He carefully removed the package from Ralph's rucksack.

It was the push up pra and stockings he'd ordered from the Andy Winters catalogue. He'd had it delivered to Ralph's because his dad was such a control freak that he'd started to intercept his post.

Simon stared at the black lace pra, fingering the tiny flowers interwoven into its tip. He'd been wearing pras for almost two years, but they were just white cotton sports ones, not the type that were so sexy that women ripped your clothes off just to see them.

Naked, he fingered the ugly rash around his genital area. He had got his first Brazilian two days before, and what had previously been a few pubes spread sparsely round smooth skin, now morphed into blotchy red lumps extending out to his thighs and stomach. He was desperate to scratch, but terrified he'd make the area even more unsightly.

He pulled the stockings on first. He quickly realised that they needed something to hold them up. He investigated the pra and noticed there were two catches either side of it. He put it round his waist, clasped it and tucked his penis into the wired cone, and was immediately aware of a restriction in his thighs and a slight pain in his dick. *"If it doesn't hurt you're not doing it right,"* Ralph had advised him. He was starting to wonder if that wasn't the mantra for all things manly.

He began to fasten the stockings to the pra. This task proved a lot more difficult then he imagined. Every time he successfully fastened one side, the other would become undone. After almost twenty minutes he was rapidly losing patience, when both sides appeared to remain up simultaneously. Terrified of knocking a clip out, he shuffled over to his mirror and admired his reflection.

Simon undressed slowly, anxious not to ladder his new

purchase. He placed the lingerie back in its box and shoved it under the bed.

Naked again, he strolled over to his wardrobe and pulled a plastic bag out from behind a pile of strategically placed jumpers.

He took out the DIY pejazzling kit and smiled, carefully laying out the cleansing wipe, the strip of jewels, the super strength skin-friendly adhesive, and the super strength skin-friendly adhesive remover on the bed. The scant instructions read:

Three quick steps to Blingtastic Balls!

1. Clean area with wipe.
2. Break seal on glue and apply a tiny dot to back of jewel, being careful not to touch the glue with your fingers.
3. Stick jewel on desired area.

Simple as that! Simon barely glanced at the back of the leaflet, which was where they put all the health warning stuff. Instead, he ripped the wipe packet open, stifling a scream as he ran the cleanser over his newly waxed willy.

The seal on the glue came off easily and, placing the cheap crystal face down on the tip of his left finger, he dripped a tiny spot of glue onto the back, and stuck the jewel on the front of his right testicle. Simon grimaced, before taking out the second crystal and repeating the process, until he had three ruby red gems on each of his balls.

He studied his willy proudly, and satisfied that he'd made an alright job of it, Simon reached for his mobile, and took a photo of his handiwork.

Wayne and Ben had retired to the sofa. Ben was nursing a

black coffee and Wayne was sipping her third whisky. She wanted to go, but every time she tried to, Ben refilled her drink. She never liked to walk away from a full glass, but she was dying for a spliff, and conscious that if she drank too much she would probably have a whitey. She moved the alcohol to one side and stood up to leave, as the doorbell rang.

Ben signalled for her to sit back down, and unsteady on her feet, she complied, reaching for her whisky as she did so.

Listening to Ben and his guest in the hall, her mind began to race. She quickly spat into her hand, and patted her hair down, whilst rolling her tongue around her mouth, making sure there were no bits of mince or lettuce stuck in her teeth.

Wayne stood up as they entered and gave George a wide grin. He didn't return it. She eyed him up and down from his flat black shoes to his lopsided white beret, and she felt her heart pound.

George wasn't much of a looker, but he more than made up for it in the bedroom. "*Ugly men try harder*," her mother had told her, and the older she got, the more Wayne found herself agreeing.

'I didn't know you had company. I'm just dropping off that shirt; I sewed the button back on for you. I'll see myself out,' George said, his face turning crimson.

'Don't go,' Wayne pleaded.

George seemed unsure what to do, his eyes darting between Wayne and Ben.

'I think you two probably need to talk, so why don't I go check on the kids?' Ben asked.

With Ben gone, they stood facing each other. George

averted his eyes and stared at the carpet. Wayne kept hers focused on him. 'I meant to call you,' she broke the silence.

'I'm sure you did,' he replied.

'It's been a really crap week. Baker died. I got suspended again...' her voice trailed off.

'Ben told me. It sounds like it's been really tough on you.'

Wayne wasn't sure if he was being sympathetic or sarcastic. That was the trouble with men, you never could tell. 'It's no excuse for not calling, though,' she ventured.

'It's actually a really good excuse for not calling.'

Wayne was confused.

'But then, your excuses are always good, elaborate, over the top, stretching the bounds of credibility, but fundamentally, good. I've never felt you didn't call me just because you didn't give a shit. You do give a shit Jane; I know you do.'

Wayne was proper confused now. It sounded like she was off the hook, but that would be too easy. George never made it easy for her, that's what she liked about him, that, and the fact that he had a great cock.

'You just don't give enough of a shit,' George continued. 'You'll always have good excuses, you'll just never stop making excuses, will you Jane?'

Wayne didn't like where this was going.

'Because I'll never be your top priority. I'll always come a poor runner-up to your job.'

'I might lose my job,' Wayne said in earnest.

'You've been losing that job as long as you've had it, and even if you did, what then? Quite apart from the fact that you'd be a nightmare to live with if you left the force, there would still be nights out with the girls, the booze, the weed, your roving eye, your aunt Stella. You'll always find someone or something to put before me. And even though I know you do this because you have a pathological fear of getting close to a man, I'll still blame myself a little. I'll start to think if I was a bit prettier, or a bit funnier, or a bit sexier, or a better cook, or a better listener, then you would want to spend more time with me. You wouldn't want me to start to hate myself, just because you never learned how to like yourself, would you, Jane?'

'No,' Wayne said quietly.

'You take care Jane, you hear?' he whispered in her ear. George's hand reached up and stroked Wayne's face and planted a tender kiss on her cheek, then fled, tears streaming down his own.

'What have you said to George?' Ben had returned, and was using his schoolteacher voice. 'Go after him!'

Wayne didn't move a muscle. She just stared at the floor. 'And say what?' she asked.

Over on the Hovenbath estate, Jeff snorted another line and collapsed on his sofa in a fit of giggles. 'This is good shit.'

His flatmate, Steve, grinned as he scrolled through music on his iPad. He found what he was after, an upbeat track, and turned the volume up full blast. Both boys danced around the living room, careful to avoid the small wooden table that held the last of their stash.

'Where did you get it?' Jeff asked.

'Some Jill gave me a bag instead of cash,' Jack replied.

'Why do you always get the coke heads? I just get middle-aged accountants, looking for a ten percent discount on a weekly arrangement.'

'I get them too. I'm like *"Listen mate, do I look like your sucking dry cleaner?"* The two boys howled with laughter.

The song ended, and Jeff's phone beeped. He read the text and his face broke into a stupid grin.

'Lover-girl?' Steve asked, his voice heavy with sarcasm.

'This one's different,' Jeff replied.

'Course she is,' Steve said. He shook his head, before bending over the table, and helped himself to one of the last two lines.

THIRTEEN

TUESDAY

Ben closed a file and used it as a pillow, as his head fell on to the desk. He needed coffee, or chocolate, or something to wake him up, after reading the latest of Professor McEwan's far flung theories. Wayne had been right about her. She was a very expensive waste of time.

He looked around the office and breathed in Wayne's absence. In a way, it was more oppressive than her presence. Ben stared at the paperwork he had spread over the desk, desperate to spot something significant. His eyes rested on the tormented face of Connor Maguire, or Vic 3, as he'd now come to be known.

He tried to recall the first time he'd seen Connor, and the horror and revulsion that he'd felt at the mutilated body. But his memory was a mesh of doe-eyed naked boys, no one standing apart from the others.

Was that what policing came down to? Becoming so desensitised that all victims looked the same? And if so, how did it help? Ben didn't have any more answers now, than he did in that first week, where his every sleep was spoiled by images of Connor's last moments.

He allowed his head to fall back on the folder and his eyes to close. His second attempt to rest was interrupted by a tap on the door and the entrance of an excitable Peachy waving a little plastic bag. 'We've got something, boss.'

Ben's eyes sprung open. His colleague had placed a bagged cuff link in front of him. He fingered it, recognising it instantly. Ben turned it over and the initials confirmed his suspicion. 'When and where did you find this?'

'The tilers handed it in this morning. Remember the bathroom was being refitted? This must have fallen into one of the tile boxes. Master Ryan said one of the plumbers found it yesterday, the first day they got back in.'

'I thought we'd searched every inch of that house, including all the building materials? Jess Christ, this is a murder investigation! How the hell can something like this take a week to show up? Right, get it straight down to forensics and then meet me out front. You and I have a lawyer to visit.'

Wayne pulled the collar of her trench coat up and the top of her baseball cap down as she buried her head in a copy of *The Shade*. She'd swapped her trademark cowboy boots for her funeral flats and, leaning back against the corridor wall, just down from the forensic lab, she was satisfied that she looked like any other overweight, middle-aged cop. Peachy skipped down the corridor and Wayne whistled at him. The young cop looked up and recognising her, his smile fell away.

'I'm so sorry,' he told her, his eyes welling up.

Wayne scanned the corridor to see if there were any witnesses to the scene. Confident that they were alone, she placed her hands on Peachy's shoulders and shook him hard.

'Pull yourself together, boy. You don't want to be seen crying like a baby, on duty.' Peachy nodded, sniffed loudly and dapped his face with the hanky Wayne handed him. As he gave it back, Peachy grabbed her hand.

'It's not fair you taking the blame for Baker. It was

my watch; I'm the one that should be facing disciplinary action. I can't eat, I can't sleep, I feel so guilty. I should go to O'Keeffe and tell her the truth.' Peachy started to cry again. Thrusting her hanky back at him, Wayne hissed.

'That's enough of that talk, P.C. McCarthy. You open your mouth now, and you'll just suck things up for both of us! You'll get done for the suicide and cover up, and so will I!' Her voice softened as Peachy composed himself, morphing back to the pouting, soft-featured fox he was.

'Look, doll, I'm on the way out. Another black mark makes no difference to an old fool like me. Trust me on this.'

'Then, you have to let me make it up to you. I'll do anything, you only need to ask.'

'Anything?' Wayne leered, placing her hand on top of Peachy's, making him blush. 'Why don't you start by showing me what you're taking to the lab?'

Wayne stood in the shadows as Dr Jackson fiddled with the lock on the basement door. It was old and temperamental and had to be turned twice to the left, and then once sharply to the right, to click into place and open. It was his fourth attempt and she heard him whisper 'shit' as he failed again.

'Here, let me,' she said, coming up behind him and smirking as he turned around. She placed her disposable coffee cup on the ground beside him and gave the centre of the door two fierce kicks. The lock gave way, as did a panel of glass, splattering all over her funeral flats and the floor. She brushed it to one side with her feet, picked up her coffee, and held open the broken door so Dr Jackson could enter.

The doctor put his books on the cardboard desk. Wayne

closed the door carefully and unbuttoned her trench coat, before hanging it on the back of the deckchair. She threw her cap on the ground beside her. She then eased herself slowly into the budget seat and drank a large mouthful of her cold coffee.

'That's quite an entrance, Jane.'

The detective grinned then returned her attention to her coffee cup, the white polystyrene emphasising the yellow staining on her fingers.

The doctor retrieved a notepad, pen and clock from his handbag. He scrawled something illegible on the first page then spoke again. 'I hadn't expected you today. Your suspension from active duty means you're not obliged to see me; you know that, don't you?'

Wayne nodded and continued to stir her almost empty cup. 'Do you want me to go? Is that what you're trying to say?'

'No, Jane,' Dr Jackson said. 'I just want to be sure that you understand that you're here voluntarily. It's quite a breakthrough, don't you think so?'

'What? That I'm seeing a shrink without a gun to my head?'

'That's a metaphor I hope, but yes, that you're seeing a shrink without a gun to your head.'

'Don't go getting too excited! I'm not committing to anything. I've decided to come today, but that will be it.'

'And why did you come today?'

'It's pissing down and daytime TV is shit.'

'Are you struggling with your suspension?' Dr Jackson asked.

'On wet days, yeah. But I've been out shooting birds most afternoons with my aunt Stella, keeping busy, you know.'

'Do you want to talk about Martha Baker?'

'What's there to say? She's dead and I killed her. Or my negligence did; case closed.'

'Had you worked with her for long?'

'My entire career. She and I go way back; we went to school together.'

'So, she was a close friend?'

'Some might say that.' Wayne conceded.

'And what would you say, Jane?' Dr Jackson asked.

'I'd say, I didn't know her at all. I thought she was good for them, you know, seven murders and I thought she might have done them. So what sort of friends were we exactly?'

'Did the evidence point that way?'

'She lied about knowing victims. She lied about sucking victims. The last one called her just before he died. We found her at a crime scene. What the suck was I supposed to think?'

'But the evidence later exonerated her?'

Wayne fumbled in her pocket for her cigarettes. As she placed one in her mouth, she saw the doctor shake his head firmly. She took it out and began tapping it against the side of the chair. 'Yeah, turns out she was just your average pervert that used hookers and sucked her friend's children, nothing special at all. Like half the force really.'

'Including you?' Dr Jackson asked. 'Do you use prostitutes?'

'See, I hate the way you educated types do that, twist words. I didn't say prostitute, I said *hooker*, but someone like you doesn't want to use the word hooker. It's too graphic. Prostitute sounds cleaner, easier on the ear. Yeah, I've used hookers; the entire force uses hookers.'

'The entire force? Really?' Dr Jackson repeated.

'Yeah,' Wayne replied. 'Except O'Keeffe, because she's afraid of catching something. And and the males on the force don't use them, obviously.'

'Obviously?' Dr Jackson repeated.

'I can tell by the look on your face that you don't approve, Doctor?'

'This isn't about me, Jane. Do you approve?'

Wayne paused to consider her answer.

'Okay, here's how it is for me, Doc. I'm in the pub, after work, having a few, and I start eyeballing some dick across the bar. If he's lonely enough and desperate enough, he might eyeball me back. We'll have a few scoops and shoot the breeze, and eventually we'll get to talking about the main subject. And we both know that's whether or not we'll suck and the rules of engagement if we do. If it all sounds casual and reasonable, we get a taxi home. He's laughing at my jokes, and saying he's never met anyone as funny as me before, and already alarm bells are ringing. A few rolls in the hay and a couple of greasy cafe breakfasts later, and he's doing my dishes, throwing out my moth-ridden cardigans, and texting me at 4 a.m. to call me out for the unfeeling cunt that I am. That's when it's hard to remember that first alcohol-soaked encounter, with its promise of newness and fun and zero expectation of anything greater than the howl of an orgasm. But I can't, because I know it was always a fantasy, never the real story. See, with a hooker, I ask him his price and he tells me. As long as I leave what they ask for, and leave if I'm asked to, and stop if they tell me to, then they're satisfied, and so am I. So, do I approve of using hookers? Hell, yes, I do, very much so.' Wayne grinned from ear to ear as she finished her speech.

She tried to read something in Dr Jackson's features but

they remained impassive.

'Does that somehow explain why you let Martha Baker down by not appreciating the normality of her actions?' he asked.

'Don't give me that psychobabble bullshit! I let her down by locking her up while she still had her tie.'

'Why did you do that?'

'I never saw Baker as the suicidal type. She was as tough as old boots. She'd survived a lifetime cutting up dead bodies, that's not for the faint-hearted. She'd beaten alcoholism, well for a few years at any rate. I just didn't think she'd go topping herself over a bit of heat. If you're sexually involved with the victims in multiple homicides, you've got to expect some heat, especially if you're not declaring an interest and performing their sucking autopsies!'

'Sounds like she brought a lot of this on herself.'

'That's because you're not listening,' Wayne replied, groping on the ground for her cap.

Ben probably shouldn't have had that second coffee, and he certainly shouldn't have asked for a double shot. He could feel his heart straining to break free from the confines of his body and he watched his hand tremor, as he pushed open the glass doors of the offices of Grisley, Glass and Green.

Inside, the evidence of a marriage of money and taste was everywhere. The open plan reception area was decorated in chic, modern furniture and contemporary art hung on the boldly painted walls. The magazine rack was stuffed with high-end glossies and the espresso machine beside it promised a more refined caffeine fix. Even the secretary looked like he was on sabbatical from his modelling job. He smiled at Ben and Peachy, revealing perfect teeth.

'Good morning, gentlemen. I'm Mark, how can I help you?' he asked.

'You can get me Gertrude Green, right now.' As Ben spoke he laid his I.D. on the gloss white desktop. Mark scrutinised it before replying.

'Ms Green isn't here. She's on a week's annual leave starting today.'

Ben fixed him with a cold, hard stare. 'Isn't that convenient? Well, get me one of the other partners then. Now.' His voice was angry and Mark looked back anxiously as he strutted down the brightly lit corridor, shaking his perfect arse as he went. As they waited, Peachy cleared his throat and offered an opinion.

'If it's alright to say, sir, do you think you're being a bit heavy handed? They are lawyers.'

'What the hell is that supposed to mean?'

'It means that if we go in there, all guns blazing, they'll shut us right down.'

'Will they?' Ben replied 'We'll see about that.'

He barged down the corridor, retracing the steps of Mark. Peachy followed a few steps behind him. They saw him come out of an office and shut the door quietly. Mark spotted them and looked as if he was about to burst into tears.

'Please, Ms Glass is in the middle of a very important meeting with a client. I'll lose my job if she's disturbed again.'

'Seven people have lost their lives. Do you really expect Withering police force to care about your silly little job?'

Ben pushed Mark aside and walked into the out of bounds office. Gail Glass sat behind a mahogany desk, her snowy white hair and wrinkly skin slightly at odds with her commanding presence.

She was scrawling her name on several sets of papers that were being passed between her and her client. Glass glanced up and gave Ben a quizzical look. 'Who the hell are you to interrupt a private meeting between a lawyer and her client?' she demanded.

Ben produced his I.D. from his handbag and flashed it, anxious to hide his shaky grip. The lawyer repeated the question, this time with an even sharper edge.

'Ms Glass, your colleague is a person of interest to us in seven homicides. We need to know her whereabouts immediately.' Ben replied.

Glass's client looked from his lawyer, to Ben, to his handbag. The client picked up his bag, but Glass signalled for him to put it back down. 'My secretary has already explained to you that Ms Green is out of the office for a week. I'm struggling to comprehend why you're still here,' Glass said.

Ben could sense Peachy's eyes begging him to leave, and he appreciated where the young cop was coming from, but there was no going back. Maybe it was the all the coffee. Maybe it was the arrogance dripping from the elderly lawyer's mouth. Maybe it was the mammoth bill for legal services after Anna bailed, but he didn't retreat.

Instead, he reached under his shirt and pulled a pair of handcuffs from his covert harness. Slamming them on the table he announced, 'Gail Glass, I am arresting you on suspicion of obstructing a police investigation. You have the right to...'

Gertrude Green checked her appearance in the mirror of her BMW and smiled. She was one sexy daddysucker. She sprayed her mouth with mint breath freshener and slicked back a few stray hairs, clicked her car locked and strolled to the bar.

Walking through the door, she clocked Fred immediately. He was sitting in a corner table, wearing a red dress as promised. Fred was even hotter in the flesh and Green cast a long, lingering eye over his luscious body. His short curly hair framed his soft, round face. His baby-blue eyes met Green's, as he broke into a smile and waved her over.

They embraced as if they were old friends and Green pulled up the seat beside him.

'What can I get you to drink, Fred?' she asked, noting approvingly that he hadn't started without her.

A wine list was brought over and Green chose a 1996 Cabernet Sauvignon. Fred giggled as she made a show of pouring the wine.

'And if you want to be really pretentious this is what you do.' Green ducked her nose almost fully in the glass and sniffed so hard that wine flowed up her right nostril.

Fred laughed out loud and seemed completely smitten.

Green filled both their glasses half way. She handed him his drink and allowed her little finger to scrape against his during the exchange. His face flushed with colour.

She clinked his glass and smiled. 'After being virtual friends for so long, it's so very lovely to meet you in the flesh.'

Ben stood outside O'Keeffe's office. He was on a major comedown from his caffeine binge and desperate for another fix or a power nap. As he waited to be summoned, he kept his body upright, but allowed his eyes to shut.

'We're not paying you to sleep on the job,' O'Keeffe

shouted in his ear.

He followed O'Keeffe into her office and waited until she bid him to take a seat. Sitting across from his boss, feeling O'Keeffe's eyes bore into him, Ben felt a shiver run down his spine.

'Why don't you start by explaining to me exactly why you arrested one of the most senior lawyers in Withering? A highly-regarded professional from the town's most prestigious law firm and for committing no crime whatsoever?'

Ben opened his mouth to speak before realising O'Keeffe wasn't finished.

'Do you actually want to be at the centre of the biggest lawsuit we'll ever have to face, is that it? Are you looking for attention? Is that your problem? Your wife leaves you and, instead of getting a hair-piece and a subscription to a dating site, you decide to go native and singlehandedly destroy the integrity and credibility of this police force?'

Ben successfully fought the urge to snort as O'Keeffe continued, 'What the suck were you thinking, Campbell?'

'I thought they might be harbouring Green,' Ben lied. He had no idea whatsoever what had motivated him to arrest Glass, except it really had seemed like a good idea at the time.

'And you really think Green is good for all these murders?'

'We can place her at the scene of the last crime, and through her relationship with Hagan, we can link her to every victim.' Ben could feel his anger rising again. Had he actually fancied a mass murderer?

'Well, arrest her then! What's stopping you?'

Ben's head was pounding by the time he was eventually excused from O'Keeffe's wrath. He found two paracetamols in his handbag and swallowed them without water. His stomach grumbled and he realised that he hadn't eaten all day. Ben wondered if he dared to risk a canteen 'meal' and decided he didn't.

He glanced up at the clock on the wall. *Shit, it was almost four!* How long had he been held hostage by the chief?

'McCarthy, we're going to pick up this slimy bitch!' Ben banged his car keys down on Peachy's desk.

Peachy jumped into action and kept pace with Ben as they headed for the car park.

Once out on the road, Ben drove like a maniac and sounded more like Wayne, as he cursed and swore at every set of traffic lights. Peachy kept his head down and his mouth shut, which suited Ben just fine.

By the time they arrived at Green's leafy suburban townhouse, Ben had calmed down slightly. There was no doubt that he was really feeling the strain of carrying the case without Wayne, and though he'd never have admitted it to her, he wished she was there. He got out of the car and locked it, as a middle-aged woman in a baseball cap strolled across the street.

'Afternoon, boys,' she said and Ben's mouth fell open. 'What the hell are you doing here, Wayne?' he snapped.

'Taking my dog for a walk,' Wayne drawled.

'What dog? You don't own a dog!'

'Crafty little beggar's done a runner,' Wayne replied, with a shrug of her shoulders. 'Anyway, forget my dog for now. I guess you're here to talk to Green?'

'How do you know Green lives here?'

'Stupid cunt has been defending Withering's scum for

ten years. And you really think I don't know where she lives?'

'You shouldn't be here, Wayne.'

'Then act like I'm not.'

'Look ma'am, we're arresting a lawyer and if Green so much as smells you, she'll have grounds to appeal the arrest. You don't want that do you?' Peachy blushed as he spoke.

'I certainly don't, sugar, which is why I won't be going in. I'll just continue walking my dog, that is, if I can catch up with her. You have a nice day, gents.' Wayne adjusted her cap and strolled down the street, occasionally shouting 'Fido!' as she went.

They were led through the crowded dining room to a table by the window that had been pre-booked. Green pulled out a seat for Fred and slipped in to hers opposite him. She watched his eyes widen as he took in his surroundings. The waiter brought some menus. Prices started at just under a tenner for a starter and Fred gave her an anxious look. She smiled at him and ordered for them both.

'So, tell me some more about yourself,' Green asked. Not that she had much interest in who Fred was, or what he had to say, or what he thought. But it was always clever to be polite and play the game.

The waiter served their starter of pan-fried scallops and oven-baked black pudding, resting on a bed of rocket.

'It won't kill you,' she promised him, as his fork danced around the dish. Fred giggled, but still he waited for his date to finish hers, before he'd take a bite.

The main course was stuffed quail and Green could tell Fred wasn't enjoying it. 'Sweetheart, don't eat it if you don't fancy it,' she said.

'I can't not eat it, how much does it cost?'

'The same, whether you eat it or not,' Green assured him. They both laughed.

Dessert was more successful. A menu was brought to the table and Green described the dishes, one by one. She picked a chocolate torte for them to share and she chose a dessert wine.

By the time Green asked for the bill, they were both fairly hammered, but in that subtle way alcohol effects a satisfied diner.

Fred excused himself to use the toilet, but felt so dizzy he had to sit down again. They both laughed some more. Green said she would accompany him to the gents.

'You're a perfect lady,' Fred slurred at her.

Ben's nose wrinkled with disgust. Strolling into Big Mamma's, he was hit with the stench of stale sweat and rampant oestrogen.

He spotted Wayne immediately. She was propping up the bar, nursing a large whisky. Beside her, on an empty stool, she'd placed a dog lead. Ben sat on it, like he hadn't noticed it or her. Peachy stood beside him. He flashed his I.D. at the scantily clad kid behind the bar, who answered to the name Angel, and demanded to see Hagan. The young lad flinched and went in search of Dennis, who vetted all who sought access to Hagan.

'She won't be in. It's Tuesday. Papa Hagan has all his children round for his hand-reared roast lamb. Last time Hagan missed it, she lost a finger,' Wayne explained.

'You shouldn't be here,' Ben replied.

'I'm a punter in a dicky bar, I've every right to be here. I think you'll find that you're the one who's out of place.'

Angel had returned with a tired looking Dennis. The death rate of Big Mamma's staff was running at an all-time high, and the strain was showing in his perfect features.

He signalled for Angel to bring him a gin and he sat down beside Ben and Wayne, addressing the latter.

'Nobody upstairs. It's Tuesday, Hagan always eats at her father's on Tuesday nights. Is there anything I can help you with?'

'We're looking for Gertrude Green. And I'm warning you, if you're harbouring her, you're looking at being charged as an accomplice.' Ben gave Dennis his most menacing stare.

Dennis De Vell looked amused. He turned to Wayne and said, 'He knows she's just Hagan's lawyer, eh? She doesn't actually live here.'

Wayne shrugged her shoulders.

'D.I. Wayne is no longer part of the investigating team,' Ben cut in. 'I would be grateful if you would address all your answers to me.'

'She doesn't live here, doll. Green doesn't even work here, you're wasting your time—and mine.' Dennis knocked back his drink, patted Wayne on the leg and excused himself.

'She's not running, Campbell. She has no reason to. It's been a week. She'll assume she lost the cufflink elsewhere.'

'How the hell do you know about the cufflink?'

Peachy's face reddened and Ben threw him a filthy look.

'It doesn't matter how I know. By tomorrow, everyone will know. Put a car outside her house, her office, and here, and go home and see your kids.'

Ben was tempted to tell her to suck off. It was his case, but he was exhausted and starting to smell. Wayne was right. If he put her under 24/7 surveillance, then what was the point in him being here?

'This is my case, Wayne, I'm in charge, I make the decisions. McCarthy, put a car on her apartment, her office, and here, and call me as soon as someone even smells the bitch. I'm going home.'

Gertrude Green drove her BMW into the private underground car park. She turned the engine and music off.

'I was enjoying that,' Fred scowled.

'You'll enjoy this more,' Green leered, leaning in and kissing him full on the mouth. 'Now come on, let's get you into the house and out of this dress.' She slapped him playfully on the thigh, and climbed out of the car, before walking unsteadily round to the passenger side and opening Fred's door.

The five-minute walk to her apartment took twice as long, as Green seized the opportunity for a quick grope in the lift.

Once they were in her apartment, Green kicked off her shoes and grabbed Fred, who was staggering towards her living room. He squealed with delight as she threw him up against the hall wall, her fingers yanking down his zip and unhooking his pra in one seamless motion.

Their foreplay was interrupted by a series of heavy thuds on the front door, culminating in it crashing down as steel toe- capped, Kevlar sporting, armed women surrounded them.

'What the suck?' yelled Green, her wandering hands firmly focused on getting her trousers up.

'Move one sucking hair and I'll blow your cunt off!'

Green went limp. Someone grabbed her shoulder, and then she was pushed to the ground. From the disproportionate weight on her right side, she guessed she was being held by two people. Cold hands frisked her body, but no-one pulled up her pants.

'Jess Christ! Look in here,' one of the team screamed.

There was a stampede of feet towards Green's bedroom.

'For suck's sake!' someone shouted. 'What the suck is wrong with this bitch?'

Green moved her eyes, the only part of her body not constricted by the thugs, and saw a middle-aged woman marching towards her. She signalled her heavies and they released their hold on Green.

The relief didn't last long as her rescuer pulled out tufts of her hair, before dragging her across the wooden floor, scraping her naked knees off the jagged edges of the oak finish.

The grip on her hair was relinquished and her arm was seized instead. Her limb was pushed so far up her back that her elbow touched her collar bone. She yelled and her assailant pushed her arm forward another inch.

'No use yelling now, you sick twisted bitch! Did he yell? Did he?' She pulled Green's face upwards so that she was staring at the mirrored ceiling in her bedroom, which captured the entire room.

Reflected, was the corpse of one of Hagan's whores, his name eluded her, but staring at his desecrated body and his lifeless eyes, Green knew she'd remember his face for the rest of her life.

FOURTEEN

WEDNESDAY

Gertrude Green hadn't slept a wink. She hadn't even closed her eyes. Her swollen arm ached and it was agony to try and move it. But her mind hardly registered the pain, as she moved from legal precedent to past cases, searching for ammunition that might be used in the lengthy proceedings that her unlawful arrest and aggravated assault would spawn. She needed to speak to Grisley.

'I have a right to a phone call,' she shouted at the sniggering voices that filtered down the empty, hollow space between her and her captors.

She'd been demanding her phone call all night. Mostly, she'd been ignored, once a voice had shouted back, 'You think anyone gives a suck about the Wringer's rights?'

'I'm not the sucking Wringer, you incompetent fools!' she wanted to yell back, but she didn't. She chose instead to conserve her energy to plan her next move.

Green had no idea how much time had passed before one of the custody team showed up carrying a cordless telephone extension and a cold cup of coffee. She had very exacting standards and drinking the piss that passed for caffeine violated all of them. There was no point in complaining, she had to remain in a state of hyper alertness and needed all the help she could get.

She spat the coffee out when she realised it actually was piss. Jess Christ, she was dealing with animals!

'I'd like privacy to make my call,' she told the laughing sergeant.

'You enjoy that privacy, you won't be seeing much of that where you're going,' the sergeant laughed some more, as she stepped out of the cell.

Green counted to sixty in her head, allowing her breaths to become deeper, and her heart rate to slow down. Her fingers struggled to press down on the keys, twice their normal size, they were operating at half their efficiency, but methodically she pushed each digit to reach her office and allowed herself a faint smile, as a familiar voice answered.

'How are you doing, Mark?' she kept a lightness to her tone.

When he didn't answer immediately, she suspected he already knew the facts. Of course, this would be highly unorthodox, but entirely in keeping with how Withering Police Station operated: inform the employers and spread gossip and rumour. That cheap trick might scare the girls in the dockyard, but they'd have to try a lot harder to intimidate members of the legal profession.

'Mark, I'm having a spot of bother, as I'm sure you've heard. Could you get me Georgina, please? And make sure you stress that it's urgent,' she instructed the receptionist

There was a significant pause before he answered. 'Ms Glass is in a meeting all day, she's not to be disturbed.' She could hear the tinge of embarrassment in his voice.

'Meeting, my arse!' Green snapped. 'Look, just put Gail on then,' she said, abandoning the mild-mannered approach.

'I can't do that, Gertrude… I mean, Ms Green. I'm sorry. Ms Glass asked me to inform you that you no longer work here. Well, not whilst you're suspected of being the… '

Mark's voice trailed off.

Green was sure she could hear him sob. *Great, just what she needed, a hysterical secretary!* She took a few deep breaths before continuing, 'Don't go upsetting yourself, Mark. It's all a huge misunderstanding, just tell Gail or Georgina, that I need representation right now.'

As she waited for a reply, it occurred to her that her secretary had been instructed to hang up. She shouted, 'Mark? Hello? Mark, are you there?' into the receiver, before pressing redial, but the phone line was dead.

'One phone call, Ms Green, you, of all people should know that.' O'Keefe was standing outside her cell door, as Peachy unlocked it, and held it open. 'I'll oversee the interview today. I assume you've got in touch with your lawyer?' The malevolent glint in O'Keeffe's eye told Green she already knew the answer.

'I'm going to need more time to find the right woman. This is a big case—suing you and this station for everything you're worth.' Green projected the confidence her day job demanded.

'Really?' O'Keeffe guffawed. 'But you're too busy to deal with that today. Because today, we're going to charge you with the murders of seven people, six of whom were minors. Now, that's a big case!' O'Keeffe grinned.

Ben couldn't believe Green had killed Jeff Stone. Of all the hookers, in all the world, why that one? He'd only met him once, but he remembered him vividly, his posturing and pouting, intended to mask his immaturity, but actually flaunting it.

The airless interrogation room was making him light-headed. He slammed the images of the murder scene down on the table as O'Keeffe entered, followed by a rough-looking Green, who Peachy pushed into the seat opposite him. Her right arm had ballooned and screamed a need for urgent medical attention. Bloody typical of the oestrogen-pumped armed response unit. Outnumbering their prey at least ten to one, and dripping in weapons, they still couldn't resist breaking a few bones. It was their calling card. But what the suck was wrong with him? Was he feeling sorry for the child killer?

'Now, are we waiting for your lawyers? Or will we start without them?' O'Keeffe smiled as she sat down.

Ben switched on the tape recorder and gave details of the time, date and names of all present.

Green seemed to be trying to make eye contact with him, but Ben ignored her.

'There has been a serious misunderstanding...' Green's signature arrogance was giving way to something much more concessionary, and once again, Ben fought his feelings of sympathy.

'That's what they all say,' O'Keeffe answered her. 'Isn't that right, Campbell?'

'It is,' Ben nodded. He began to lay out a series of the crime scene photos in front of Green, scrutinising her features as she inspected each one. He could see flashes of shock and fear, but for the most part she remained composed. Was it all part of her training as a lawyer? It was as if she was flicking through a furniture catalogue, not the uncut footage of what could have come from an 18-rated horror movie.

'These are very shocking images, but they're nothing to do with me,' the lawyer said, pushing the last one, a close-up of Jeff's torn anus, back towards Ben.

O'Keeffe shoved it forward, until it was in front of Green again.

'Except for the fact that it was taken in your bedroom.' O'Keeffe smiled as she spoke.

'A fact I can't yet explain. But given that I did not put him there, or harm him, or even know him, except in passing, then we can ascertain that there is an explanation for this occurrence. I'm sure you'll find further investigation of the crime scene and all other relevant data will no doubt make sense of this mess.'

'Is that it?' Ben surprised himself by snapping at her. 'I didn't do it. It's nothing to do with me. Why don't you figure it out? My five-year-old could come up with better than that.'

'Yeah,' O'Keeffe echoed. 'His five-year-old could come up with better than that.'

If Green was dejected by O'Keeffe's taunts, she didn't show it.

'And what exactly do you mean that you know him in passing?' O'Keeffe asked. 'As in passing trade? Is that some fancy lawyer's way of saying you paid him to suck you?"

'No, it's exactly as it sounds. I had seen him around.'

'Around where? Your house? Where we found his dead body? Is that where you knew him from?'

'I didn't know him, I knew of him, from Big Mamma's. He was one of Hagan's whores.' Green's voice was definitely getting louder. She used her working hand to brush sweat-stained hair from her face.

'How did you know he was a whore?' O'Keeffe asked. 'Did you use his services?"

Ben studied Green's reaction closely. Water glinted on her forehead, but her eyes gave nothing away.

'Did I say "whore"? Forgive me, it's the stress of being awake all night, combined with the pain from my untreated injuries, and the trauma of how they were sustained. Let me be clear, I recognised him as being an employee of one of my clients, Harriet Hagan. He was a dancer, I believe, possibly a waiter,' Green replied, her volume now in check.

'He was a whore,' O'Keeffe screamed so forcefully it hurt Ben's ears. 'But now he's a dead whore because you killed him. Why don't you just own up? There's no way you're getting out of this!' She brought her fist down on the table.

'I appreciate how much easier your job would be, Ma'am, if every suspect simply confessed at the first hint of police brutality. But as we're both well aware, many don't, for a number of reasons, not the least of them being that they are innocent of whatever crime they stand accused of. I am one such woman, and there is nothing you can do or say that will make me confess.'

'Nothing?' O'Keeffe said the word slowly and softly. She stood up and walked round behind Green. Ben watched, aghast, as she grabbed Green's hair and used it as a lever to smash her head into the table. He couldn't decide which sound was more disturbing, Green's wail, or the thud or her skull hitting the metal table.

'I need a piss,' he heard himself say, pushing his chair back and fleeing the room.

Ben kept throwing cold water onto his face, in the hope that it might change his perspective. It wasn't working. He hadn't needed to piss; he'd needed to puke. He literally didn't have the stomach for any more of O'Keeffe's thuggery, but then, how do you go about extracting the truth from a serial killer?

Green wasn't going to crack easily, if at all. They'd already broken her arm, and the force of O'Keeffe's latest assault would probably leave her bruised, if not more seriously injured. Ben's thoughts turned to the victims and their brutal desecration. Why the suck was he wasting time feeling sorry for a dangerous bitch?

He could hear Wayne's voice in his head, *"You know what your problem is, Campbell? You're too hung up on the rights of the accused. Leave that sort of stuff to scumbag lawyers and bored, middle -class, house-husbands."*

He splashed his face one last time, and wiping the water away with wads of toilet roll, he took a deep breath in, pulled his shoulders up and strolled back to the interrogation room.

It was empty! What the suck? He ran back into the main office in search of Peachy. The gossipy-but-sombre vibe that had pervaded all morning had shifted to what could best be described as a party atmosphere. A radio was blasting out dance tunes and voices competed to be heard, like closing time at the pub.

He spied Peachy at the desk closest to Wayne's office. He was pulling his hair out from a tight bun, and swaying his mane forward and back, as if he was in a shampoo advert.

'What the hell's going on? I've just come from the interrogation room. Where's Green?'

'We've charged her, sir!' Peachy shrieked. He'd tipped his make-up bag out on the desk and was rummaging through at least half a dozen lipsticks.

Ben slammed his hand on the shade Peachy had finally chosen.

'Leave that for a minute. What do you mean, charged her, when, how?

'O'Keeffe did it, about five minutes ago.'

'O'Keeffe, about five minutes ago? But I only went to the toilet. How could she do that? Did Green confess?'

'Nope. But who needs a confession when you've got a dead body in her bedroom? Do you think a jury needs to hear more than that?'

Ben shook his head.

'What did she charge her with? Jeff's abduction and murder?'

'All the murders.' Peachy seemed positively thrilled to be the bearer of such huge news.

'All the murders? But, other than the cufflink and the dead body, we've got nothing.'

'But we've got a dead body in her bedroom, do you think a jury needs more than that?'

'I'm guessing you got that line straight from O'Keeffe?'

Peachy blushed, then bent over the desk, found his lipstick and applied it freestyle. 'I'm doing the off-licence run. The chief's buying. What are you having?' he asked, applying a second coat.

'I'm good,' Ben replied, skulking away to Wayne's office and curling up on the chair.

He couldn't quite understand what had just happened. All those weeks and weeks of adrenalin, all the sleepless nights and the endless days, and the hours and hours of pointless interviews, and all the testing of this and the checking of that, and for what? He takes a toilet break and returns to find the crime of the century is effectively solved. It was as if the last gift under the tree had given up its secrets, and there was nothing left of the day, except the kids' meltdowns, the toys' breakdowns and the Queen's speech.

What the suck was wrong with him? It's a result. We've got the bitch! She can't hurt anyone else now. It's over!

He leapt off his seat, and threw open Wayne's office door. Peachy was still at his desk, dusting his cheek bones with a layer of blusher.

'I'll have a can of lager,' he beamed at the junior officer.

There were grey clouds gathering as Ben parked beside the railway. He pulled his coat up around his neck as he got out of the car. He approached the newsagent's adjacent to the station and ordered two packs of Wayne's cigarettes.

The local rag immediately caught his eye. Green's mugshot took up most of the front page next to the headline: LUSCIOUS LAWYER IS SERIAL STRANGLER.

He glanced at his watch. It was five minutes past midday. O'Keeffe must have contacted the papers before she'd even charged her. He took a copy, placed some loose change on the counter, and stuffed it into his handbag.

He walked past the main house and down the back to the basement flat. The door was slightly ajar, so he pressed the doorbell and waited. He rang twice more and when he got no reply, Ben pushed the door open and hesitantly entered.

'Wayne,' he called, walking into the empty living room. 'Are you at home, Wayne?'

'Do you usually just walk into people's homes uninvited?'

The voice came from behind him and he turned around to find Wayne standing in the doorway. She had a shotgun in one hand and two dead birds in the other. There were flecks of dry blood on her coat where the fresh prey had rested.

'Shit! I'm sorry, Wayne, I...'

Wayne laughed. 'Don't go getting your knickers, or whatever politically correct thing you wear down there, in a twist. There's nothing worth nicking here, that's why I leave my door open. I really couldn't give a shit who comes in.'

Wayne put the birds down on her kitchen counter and grabbed a load of washing that was heaped on one of her armchairs. She flung it on the floor and beckoned Ben to have a seat. He did so and handed Wayne the cigarettes he'd just purchased.

'That's kind of you, Campbell,' she said. 'Right, I've no coffee or the like, so it's vodka neat, vodka with water, or I can make you a hot vodka, I suppose.'

'Not for me, thanks. I've already had a can of lager today, anymore and I won't be able to drive.'

Wayne glanced at the clock on her wall. 'I take it from the lager drinking that you've charged her?'

'About an hour ago,' Ben replied.

'Well, congratulations, Campbell. You caught the Withering Wringer! You can probably make a living now, on documentary fees alone.'

Ben smiled. He'd never even considered that. He was just looking forward to spending some time with the kids, without always having one eye on the phone.

'Baker's autopsy was today. You know the results, I suppose?' Ben asked.

'I didn't feel the need for a rerun. I was there for the live event.'

'But didn't you have to give evidence?'

'Nope. O'Keeffe was very insistent that I stay away. She got me a sick note.'

'She didn't kill herself,' Ben blurted out.

'Sorry, you've lost me, Campbell. I was there, remember?

I cut her down.'

'Well, what I mean is, hanging herself didn't kill her. She had a massive heart attack seconds before and would have died before she started to swing.' Ben recoiled at his crass terminology.

Wayne burst out laughing. She was laughing so hard that she had to hold her sides and tears fell from her eyes.

'Good old Baker,' she declared. 'She'd have loved that!'

Ben didn't know what to say. Her reaction wasn't normal, but then Wayne wasn't normal, so maybe it was. Should he commiserate with her? Should he laugh as well?

As if reading his mind, Wayne said, 'You know what your problem is, Campbell? You worry too much about what other people think. Like right now, you just want to laugh, but you're afraid it's inappropriate. A good detective learns to laugh at every inappropriate opportunity she gets. How else are you supposed to get through the horror and the bloodshed, the beaten families and the broken people? Now, let me ask you this, are you happy that this is the Wringer?'

'What's that supposed to mean?'

'This business of the body in her bedroom? Young Jeff, that doesn't strike you as odd?'

'The whole thing strikes me as odd. She was a sucking maniac, who strangled young guys then mutilated their corpses. The fact that she did this in her bedroom is actually the least unusual thing about her, wouldn't you say?'

'She never did before, though, did she? Not one of the previous victims had been moved. They were all killed exactly where they were found. Was Jeff?'

Ben flushed. He didn't know. The post mortem results weren't even in.

'Pay no heed,' muttered Wayne. 'What does an old girl like me know?'

'Too bloody much,' retorted Ben. 'This isn't even your case anymore; you're not even a cop right now. I shouldn't even be here.'

'True,' agreed Wayne.

'You just can't bear the thought that I solved this without you. Isn't that it?'

'Interesting. Was it you who charged her?' Wayne asked.

Ben hesitated. 'Not exactly, it was O'Keeffe who led the interview.'

'Well, that solves it then. It's not as if O'Keeffe will have conducted anything but a thorough investigation. We can sleep easy with that knowledge.' Wayne's eyes twinkled as she spoke.

'Exactly,' Ben nodded. 'I've got to go, I shouldn't have come.'

He shut the door behind him and walked slowly back to his car. Rain was just starting to fall as he opened the door. He threw his handbag onto the seat and walked towards the car park wall. He lifted his foot and smashed it into the concrete. The kick was so fierce, chips fell onto the tarmac and his second kick scattered some more. An old man, dwarfed by a giant umbrella, yelled at him.

'Hey, you, leave that wall alone, or I'm calling the police!'

Sweat poured down Wayne's face as she sat in Rita Ryan's sweltering flat. She had stripped down to her shirt and she reckoned she could still lose another layer. She wiped her brow with her already damp shirt.

'It's very good of you to come and fill me in, Inspector. Very good indeed,' Ryan said, lifting the teapot and pouring the first cup. She shook so much that tea spilled on to the biscuits and the plate they sat on. She looked embarrassed as Wayne removed the pot from her and finished the job. 'My hands aren't what they used to be. I was a mechanic before I went into the rental business. In days gone by, I could resurrect any engine in a couple of hours. Now look at them.' The old girl stared at her gnarled fingers.

Wayne handed her a cup, let her take a sip and then put it back on the table. 'Anyhow, more importantly, you've got her then, the Wringer. This nightmare is over?'

'That's what they tell me. It's not actually my case anymore.'

'But you are able to tell me who it was? Would I know her?'

'Have you heard of Gertrude Green?'

Ryan scrunched her eyes up and thought, then nodded her head. 'Wait a minute, is she a lawyer?'

'She is indeed.'

'Grisley, Glass and Green. They handled his estate when Melvin's uncle died a few years back, I think. I'd have to check my papers to be sure.'

'I don't think it really matters much at this point,' Wayne replied.

'Is that how she got into our computers?'

'Hard to say. Don't forget, they have girls that can break into the systems of banks and government offices. It's not difficult to hack into an amateur's files.'

'And has she confessed?'

'No, but she's a lawyer. I wouldn't expect her to, would you?'

'Very true,' Ryan agreed.

There was a knock on the door and a middle-aged

man in a dark brown dress, swamped by a beige cardigan, shuffled into the room.

Wayne had seen him before, at McEwan's house. It was the deranged bachelor brother. She registered a flash of recognition in his eyes as he walked hurriedly over to Ryan and handed him the keys.

'I'll see you Monday, Rita,' he said, keeping his voice low, before scuttling out of the room.

'What's he doing here?'

'Who, Paul? He's our accountant. He comes to do the accounts because it's not easy for me to get out these days.'

'But you didn't mention him on any staff list?'

Ryan shrugged. 'He's not on the books. He just gives Ronnie's figures a quick once over to put my mind at ease. He doesn't even charge for it. We go to the same church.'

'Which church is that?'

'St Joan's,' Ryan replied.

'The one next to the youth hostel for vulnerable boys?'

Ryan nodded. Wayne leapt out of her seat and scrambled for the door.

'Inspector,' Ryan called after her. 'Where are you going? You haven't finished your tea.'

Ben had taken a detour via a local school supplies shop and picked up the various garments and sports equipment his kids needed. He'd figured nobody would notice his absence, but now, returning to the main office, which currently served as a temporary bar, he wished he had stayed away longer.

The party was in full swing. Peachy and Johnston were dirty dancing on top of one of the desks and a couple of the girls were playing drinking games with a bottle of Southern Comfort.

O'Keeffe spotted him straight away and made a beeline for him. 'We got the bitch!' she bellowed, even though she was right beside him. 'What are you drinking, Campbell?'

'None for me, Ma'am, I'm driving.'

'I said, what are you drinking, Campbell?'

He regretted his first mouthful of whisky instantly, but the second made up for it. He unbuttoned his shirt at the top. Someone had put on Abba, and as Peachy beckoned him to jump up on a desk, he knocked back another whisky and climbed up.

Much later, he held back Peachy's hair in the gent's toilets. Peachy kept mumbling thanks between moans about the last shot he'd had, as if the twelve that preceded it hadn't been a problem at all.

He eventually stopped puking and slowly staggered to his feet, using Ben as a lever. He looked around for his handbag. Ben handed it to him. Relief washed over his washed-out face. He emptied the bag on to the side of the sink. Out fell his purse, his keys, his phone, a picture of his cats, a picture of himself wearing very little clothing, and more make-up than Ben had ever imagined could be contained in one handbag.

'You have to help me, Sir. You have to put my face back on.' There was desperation in Peachy's voice.

Ben wanted to tell him to get real, to get a taxi and to get his head down, but he wasn't so completely removed from the life he'd once lived.

Instead, he set about deftly recreating Peachy's usual look. When he had finished, Peachy began to drunkenly rub his fingers along Ben's jaw line. 'You've got great bone structure, you know,' he slurred. 'You should borrow some of this slap.'

The rain pounded down on the back of the building, making it almost impossible for Wayne to smoke. But nonetheless she tried, bringing the dripping joint to her mouth and cursing as the damp paper refused to light.

After three attempts, she tossed the spliff on the ground and stepped furtively into the police station, through the fire exit door one of the girls had unlocked for her. She shook herself and a puddle of water hit the cheap lino beneath her.

She kept her head down as she weaved her way down the corridor, past her drunk, unobservant colleagues, towards O'Keeffe's office, which she correctly guessed would be both empty and locked. She punched in the four-digit code she'd memorised several years earlier, scanned the hallway, and crept in closing the door behind her.

It wasn't difficult to hack into O'Keeffe's computer using a password that Florence from the fraud squad had provided and she typed McEwan's name into the system.

Wayne scrolled down the three Lottie McEwans that had been arrested in the past twenty years, since computer records began, registering that none of them were the McEwan she was looking for. She tried Charlotte McEwan and got two more hits, but again neither were the Cambridge cock. She tried Paul McEwan and though seven people had been arrested with that name, all for shoplifting, not one of them matched his age and description.

She was about to log out, when she decided instead to search for McEwan online. Here, she found her, at least. She had her own website on comparative religious study and she was also referenced in several other sites on the subject. Wayne downloaded the photo that accompanied her biography and printed it out. Then she turned off the printer and computer, placed O'Keeffe's seat exactly where she'd found it and slipped out of the office.

She could hear the drunken karaoke of her colleagues from the other side of the building and she smiled as she made her way downstairs to the holding cells.

Baker's death had prompted an increase in security and two police constables womanned the main desk. They were sharing a beer that someone had snuck down for them, but quickly pushed it under the table as the senior officer approached. 'Good to see you back, Ma'am,' one of them volunteered.

'I'm not back,' Wayne replied. 'You didn't see me, you definitely didn't give me access to the cells and I didn't notice you drinking on duty.'

She waited as the two officers weighed up their options. One of them quickly handed her a set of keys and she rewarded them both with a wide tobacco stained smile.

She unlocked the first gate and walked quietly towards the bottom cell, where the most famous prisoner Withering had ever housed, sat silently staring at the wall.

Stripped of her fine clothes and status, Green looked like any one of a hundred clients she'd represented, and Wayne allowed herself a grin. The pair locked eyes and she registered the fear in the lawyer's face.

'What the suck are you doing here?' Green asked, backing herself further into the corner of her tiny bed, as Wayne unlocked the cell door.

'Now, is that anyway to talk to the only copper in Withering who knows that you're innocent?' Wayne asked.

She locked the cell door behind her and took a seat on the opposite side of the piss-stained mattress.

'Are you trying to be funny?' Green countered. Her eyes

darted from Wayne to the cell door and back to Wayne.

'Seven murders,' Wayne continued. 'And nothing, not a single lead. But then, suddenly, we have a cufflink and a body and a whole trail of evidence that leads us right to you, like breadcrumbs my pigeon-headed colleagues swallowed whole.'

'What are you trying to say, Wayne?' The previous angry tone had been replaced by a more conciliatory pitch and Green leaned forward.

'Look, you're a lawyer who represents low-life scum, and I would happily see you raped daily in an overcrowded jail wing. But you're not a killer, and even if you are, you're not the Wringer. I'd stake my aunt's pension on it.'

'Thank you, Wayne, that's probably the nicest thing you've ever said to me.' Tears gathered at the edge of Green's eyes and she blinked furiously.

Wayne pretended not to notice, as she emptied out her pockets, searching for the photo she'd downloaded from the net. She handed the lawyer a crumbled page that unfolded into an image of McEwan.

'You ever seen her before?'

Green nodded. 'That's Lady Lottie McDougall. I was part of her mother's defence team, it must be a decade ago now. I'd just started out and her mother was charged with corporate fraud. Huge figures were involved, we're talking millions. You must remember it?'

Wayne shrugged her shoulders. 'It's not my type of crime, rich bitch steals from another rich bitch. I mean, who cares?'

'The rich bitch that's been had,' Green replied. 'We thought we'd nailed it, but there was an eleventh-hour surprise witness, some computer geek who alleged she'd been paid by McDougall to hack accounts. The team let me question her because I was the only one with a computer background, but my A Level in I.T. was no match for her considerable expertise and she came off looking very credible. McDougall was sent down for eighteen months, but she never served a day.' Green cast her eyes downwards before continuing, 'She topped herself within hours of the verdict. I was really shaken up. It was my first big case and to lose with such devastating consequences was a huge blow, but Lady McDougall couldn't have been more understanding. She said the prosecution was airtight and I shouldn't blame myself.'

'Well, guess what?' Wayne drawled, a smirk spreading across her face. 'She was lying!'

Ben found Peachy's keys at the bottom of his well-stocked handbag and opened his front door. The task proved difficult, as Peachy kept grabbing his arms, attempting to cajole him into a duet of *I Will Survive*.

Once inside, he located the bedroom in Peachy's pokey flat and dragged his reluctant colleague in its general direction.

'Just one more drink, boss, we got the bitch!' Peachy begged, pulling free from Ben's grip. He staggered across the living room to what an estate agent would probably have called the kitchenette. It was little more than a few cupboards with a sink, and a mini microwave balanced precariously on an even smaller fridge.

Peachy could do better than this on a PC's salary, Ben reasoned, sizing up the impoverished living space. He glanced at the armchair in the living room. It was overflowing with new clothes, many of them with their labels still intact. *Perhaps not!*

Peachy opened one of the cupboards and pulled out a bottle of Pear Schnapps. Ben groaned as he filled two mugs with the foul looking liquid. He handed one to Ben and sipped the other, as he tried to hook his phone up to his speakers. He managed it, but then knocked over a small wooden table he was trying to balance the speaker on.

'Shit,' he slurred, trying to pick it up, before abandoning the tidy up, in favour of collapsing on his sofa. Peachy shut his eyes, and within seconds he was out cold.

Ben hauled the duvet off his bed and placed it gently over him. He emptied the schnapps into the sink and filled the mug with cold water, which he placed on the grotty carpet beside him. With one final check on Peachy, he switched off the table lamp and tip-toed out.

Ben reversed out of Peachy's street carefully. He really shouldn't be driving, but that was the only advantage of working in a rural backwater like Withering. The truth was that no cop would ever pull another, add to that the fact that the entire force was pissed and doing the can-can when he left, he felt fairly safe. Two hours of dealing with Peachy had sobered him right up.

His phone rang. He reached into his handbag for his mobile, but couldn't find it before the ringing stopped. Pulling over, he threw the contents of his handbag onto the driver's seat. Drea had called him. His heart thumped as he saw it was the sixteenth missed call from his daughter. Sucking hell! He dialled her number. The line went dead. Shit! He'd run out of charge and the screen went black. Ben turned on the engine, placed his foot on the accelerator and screeched down the street.

Rain pelted the windscreen, as Ben pulled up outside his house. There was an ambulance and two police cars in his drive. Through the rain, it looked as if it was Wayne who was walking towards one of the cars, carrying something. He lunged out of his car as he realised it was Val.

'What's going on?' he screamed, as Wayne placed his youngest child in a police car. He looked inside and saw Val nestled into Drea, an officer either side of them. He smiled weakly at his kids, then turned to Wayne. 'What's happened? Where's Simon? Where's George? Where are you taking the kids? Why are all these people at my house? What the hells happened?' Ben grabbed Wayne by the sleeve of her trench coat.

Wayne tapped the roof of the car and it drove off. Ben let Wayne's hand on his back gently guide him slowly towards the house. Once inside, he lost count of the number of officers milling around his home. The same people he'd left dancing on desks an hour ago, were now pulling out his drawers and rifling through his laundry. Wayne led him past his strangely sober colleagues to the bathroom, and locked the door behind them.

'Simon's been taken, so has George,' she whispered, her words hitting Ben like blows from a cricket bat.

'Taken? Taken by whom?' Ben was struggling to breathe.

'The Wringer. The real Wringer, Lottie McEwan—or McDougall— as she's actually known,' Wayne continued to whisper.

'McEwan has my boy! But Green's the Wringer, I don't understand. What's been done? Have they sent an armed response unit?'

Wayne opened the door slightly and stuck her head out before she closed it again and pulled Ben close.

'They're doing nothing,' her whisper felt warm against his ear. 'Because I haven't told them about McEwan. They only know that they've both been abducted. Drea witnessed the whole thing. But she's never met McEwan, and was too shocked to get a plate number. Simon was trying to sneak out to meet the Cambridge cock in her car, but George clocked him and tried to stop him. He even jumped on the car, but was run over by the cock, and then shoved in the car. Listen, Campbell, she's got George, *my* George, and your boy. Do you really trust their safe return to the trigger-happy freaks from A.R.U., who are currently half pissed?'

Ben's insides could take no more. He hurled up half a dozen whiskies over Wayne's shoulders.

'For suck's sake!' Wayne muttered. 'I just got this back from the laundry.'

'I don't give a shit about your coat, Wayne,' Ben hissed. 'I just want my son back. If we're not calling the A.R.U., then who?'

'Me, that's who. Look, I've already been to her place, so I have a rough idea of the layout. If she sees a whole team, then she'll kill everyone 'coz she's nothing to lose. The best chance we have is for me to ambush her. You stay here, and if I'm not back by morning, you can tell O'Keeffe everything.'

'Like hell I will. If you're going, I'm going too,' Ben's voice had increased in volume, and Wayne clasped her hand over his mouth.

'Get a grip, Campbell. This is one serious psycho. She's already killed your kids' mother. How am I supposed to live with myself if I let her kill you as well?'

'Then you better make sure she doesn't!' Ben whispered as Wayne loosened her grip on his mouth.

FIFTEEN

THURSDAY

There were so many people coming and going from every room in the house, that it was easy for them to slip out the front door unnoticed, and run towards the car. Ben took the wheel, as Wayne climbed into the passenger seat, and they sped through the rain drenched streets.

'You shouldn't blame yourself,' Wayne told Ben. 'It's a classic rookie mistake. Seen it all before, hire the murderer as a freelance expert, give her access to all the crime scene data, and regular updates on the pace of the investigation. To be fair, this could happen to anyone...'

Ben wasn't listening, his body was there but his mind was elsewhere. It was summer and they were in their flat share in Spain. Val wasn't born yet, so it was only the four of them. Simon had finally learned to ride his bike, and he was wobbling down the seafront. His son was trying to catch up with some kids he'd met, whilst he and Anna strolled behind them. Though Drea was old enough to walk, she wasn't up for it, and Ben's skin dripped with sweat, carrying her on his shoulders through the midday heat.

A skateboarder flew past and crashed straight into Simon, knocking him off his bike. The teenager ran over Simon's hand and then skated off, without a backward glance. It happened so fast, he could vaguely recall the details. But the interminable amount of time between Simon hitting the ground and letting out a piercing scream, was burned forever into his brain. Ben screamed, threw Drea at Anna and ran towards his injured son.

When the cry finally came, it was nothing like any sound Simon had made before. He kept it up, a singular pitch of pain, the whole way to the hospital, where the x-ray showed Simon had broken three fingers. Sitting in the recovery room, stroking Ben's face with his good hand, he told him, 'My fault, Dad, I wasn't looking.'

'Now you listen here,' Ben replied, pulling him close. 'It was *my* fault. I'm so sorry, I promise that I'll never let anything bad happen to you again.'

'What the suck, Campbell, look out!' Wayne screeched.

The car coming towards them had its headlights on full beam. Ben swerved to avoid it, and crashed into a pole.

'Sucking man drivers,' the driver yelled back, before honking her horn and giving them a two-fingered salute.

'Sucking hell! Wayne, are you alright?' Ben asked, his adrenalin pumped body distracting him from his own bleeding forehead.

'I'm fine. You're not though,' Wayne replied, pulling down the driver seat's mirror, and turning on the light.

Ben looked at the trickle of blood running down his face. His eyes welled up, and as his tears started to fall, his mouth released a wolf-like howl. He cradled his head in his hands to muffle the sound.

'Snap out of it, Campbell. Nervous breakdowns have to be on your own time, it's on page one of the copper's manual.'

Wayne's pep talk fell on deaf ears, as Ben's relentless howling continued unabated. She tried a different approach.

'Campbell, your son's been kidnapped by a psychopath, who you hired, it's very stressful but ...'

Ben's wails stopped abruptly, he turned to her and whispered, 'Oh Jess! You're right, I hired her, against your advice. I did this, it's all my fault. And I promised him I'd always protect him.' More tears followed the revelation and Wayne sighed.

'Get out. I'll drive,' she instructed him.

'But you can't drive,' Ben replied.

'Who told you that? I don't drive, which is not the same thing.'

A more together, almost stoic Ben climbed into the passenger seat. Placing her hands on the wheel of a car for the first time in almost thirty years, Wayne wondered if she hadn't been a bit hasty.

The steering wheel was a bit too far away, and as she adjusted the seat, she reluctantly conceded that Campbell was probably taller than her. She placed her hands on the gear stick and satisfied it was in neutral, she turned the key.

The engine fired into life, emitting a barely audible hum, in marked contrast to how engines used to sound. She had a quick glance in the mirrors, checked her blind spot, put it in to first and pulled away. Jess Christ! It's like riding a bike…

'I can't believe you can drive,' Ben said. 'That's bloody typical of you.'

The rest of the journey was spent in silence, punctuated by the odd whimper from Campbell. Wayne cursed herself for having agreed to let him come. She kept her eyes on the road, and both hands on the wheel, as she chugged along in the hazardous weather. Keeping the speedometer below fifty was the only way they were going anywhere tonight.

The absence of conversation allowed her to focus on McEwan. *How the hell had she missed her?* She tried to recall the handful of times they had crossed paths. Wayne had been so keen to expose her contempt for the wasted time and resources, that she'd never looked closely at McEwan, which was exactly what the Wringer had counted on.

Wayne had always hated educated types, especially cunts from Cambridge and Oxford. McEwan couldn't have known that, but she'd have guessed quickly. McEwan had played her. *Would Baker still be alive if she'd seen through the charade earlier? Would Jeff?*

Torrential rain poured down faster than the wipers could wash it away, and Wayne struggled to see more than a few feet in front of her.

'Campbell, get out the map, I don't have a sucking clue where we are.'

'We passed a garage about a mile ago, remember the sign?' Ben replied. 'That means we keep going till we reach a fork in the road, about two miles on, at a guess. Then we turn right, and the gates of the estate are about 500 metres away.'

'How the suck can you remember that? We've only been here once?' Wayne asked.

'I pay attention.'

Reaching the junction, Wayne turned right, and they drove down hill, stopping a few feet from the gates. 'We're on foot from here,' she informed Campbell.

'Yeah, I know, I'm the one giving you directions.'

He buttoned his jacket up right up to the neck and turned the collar up, then he took a deep breath.

'It's not too late to change your mind, Campbell, you can wait here.'

'Like hell I will.' Ben pushed his door open and jumped out, straight onto fresh deer shit. He shone a torch either side of the entrance, trying to figure out the best route over the thick bramble bushes that flanked it either side. There wasn't one.

He took one side, and Wayne picked her way through the other, and they both wound up bleeding and scratched. He ripped a thorn out of his hand and ran the torch over the vast fields that lay between them and the house. The dim light and the heavy rain meant that they could barely see in front of them.

On and on they trekked, up the narrow country lane. Wayne punctuated the silence with swear words, which Ben took to mean she'd stepped in deer shit too.

'Oh, grow up, will you? A bit of deer shit is the least of our problems,' he snapped.

'You would say that, you're wearing brogues. Do you know how much these boots set me back?'

Ben was about to reply that he couldn't care less, when Wayne signalled for him to turn out the light. He did as he was told, and became vaguely aware of some voices in the distance.

He turned the light back on, and off again quickly, as he saw the walled perimeters of the house a hundred yards ahead. They hunkered down outside the walls, and listened. The voices had stopped.

Ben switched the light back on and followed the wall eight feet up, to its top, which was covered in barbed wire. He couldn't see either of them scaling that, but Wayne had already hooked the cap of her boot between two bricks and her other boot quickly followed.

Buoyed by her confidence, Ben tried to shove his brogue into a crack in the wall. It was too large and round to grip anything. Wayne swore, cutting herself on the wire at the top, and Ben tossed his shoes off, finding his toes could easily make the ascent. He kept chipping his feet against bits of stone, and losing his grip as water beat on his already drenched body. But he didn't give up, and suffered cuts to his hands and feet on the barbed wire, before throwing himself off the top, and crashing to the ground of the cobbled courtyard.

Wayne was leaning against the wall, using her trench coat as a tent, so she could smoke a fag under it.

'What took you so long?' she asked. Then putting her coat back on, she led them both in the direction of the stables and sheds. 'We need to split up,' she informed him. 'You take the backyard, I'll go round the front.'

Ben nodded, although he didn't think it was the best of plans, largely because he was terrified. He hauled himself up straight and walked painfully towards the yard, stopping in his tracks as a sensory light was set off. It illuminated the entire space between Ben and the back door. He watched in horror as the large, wooden door was pulled open.

'Who's there?' A man's voice called. It was McEwan's brother, Paul. He recognised Ben at once. 'Inspector Campbell, is it yourself?' he shouted. 'Come in, quickly, you'll catch your death in this weather.'

Ben couldn't believe his luck, he hadn't a trace of suspicion in his voice. He ran towards the entrance, his feet hitting off stones and chips, but by then they were strangely anesthetised to pain.

'You're not wearing any shoes, Inspector,' Paul observed. He had shut the door and was staring at Ben's feet.

'Low pulls,' Ben explained. 'Bloody low pulls, I'm too old for them. But I insist anyway, don't I? So after two hours of them pinching at my feet and ripping my calves to shreds,

I said to myself, "*that's it, I've had enough, these are coming off*". You probably think I'm mad, walking round in the rain barefoot, but I tell you the balls of my feet wouldn't agree.'

Less was more, when it came to lies, but he couldn't seem to help himself as he continued. 'Of course, I hadn't expected to be coming here, that was all very last minute. But I have a few details I wanted to clear up with your sister about the case she was working on with us. It turns out that the Wringer is Gertrude Green.'

'You're shivering, Inspector, let's get you warmed up.' He ushered Ben towards the open plan kitchen, and pulling a towel off the rail on the Aga, he handed it to him. 'Draw up a chair, I'll get you a cup of cocoa.'

Ben hardly dared to breathe, as he watched Paul potter about the kitchen. There didn't seem to be a trace of doubt in his weather-beaten features. Maybe he was better at this lying game than he gave himself credit for, and also maybe Paul knew nothing of his sister's alter ego.

Ben read about it all the time, men who lived with serial killers and had no idea. He'd even watched a TV series on it last year, called, *I Lived with a Serial Killer and had No Idea!*. One bloke said the first he knew was when he saw his wife had been arrested on TV. If Paul didn't know, which seemed likely, then Ben would have to tell him, and pray his sense of common decency would come before any misplaced sense of family loyalty.

'There you go,' Paul said, handing him a mug of milky cocoa.

Ben swallowed half of it in two mouthfuls, its warm sweetness reminding him how his body ached and shivered. How do you tell someone who's just made you hot chocolate, that their sister is a homicidal maniac? He wondered, giggling before slumping forward as his head fell onto his lap.

Wayne was standing on the outside ledge of the bay window on the second floor. She was starting to feel more like Spiderwoman with every climb, and with rain pelting across her back, she shuffled across the ledge, trying to open each sash window as she went.

The fourth window moved a little, and balancing herself carefully, she put all her strength into a second, then third pull, which pushed the window two feet up. She hurled herself into the opening, landing head first on the floor.

She groaned, then fiddled around in her pocket for the torch. Her fingers hurt and she struggled to turn it on.

When she finally pushed the switch down, it threw a circle of light on to the top half of a huge portrait painting of what was probably some rich ancestor of the Wringer.

Wayne was no expert, but the subject was so ugly and the brush work so shoddy, she figured only a deluded relative could have found any merit in hanging the piece.

She threw the light a few inches to the right and illuminated the Cambridge cock, pointing a shotgun at her head.

'Is the doorbell not working?' the Wringer asked, holding the weapon steady.

'Seemed a little late to disturb you,' Wayne replied. She dropped the torch and reached her hand into to her pocket, to retrieve her loaded pistol. Her arm went limp, as she felt the barrel of a shotgun pressed against her temple.

'Spread both your arms out,' the Wringer commanded. Keeping the gun pressed to her head, she patted her down, pulling a pistol from one pocket and her mobile from the other. She then pulled the coat off Wayne and began groping her ample frame, finding a Stanley knife attached to her hairy leg. Wayne yelped as the duct tape securing it was ripped off.

'Move,' the Wringer ordered.

'Give it up, McEwan, or should I say, McDougall. The A.R.U. is on its way, your estate is probably crawling with them as we speak.'

'Really? Which is why, you're jumping through second storey windows, and your partner is stumbling barefoot around our stables.'

The Wringer pushed Wayne out of the room, down the hall, downstairs, through a door into the kitchen, and past it into the scullery. As she opened a laundry room to toss the weapons she'd just seized inside, Wayne noticed two dead deer hanging either side of a huge washing machine and tumble drier. Jess Christ! Was there anything this woman didn't kill?

Following the line of her eye, the Wringer asked, 'Have you ever eaten hand-reared, organic venison, marinated in 1963 Merlot, before being slowly chargrilled over a spit, Inspector?'

When Wayne didn't respond the Wringer continued, 'That's a shame, because now you never will.' Her face contorted with laughter and if it wasn't for the gun at her head, Wayne would have kicked her in the cunt.

'I've made your night cap, Lottie,' the deranged bachelor shouted through from the kitchen.

'Thanks, Paul,' the Wringer replied, before shoving Wayne towards the large walk-in larder at the back of the kitchen.

In single file, they negotiated their way past enough

food to keep a large family fed for a year, assuming the family had expensive tastes and a strong constitution. There were shelves lined with chutneys and pickles and every conceivable type of spice and herb. Most of the supplies were so exotic that Wayne had never heard of them.

'Who the suck uses truffle oil?' she muttered.

The Wringer pressed the gun hard into Wayne's neck, by way of reply.

At the back of the storeroom, out of place among the decadence, stood several sacks of deer nuts.

'Pick them up and shove them aside.' The Wringer barked the order. Wayne did as she was told, revealing a door behind them. 'Open it,' the Wringer said, handing her a key. Once she did so, she was plunged down a set of rickety steps, and the door was bolted shut.

Wayne moaned at the cumulative effect of three crash landings in as many hours. She consoled herself that at least the wooden floor beneath her was marginally softer than the previous two, and eased her limbs into a standing position.

Wayne retrieved a Zippo lighter that the Cambridge cock had missed when searching her trouser pockets. She illuminated a tiny section of the cellar and saw it was filled with racks of wine. Her eyes lit up, as she waved the lighter back and forward over at least a dozen identical rows. Reaching the last one, she heard the sound of laboured breathing. She paused, hunkered down and cast the slice of light over an unconscious Campbell. Kneeling, she shuffled up towards his upper body and shook his shoulders.

'Campbell, wake up!' He didn't move. She gave it another couple of attempts, before sliding her hand down his body and fiddling about in his trouser pocket.

'Wayne, is that you? What the suck are you doing?' he sounded groggy and confused.

'I need that Swiss army knife I gave you earlier,' Wayne explained, as she pulled it out of his pocket, and shifted the Zippo's glow back towards his face.

'My head hurts,' Ben said, lifting it and his body up into sitting position.

'I'll get you something for that,' she assured him. 'Here, hold this and shine it up there.'

'There must be a light switch,' Ben said, leaning on his hands, and using them as a lever to stand up. 'I'm going to find it.' He handed the Zippo back to Wayne, and placing his hands in front of him, Ben began to slowly negotiate the pitch-black cellar.

Wayne barely noticed as she fiddled with the Swiss army knife until she located the cork screw attachment. She groped the dusty bottles of expensive, potent wine and pulled one out of the rack. Wayne placed it between her legs and guided her hands up the bottle until she reached the cork, before plunging the cork screw into it.

A light bulb in the centre of the room came on and Wayne closed her eyes to adjust to the sudden glare. Opening them slowly, she saw properly for the first time the vast alcohol collection the Wringer had amassed, and she resisted the urge to scream with delight, guessing Campbell might think it insensitive. She turned her attention back to the wine between her knees and twisted the cork screw expertly, before removing it completely with one clean pull. She smiled triumphantly at Campbell.

'Please tell me you're not going to drink that,' Ben said.

But Wayne already had the bottle to her mouth. She drank like she was in the desert and had stumbled across a fresh water spring. Clearing over half its contents, she handed the wine to Ben.

'I don't want wine,' he shouted at her. 'Are you completely insane? Some crazy bitch has Simon and George, and this is the best you can come up with? Getting wasted!'

'You've got to ask yourself, Campbell, how many times in an average life are you going to get locked in a loaded wine cellar?' Wayne was feeling mellow, as she took another large gulp. She then placed the bottle on the ground and grabbed the army knife, before walking towards the stairs.

She climbed them slowly, her eyes searching each step for nails loose enough to be pulled out. She found two, that with the help of her knife, she could prise from the wood. She continued up the stairs stopping three before the top. 'Campbell, give me your pra,' she shouted at Ben.

'What?' Ben replied, 'Seriously, Wayne? I'm really tiring of your inappropriate comments.'

'I am being serious. I need it.'

'What for?' Ben asked, moving towards her.

'I'm going to use it to make a trip wire, which the deranged bachelor will fall down, when he comes to check if we're okay.'

Ben stopped in his tracks. 'You do know that he's an accomplice in his sister's crimes? I'm not sure he'll be bringing us tea and biscuits any time soon.'

'Wrong! That's because, although you are one, or perhaps because of that, you know very little of the male mindset. Do you remember when we came to pick up that letter? He made us that feast of scones, jam and fruit cake. I've been to wakes with less generous spreads. Do you want to know what that says about him?'

'That he's clinically insane, but hospitable?'

'Exactly! He's ugly as sin, right? So, he has to compensate in other ways, to at least try and avoid his unavoidable fate of bachelorhood surrounded by cats. Now, give me your pra. He's probably stewing the tea as we speak.'

Ben slipped his hands down his front, unfastened his pra, slid his penis out of it, and handed it to Wayne. Using the nail, she made a tiny hole in the stitching and attached it to one side, stretched it across the step, and did the same on the other side. Wayne strolled down the stairs, smiled at her red-faced colleague, and retrieved the remainder of the wine from its resting place.

'What do we do now?' Ben asked.

'You turn off the light. I drink wine. And we wait.'

The Wringer sat back as the snivelling prick opposite her shoved his oysters around the plate, his heavily made-up face almost sliding off, as pools of sweat and tears ran down his brow.

The stupid little sucker could hardly be more afraid if he was tied to a cross, awaiting almost certain death, and she felt deprived of an entire stage in the game. Fear was the ultimate destination, obviously, before the final one. But she loved to start with innocence and hope, and watch their transparent features betray their gradual realisation that all was not well, before the desperate truth slowly dawned on them.

There was no hope left to crush with this kid. Once he'd seen her use a hammer on the skull of George the manny, all reasonable expectation that he was getting out of here alive had vanished. There seemed little point in small talk, so she tried another approach.

'My brother found your father running around outside

barefoot, so I've put him in the cellar, with that renegade misfit he calls a partner. When we're finished here, and I'm finished with you, I'm going to give them a blow by blow account of what's happened to you, before throwing a bucket of petrol on them, and burning them alive.'

It was entertaining to observe his terror multiply, and his heart rate increased so much that his naked chest jerked in and out. The ultimate fear threshold had not yet been reached, she observed, there were still more games to be played!

Wayne and Ben sat in darkness, about halfway down the cellar. Ben shivered as the dampness set into his body. Wayne, getting nicely through her second bottle of Merlot, showed no awareness of the cold.

'So much for your intuition about men, Wayne.'

'He'll come soon enough, like night follows day, you mark my words,' Wayne replied.

Ben snorted. As his body temperature continued to plummet, Ben leaned in to Wayne's fleshed-out frame, and rested his head on her shoulder.

'You know the best way to conserve body heat, don't you?' she leered at him.

He broke free from her and was just about to launch into a tirade, when the upstairs latch moved. They both stayed perfectly still, hardly daring to breathe.

The door opened and the light switch was flicked on. Paul stood at the top of the stairs, a shotgun in his right hand. He glanced down at the hostages before wedging his foot in the door, and picking up a tray laden with mugs of tea, and hot buttered crumpets in his left. Ben's eyes almost popped out of their sockets.

'I'm armed, so don't try anything silly,' he called, taking the first, then second step down. On the third, his heavy black shoe got caught in Campbell's pra, and he tumbled headfirst down the next ten, dropping the gun and the tray as he went. Tea, crockery and crumpets bounced off the ground, as Ben and Wayne leapt into action.

Wayne grabbed the gun, and Ben threw his weight on top of the dazed Paul. Ben ran his fingers down Paul's body, and pulled a massive ring of heavy keys from his apron pocket. Working his way up to his head, he realised he was unconscious, blood starting to seep from his head.

'I think he needs an ambulance,' he told Wayne.

'You know what, sugar, probably best to leave the thinking to me,' Wayne replied.

The Wringer had moved up to her bedroom. She had tied her hostage face down onto a cross, and was giving her suitcase a once over, before moving in for the final act.

She checked her wallet, her passport, and her plane tickets, zipped the front of the case closed, and wheeled it beside the door. By this time tomorrow, she would be someone else and living somewhere new. Her plan was to lay low for a few months, whilst she created the contacts to match her credentials, and then she could start all over again. She would burn the house down, leaving the incompetent police force, with whom she'd once shared an office, to try and piece it all together.

She wondered if her husband had finished packing. He'd been whining all day about how afraid he'd become of her, how he thought she needed professional help. The stupid dick was becoming a liability. She'd seriously considered adding him to the casualty list, but it was so much easier to ingratiate yourself in the right society if you had a pretty husband. She'd take him with her for now, and if he continued to be a pain, she'd deal with him.

'What are you going to do with me?' The whinging whore stuttered from the cross.

'Teach you how to enunciate your words better, for a start,' she replied, slashing his buttocks with a cane.

After locking Paul in the cellar, Wayne and Ben sped through the scullery and kitchen and into the expansive main hall. Ben hit a light switch and two chandeliers at either side illuminated the space.

'She'll be upstairs,' Wayne said.

'What makes you say that?'

Wayne shrugged her shoulders, 'We have to start somewhere. Come on, we're wasting time.'

Taking the stairs two at a time, they found themselves in another huge hallway.

'You take the left side,' Wayne instructed, turning into the first room on the right. It was an impressive portrait gallery, with floor to ceiling paintings of some of the least attractive human beings Wayne had ever laid eyes on. Centuries of inbreeding had created a succession of equestrian featured mutants. If she'd been related to any of these people, she sure as hell wouldn't advertise it. Satisfied that there was nowhere to hide, she moved swiftly on, running into Campbell in the hall.

The second room was lined with glass cabinets, filled with fine bone china. She quickly ascertained that there were no secrets for the space to give up, so she hurried out to the next room.

Stepping into the library, she scanned the rows of shelves

before creeping, slowly between them. She turned into the final row and saw the Wringer's husband, leaning against the back wall, his sobbing face obscured by his hands. She leaned her gun carefully against the shelf, and shuffled down towards the dude in distress.

'It's not that bad, you know,' she told him. 'Anyone would think you'd married a serial killer.' To her immense surprise, he burst out laughing.

'I love a woman with a sense of humour,' he said. 'That's what first attracted me to Lottie, that, and the fact that she was stinking rich.' His manic laughter chilled Wayne.

'Are you hiding here, Ivan?' Wayne asked.

Ivan looked up and nodded. Taking his hands away from his face, Wayne couldn't fail to notice the recent bruising around his eye, that his make-up hadn't fully hidden.

'Did Lottie do that?' she kept her voice low.

Ivan nodded again.

'Does she do that often?'

Ivan stared blankly at Wayne.

'Do you know where she is right now?'

Ivan didn't reply.

'I think you do know,' Wayne's voice remained low. 'And I think you want to tell me, but you're scared.'

'She'll kill me if I do,' Ivan whispered.

'I think it's come to a point where she'll kill you if you don't.' Wayne held his gaze.

'What will happen to me? Will I be charged?' He bit his bottom lip as he spoke, and tears began to fall from his fear-stricken eyes.

'Not if I can help it,' Wayne promised him. 'But if you give us the information that leads to her capture, that will go a long way to helping your defence.'

'She's in the last bedroom on the left, on the next floor,' Ivan said, then he rooted around in his handbag and retrieved a heavy iron key. 'You'll need this. She always keeps it locked.'

'Right, we're going in right now. This is what I need you to do. Call Withering police station, tell them I told you to call, tell them where we are, tell them to send an ambulance and tell them to sucking hurry!' Wayne grabbed the gun on her way out, and ran down the hall, in search of Campbell.

'We've got her, next floor, follow me,' she ordered.

The Wringer ran her fingers up Simon's naked spine. The smell of his fresh urine and even fresher fear aroused her greatly, and she regretted how hastily the evening was speeding along. She checked the antique clock at the side of the bed; she had four hours before she had to be at the airport, and a lot to achieve before leaving.

'Please, don't hurt me anymore,' Simon pleaded from the bed. She was impressed he could still talk.

'Don't worry, I'm not going to hurt you,' she replied. 'I'm going to kill you.' She measured out around two metres of wire and cut them, laying the pliers carefully back on the dresser.

Coming over to the bed and using his hair to lever his head up, she pushed the wire under him. She then mounted him and grabbed a side of the wire with each hand. Closing her eyes she pulled the wire tight. He screamed so loud she let go of the right side and slapped him hard across the head.

Satisfied he'd be a bit quieter next time, she found the end of the wire and again tugged it tight. A key was being inserted in the door and the lock being turned, and she wrapped the wire tighter around each fist, and began to pull it upwards.

The door sprung open, and there was the click of a shotgun. Something hit her just below her chest, and she screamed in agony, as she was propelled forward on top of Simon.

'Get her off me! Get her off me,' Simon screamed.

Wayne dropped her gun and hauled the Wringer off him, before throwing her on the floor.

Ben rushed to his son's side. He wanted to vomit when he saw his child's bleeding neck and bruised and beaten body.

'It's going to be okay, Simon, I'm here,' he whispered to his son, searching the room with his eyes for anything that might protect his modesty. 'Wayne, pass me that dressing gown,' he told her, pointing to a long, white, silk robe that hung on the back of the door. He threw it over Simon, then started to untie his outstretched arms.

All the while, Simon lay there softly moaning, and Ben wondered if his child would ever be the same again.

'One more minute, boy, and you could have been mine,' the Wringer croaked. 'I would have made you famous; no-one every remembers the one who got away.'

'She's alive! Jess Christ! She's alive,' Simon screamed. 'Do something, Dad, do something!'

Wayne was already on top of the Wringer, shoving her knee into her stomach, 'Where the suck is George?' she screamed at her. 'What the suck have you done with George?'

The Wringer opened her mouth and whispered, 'He's outside in the...' Wayne leaned in, and then let out a piercing scream.

'She's stabbed me! The crazy cock has stabbed me!'

Wayne's body was thrown backwards with the force of the injury, and blood spurted from her upper leg. The Wringer raised her hand to plunge the knife into Wayne for a second time.

Ben snatched the gun from the side of the bed and pointed it at the Wringer's forehead. She caught his eye, and her face broke into a wide smile. He pulled the trigger and watched aghast, as the grin and half her face was wiped off.

Wayne pulled herself up, and stared at the blood splattered Stanley knife that had fallen at her feet.

'Jess Christ! The bitch stabbed me with my own knife!'

Wayne inhaled her cigarette deeply and pushed away a paramedic who was trying to move her to a waiting ambulance. 'Get your hands off me!' she shouted. 'I'm not going anywhere till we find George.'

Ben had been taken to hospital with Simon. It had been half an hour since the Wringer had stabbed Wayne, and she was losing a lot of blood. The manor was overrun with cops and ambulances, forensics and photographers. Wayne caught sight of O'Keeffe talking with the medical examiner and she crouched behind the paramedic.

'Over here,' a cop called from one of the barns. 'I need help over here right now.'

Wayne hobbled towards the direction of the voice, a paramedic trailing after her.

'Please, Ms, you've lost a lot of blood. We need to get you to a hospital.'

'Back off!' Wayne snarled, pushing the paramedic away, and continuing to the barn, where a large part of the team was now gathered. She stopped just outside, drew her breath and winced in pain. Wrapped around her leg was the shirt that Campbell had ripped up and used as a bandage. It was now bright red, as was most of her left trouser leg.

Ignoring her injury, she pushed through the crowd. In the middle, lay George. He was stretched out on a stack of hay, one paramedic listening to his heartbeat, another attaching a drip to his arm. His face was bulging from where he had suffered a series of blows to the back of the head. He was still wearing his apron, and splatters of his blood mixed with its cupcake pattern almost seamlessly.

She shuffled forward until she was standing over him. Wayne thought she could see a flicker of recognition in his half-closed eyes and she grabbed his hand. He flinched, she felt it, he definitely flinched! There was hope.

'We need to get you to a hospital, doll,' she whispered to him. His eyes moved again and then his body started to convulse.

'What's happening?' Wayne shouted, watching helplessly as George thrashed about, and a medical team barked orders at each other. One of them grabbed her by the shoulders, and pushed her to one side.

More running, another drip. Wayne felt like she was trapped in some god-awful nightmare. More orders were shouted. Were those paddles they were using on him?

'One, two, three and clear. And again. One, two, three and clear.'

Wayne was properly panicked now. She waited for the next count, but they had stopped.

'What's happening? George?' she yelled.

'Ma'am, we need to get you to hospital now.'

By this time, a group of four medics surrounded Wayne. The frantic movements of the medical team had ground to a halt and she watched as a young woman closed George's eyes.

'No,' Wayne howled and, with all the strength she had left, willed herself back towards her lover. She fell to her knees at his feet and began pulling at his limp hands.

'Wake up, George, will you? For suck's sake, George. Will you just wake up?' She stopped shouting at him and she stopped pulling at him and instead, allowed her head to fall at his feet.

'She's unconscious,' a paramedic yelled. 'Quick, let's get her out of here before she wakes up!'

SIXTEEN

MONDAY

SIX WEEKS LATER

Ben opened the oven and poured another generous glass of red wine over the bubbling beef stew. It wasn't part of the recipe, but Wayne always ate more when she knew the food had alcohol, and he wanted to help build her strength up.

It was six weeks since she'd been stabbed and she was still a shadow of her former self. He did a quick recount to make sure he had enough plates, and stacking them at the side of the cooker, he began to lay the cutlery on the table. A gunshot made him jump, until he remembered that Wayne was teaching Drea to shoot in the back garden. They'd been out there every afternoon since Wayne had been discharged from hospital, but Ben still couldn't get used to the sound of gunfire so close to his home.

He'd been absolutely opposed to the idea, but Drea kept on and on at him. She'd been severely affected by her brother's abduction, and George's murder, and shooting practice was providing a release for her feelings. At least that's how Wayne had sold it to him, and though he hated to admit it, she was right. Drea was much happier after she'd been shooting at something, and so was Wayne. His colleague's state of mind was Ben's responsibility as Wayne had been staying with them since her release from hospital. A community health team had given her basement flat a definitive *thumbs-down* after a glance at what Wayne called home. A condition of her discharge from hospital was that she found alternative accommodation and Ben had volunteered to share Val's bedroom, and turn his own bedroom into a temporary guest room.

Initially, he'd dreaded the arrangement. Wayne was hard enough to work with, living with her was going to be even harder! But his fears, in the main, proved unfounded. She'd been somewhat subdued since George's death, and as a consequence, not her usual deeply offensive self.

If the truth be known; he was getting quite used to having a woman around again. She'd fixed a pipe in the bathroom, grouted the shower tiles, and neatly nailed all the loose internet wires to the living room wall. In addition to this, her very presence instilled a sort of subconscious respect for authority in the kids, and they did what they were told more often. Best of all, she didn't expect to suck him, and as far as he could make out, she was vaguely repulsed by him, which suited Ben just fine. He was surprised to realise how much he'd probably miss her when she left.

He switched the oven off just as the back door swung open, and his eldest daughter and Wayne returned from shooting wild birds, or anything else that had the misfortune to stray into their territory.

As usual, they were empty-handed, as there was a distinct lack of prey flying above or roaming the streets of suburban Withering. Ben had drawn a line at the two heading further afield with Drea's new-found hobby. Wayne tossed her mucky boots into the box beside the fridge that Ben had designated for them, and hung her coat on the stand in the hall. Ben felt quite smug, convinced he had played a pivotal role in her domestication. Wayne returned to the kitchen and sniffed the aroma of the marinating meat. Saliva dripped from the side of her mouth.

'Will I open the wine?' she asked, unscrewing a claret that she had just procured from the local off-licence. Ben was about to protest, but remained silent as the liquid splashed against the side of the glass, and resigned himself to another night of drunkenness.

'Can I have a glass?' Drea asked.

Wayne grabbed a third glass from the shelf and began to pour wine into it.

'What are you doing? Give me that, Wayne! She's thirteen!'

'Which is as good an age as any to have your first drink. If she lived on the continent she'd be an alcoholic by now.'

'Yeah,' Drea agreed. 'It's civilised to drink at my age in Europe.'

'And if you lived in Africa you'd be a child soldier by now. Go upstairs and wash your hands,' Ben ordered, before turning to Wayne. 'What the hell do you think you're playing at? What kind of example is that to set? She sees you as some kind of role model, doesn't that bother you?'

'Not in the slightest,' Wayne replied. 'But I can see how it would scare the shit out of you. Anyway, the good news is I got the all clear from the consultant this morning, so I'll be out of your hair after dinner.'

'What do you mean by *all clear*?' Ben hoped his voice sounded neutral.

'The wound's healing nicely. They reckon I can lose the stick in about a month, and there's no reason I can't return to my own gaff, especially now it's been given that deep clean, courtesy of Peachy. So, I'll be making tracks this evening.'

'Of course,' Ben replied. 'That's really great news, it'll be good to get my room back.' He reached up to the cupboard which held the dinner plates, fixed his eyes on a glass tumbler, and blinked back the tears.

Wayne sat at the table and gulped her claret. She was glad to be going home, but she was going to miss this way of life. The smell of freshly cooked food, the noise of the kids upstairs, the sight of a lived-in, loved, looked after house—a home. She'd had something similar with George at one point. When George's lad would come back from uni for a weekend, he'd go all out on the cooking and the cleaning, his nesting instinct kicked in. Wayne felt as if she was in a fifties movie, not one she'd normally watch because there was no blood or guts or action, but one she liked being in, none the less. Of course, she'd sucked that up. There was no chance of ever starring in that movie again.

It would be easy to blame the Cambridge cock, but the fact was that the cosy fantasy was dead before George died. George had been on the ball when he said she was shit at relationships. It wasn't as if George was the first man to make that observation. Her maudlin thoughts were interrupted by a toy car crashing into her ankle.

'For suck's sake!' she screamed, and instantly regretted it as the toy's owner burst out crying.

'I'm sorry,' Val sobbed. 'I meant to shock you, not hit you.'

'Of course you did,' Wayne's tone altered completely, as she scooped the young girl into her arms. 'And guess what? Hitting me was a real shock, so you did well, kid.'

Val grinned from ear to ear. 'I'm sitting beside Wayne,' she declared climbing down from her knee and onto the seat next to her.

Drea and Simon ran down the stairs and Drea hopped over the couch and into the seat on her other side. Wayne quickly refilled her wine glass and downed it in one, as they waited for Ben to serve up dinner.

When the meal was eaten and everyone had cleared their plates, Ben turned to her, 'Will you have that chat with Simon like you promised, before you leave?'

'Ah, Jess, do I have to?' Wayne replied.

Ben nodded.

'Well, I'm making myself a spliff before I do.'

Simon lay on his bed and stared at the ceiling between fielding texts from half the school. His brush with notoriety and his status as the only survivor of the Wringer had done wonders for his street cred. He was one of the most popular kids in school now. All the boys wanted to befriend him, and all the girls wanted to do much more than that, and he was loving his newfound celebrity. But he was taking things nice and slowly. Despite countless invitations, he still hadn't been out at night since it all happened. The days were okay, but come dusk a panic would start to descend, and he didn't feel safe unless he was at home, under the same roof as his dad.

He'd developed a new respect for his dad in the wake of the tragedy. He'd also developed a greater understanding of why his dad hated women. If all women were like the Wringer, and his mother, then he'd hate them too. She hadn't even come to the hospital to see him. He'd made his dad try every old contact he had in an attempt to locate her, but he'd drawn a blank. *"She doesn't want to be found, kid, so you won't find her"*, Wayne had told him. And she was so right. He felt kind of sad Wayne was leaving, he'd liked having her around. His dad was more mellow in Wayne's company, or maybe that was just all the wine they drank.

There was a loud tapping on his bedroom door and he opened it to find Wayne standing outside. She was rubbing her wounded thigh, between winces.

'Are you coming in?' he asked.

Wayne hobbled into the room and over to Simon's desk that sat beneath the window. With care, she lowered herself into his chair, her face affecting a look of pain.

'Wayne, are you sure you're alright to go home? Dad would love to have you stay for a while longer. We all would,' Simon said, giving her a warm smile.

'Got to go sometime, kid,' she replied. 'Speaking of your dad, he's got it into his head that I'm some kind of mother figure to you all. And on that basis, he wants me to have a word with you about your recently acquired habit of smoking marijuana.'

'I don't smoke marijuana,' Simon retorted too quickly, as his cheeks reddened. 'What gave him that idea?'

'The weed he found under your mattress,' Wayne answered.

'I'm minding it for a friend,' he responded, then changing tack added, 'Anyway, what's he doing looking under my mattress? He's no right to be searching my room.'

'Look, kid, you were abducted and almost killed by a psychopath, who you had been talking to online for months. The price of your survival is a neurotic father, who will rake over every inch of your life, from now until you leave home. It's his desperate attempt to be ahead of the game, in the highly unlikely event that another psychopath tries to abduct and kill you. It's not logical, but he's a man, and someday you'll grow up and be just as crazy.'

'I don't care what you say, he has no right searching through my stuff. Anyway, I told you it belongs to a friend. I don't smoke marijuana.'

'That's right, you don't,' agreed Wayne, reaching into her pocket and pulling out the joint she'd just made. She sparked it up and Simon yanked the window open.

'You smoke shit; I don't know who is selling it, or what they are charging you for it, but you are being ripped off, big time. Here, try this.' Wayne handed him the spliff.

Simon stared at it, unsure what he should do next. He reckoned it was probably a trick and he handed it straight back to Wayne repeating his mantra.

'I don't smoke. I keep telling you.'

Wayne acted like she hadn't heard him and offered him the joint again. This time, he accepted it, inhaling and keeping it in for the count of fifteen. When Simon eventually exhaled he almost coughed up his lungs. Undeterred, he took another toke and grinned as he handed it back to her.

'You're right,' he laughed. 'I do smoke shit!'

'Here's what you're going to do, kid…'

Wayne was scrawling a number onto his maths folder. 'When you need a smoke, give Harriet the hippy a call. She keeps me going between raids. Tell her I sent you, and tell her if she tries to rip you off, I'll rip her head off.'

Wayne took another few draws on her joint before handing it to Simon. She pulled herself up, and grinned at him. Wayne turned back just before leaving the room, 'It's been good talking to you, kid. You and I should do this again.'

Wayne negotiated the stairs slowly, pausing for breath at the bottom. Catching a glimpse of a worn-out Campbell, half asleep on the living room couch, she smiled. He had never regrown his beard since he'd shaved it, and as a result Wayne found him much easier on the eye.

'It suits you, the clean shaven look, it's more...' she heard herself say the words and stumble as the sentence continued.

'Normal?' Ben offered.

'I was going to say sexy,' Wayne lied as a deep flush ran up her face. Ben blushed as well and poured the last droplets of wine into his glass.

'I've another in my bag,' Wayne offered. She limped towards her holdall, which she'd stored in the hallway, and hobbled back with a second claret. Wayne filled two glasses to the brim and handed one to Ben.

She stood beside him awkwardly fingering the memory stick in her pocket. Quickly, before she had time to talk herself out of it, she whipped it out and banged it down on the table.

'This belongs to you,' she told him.

Ben fondled the tiny piece of hardware. He looked confused.

'We found it amongst your ex-wife's belongings.'

'This was Anna's?' his voice became louder as he continued. 'I don't want it. Why the suck would I want anything belonging to her?'

'Okay, fair enough,' Wayne nodded, grabbing back the memory stick.

She had almost returned it to her pocket when he asked, 'What's on it?'

Wayne hesitated and shuffled her feet, wincing every time she put weight on her sore leg.

'You. Her. And a... watermelon.' Wayne's eyes darted from left to right and back again as she avoided making contact with Ben. His face turned crimson and his hands began to shake.

'You watched this?'

Wayne considered denying it, but she'd said too much already and there was no going back.

'I had to,' she rushed her words together. 'It was evidence. We didn't know what was on it, and it had to be investigated.'

'We?' Ben shouted at her.

'Baker found it. She watched it first, before passing it on to me.'

'I see, so you and that dirty old bitch watched me and her, did you? Bet you both got off on that!'

'Oh, get over yourself, Campbell.' It was Wayne's turn to shout. 'Do you have any idea of the serious shit Baker was into? You really think some grainy amateur footage of your cock and tongue can compete with that?'

'So, what you're saying is that I look like shit naked?'

Wayne was very conscious that she was talking to a man and that it was impossible to say the right thing.

She lifted her glass to her mouth and sank back half of it, stalling for time before carefully continuing.

'I'd do you,' she said. 'Since seeing the footage, I mean, before that—no danger. Baker would have though, done you, either ways, at any time. She always thought you were a natural beauty.'

'I don't need your approval to render me sexually valid.' Ben declared. 'And I sure as hell don't need Baker's!'

"Give me a break, Campbell!' Wayne snapped. 'How could I possibly know that there was nothing relevant to the investigation on that footage without watching it?' Wayne finished her drink in one mouthful and helped herself to an immediate refill.

'When you put it like that, I can see your point,' Ben conceded.

Wayne reached out her hand to give him the memory stick, but then she had a better idea. She shuffled over to wastepaper basket and dropped it in.

'Best place for it,' she told him and was rewarded with a weak smile. Exhausted, she allowed herself to flop in to an armchair, and held out her hand for Ben to pass her glass of wine.

'I got you something,' Ben said. He was like an excitable child, as he pulled a box from behind the couch and handed it to her.

Wayne peered inside and her face creased with laughter. 'Campbell, I could kiss you,' she announced, pulling out a pair of the snazziest cowgirl boots she had ever seen. The scuffed boots that adorned her feet currently, paled next to this new, shiny, tan pair. The feet were decorated in a snakeskin pattern, that was the slightest shade darker than the body of the boot. She brought them up to her nostrils and inhaled the smell of brand new leather. Leaning down cautiously, she pulled first her right, and then her left boot off, and marvelled at the ease with which her aching limbs settled into the new pair.

'They fit like a glove,' she beamed at Campbell. Her mobile beeped. 'That'll be my taxi.'

'Already?' Ben said.

'Can you grab my trench coat from upstairs?' she asked him.

'Of course I can.'

Wayne hobbled back over to the wastepaper basket. She leaned down, retrieved the memory stick, and slipped it into her trouser pocket. She was putting her old boots in the shoe box, when Ben returned empty handed.

'Not in the bedroom,' he informed her.

'Did I hang it up in the hall?' Wayne scratched her head.

Ben nodded, grabbed it with one hand, and took her holdall in his other. 'Now, is there anything else you need me to fetch?'

'Nope,' Wayne grinned at him, 'I've got everything I need.'

ACKNOWLEDGEMENTS

Thank you Valarie Scouten for running the best creative writing class in Edinburgh, and to fellow classmates Victor and Michael for championing *Nailing Jess* from the very start.

I'm very grateful to Linsey Young and Veronica Kidd for all their hours reading and editing the first draft, and to Julie MacPherson, my go to writer in times of fatigue and self doubt. And to my lovely friends Louise, Diane, Debs, The two Montses, Kenny, Morna and Ashley.

Huge thanks to my publishers/editors at Cranachan Publishing, Anne Glennie and Helen MacKinven, for taking my rough idea and editing it and editing it and editing it! Thanks also for taking someone that didn't fit the profile of debut author and making her one.

Biggest thanks of all to my best friend Norm and my wonderful son, Mikey.

ABOUT THE AUTHOR

Irish-born Triona lives in Edinburgh with her son, Mikey. *Nailing Jess* is her debut novel.

Triona blogs at trionascully.com

THANK YOU FOR READING

As we say at Cranachan,
'the proof of the pudding is in the reading'
and we hope that you enjoyed *Nailing Jess*.

Please tell all your friends and tweet us with your
#nailingjess feedback, or better still, write an online review
to help spread the word!

We only publish books which excite and inspire us, so if
you'd like to experience other unique and
thought-provoking books, please visit our website:

cranachanpublishing.co.uk

and follow us
@cranachanbooks
for news of our forthcoming titles.